The Witching Time
Tales for the Year's End
(1886)

The Witching Time
Tales for the Year's End
(1886)

11 Short Stories & Verses
of the Supernatural & Weird

Henry Norman

LEONAUR

The Witching Time
Tales for the Year's End (1886)
11 Short Stories & Verses
of the Supernatural & Weird
by Henry Norman

First published under the title
The Witching Time
Tales for the Year's End (1886)

Leonaur is an imprint
of Oakpast Ltd

ISBN: 978-0-85706-787-6 (hardcover)
ISBN: 978-0-85706-788-3 (softcover)

http://www.leonaur.com

Publisher's Notes

Contents

In Witching Time
By Austin Dobson

In Witching Time when, sparkling higher,
The last log crumbles in the fire,
And through the midnight's creeping cold,
The shadows lengthen, fold by fold,
And in the settle nods the sire,
And the dame droops, and maids draw higher,
Each to the man of her desire,
(So do the bashful seek the bold
In witching time!)
E'en as this hour, when revels tire,
And the spent mirth and mood require
Something to stir the sense, or hold
The soul in awe, these tales were told—
Told, while the flickering flames expire,
In witching time!

By the Waters of Paradise
By F. Marion Crawford

1

I remember my childhood very distinctly. I do not think that the fact argues a good memory, for I have never been clever at learning words by heart, in prose or rhyme; so that I believe my remembrance of events depends much more upon the events themselves than upon my possessing any special facility for recalling them. Perhaps I am too imaginative, and the earliest impressions I received were of a kind to stimulate the imagination abnormally. A long series of little misfortunes, so connected with each other as to suggest a sort of weird fatality, so worked upon my melancholy temperament when I was a boy that, before I was of age, I sincerely believed myself to be under a curse, and not only myself, but my whole family and every individual who bore my name.

I was born in the old place where my father, and his father, and all his predecessors had been born, beyond the memory of man. It is a very old house, and the greater part of it was originally a castle, strongly fortified, and surrounded by a deep moat supplied with abundant water from the hills by a hidden aqueduct. Many of the fortifications have been destroyed, and the moat has been filled up. The water from the aqueduct supplies great fountains, and runs down into huge oblong basins in the terraced gardens, one below the other, each surrounded by a broad pavement of marble between the water and the flower-beds. The waste surplus finally escapes through an artificial grotto, some thirty yards long, into a stream, flowing down through the park to the meadows beyond, and thence to the distant river. The buildings were extended a little and greatly altered more than two hundred years ago, in the time of Charles II., but since then little has been done to improve them, though they have been kept in fairly good repair, according to our fortunes.

In the gardens there are terraces and huge hedges of box and evergreen, some of which used to be clipped into shapes of animals, in the Italian style. I can remember when I was a lad how I used to try to make out what the trees were cut to represent, and how I used to appeal for explanations to Judith, my Welsh nurse. She dealt in a strange mythology of her own, and peopled the gardens with griffins, dragons, good *genii* and bad, and filled my mind with them at the same time. My nursery window afforded a view of the great fountains at the head of the upper basin, and on moonlight nights the Welshwoman would hold me up to the glass and bid me look at the mist and spray rising into mysterious shapes, moving mystically in the white light like living things.

"It's the Woman of the Water," she used to say; and sometimes she would threaten that if I did not go to sleep the Woman of the Water would steal up to the high window and carry me away in her wet arms.

The place was gloomy. The broad basins of water and the tall evergreen hedges gave it a funereal look, and the damp-stained marble causeways by the pools might have been made of tombstones. The gray and weather-beaten walls and towers without, the dark and massively furnished rooms within, the deep, mysterious recesses and the heavy curtains, all affected my spirits. I was silent and sad from my childhood. There was a great clock tower above, from which the hours rang dismally during the day, and tolled like a knell in the dead of night. There was no light nor life in the house, for my mother was a helpless invalid, and my father had grown melancholy in his long task of caring for her. He was a thin, dark man, with sad eyes; kind, I think, but silent and unhappy.

Next to my mother, I believe he loved me better than anything on earth, for he took immense pains and trouble in teaching me, and what he taught me I have never forgotten. Perhaps it was his only amusement, and that may be the reason why I had no nursery governess or teacher of any kind while he lived.

I used to be taken to see my mother every day, and sometimes twice a day, for an hour at a time. Then I sat upon a little stool near her feet, and she would ask me what I had been doing, and what I wanted to do. I dare say she saw already the seeds of a profound melancholy in my nature, for she looked at me always with a sad smile, and kissed me with a sigh when I was taken away.

One night, when I was just six years old, I lay awake in the nursery. The door was not quite shut, and the Welsh nurse was sitting sewing in the next room. Suddenly I heard her groan, and say in a strange voice, "One—two—one—two!" I was frightened, and I jumped up and ran to the door, barefooted as I was.

"What is it, Judith?" I cried, clinging to her skirts. I can remember the look in her strange dark eyes as she answered:

"One—two leaden coffins, fallen from the ceiling!" she crooned, working herself in her chair. "One—two—a light coffin and a heavy coffin, falling to the floor!"

Then she seemed to notice me, and she took me back to bed and sang me to sleep with a queer old Welsh song.

I do not know how it was, but the impression got hold of me that she had meant that my father and mother were going to die very soon. They died in the very room where she had been sitting that night. It was a great room, my day nursery, full of sun when there was any; and when the days were dark it was the most cheerful place in the house. My mother grew rapidly worse, and I was transferred to another part of the building to make place for her. They thought my nursery was gayer for her, I suppose; but she could not live. She was beautiful when she was dead, and I cried bitterly.

The light one, the light one—the heavy one to come," crooned the Welshwoman. And she was right. My father took the room after my mother was gone, and day by day he grew thinner and paler and sadder.

"The heavy one, the heavy one—all of lead," moaned my nurse, one night in December, standing still, just as she was going to take away the light after putting me to bed. Then she took me up again and wrapped me in a little gown, and led me away to my father's room. She knocked, but no one answered. She opened the door, and we found him in his easy chair before the fire, very white, quite dead.

So I was alone with the Welshwoman till strange people came, and relations whom I had never seen; and then I heard them saying that I must be taken away to some more cheerful place. They were kind people, and I will not believe that they were kind only because I was to be very rich when I grew to be a man. The world never seemed to be a very bad place to me, nor all the people to be miserable sinners, even when I was most melancholy. I do not remember that anyone ever did me any great injustice, nor that I was ever oppressed or ill treated in any way, even by the boys at school. I was sad, I suppose, because my childhood was so gloomy, and, later, because I was unlucky in everything I undertook, till I finally believed I was pursued by fate, and I used to dream that the old Welsh nurse and the Woman of the Water between them had vowed to pursue me to my end. But my natural disposition should have been cheerful, as I have often thought.

Among the lads of my age I was never last, or even among the last, in anything; but I was never first. If I trained for a race, I was sure to sprain my ankle on the day when I was to run. If I pulled an oar with others, my oar was sure to break. If I competed for a prize, some unforeseen accident prevented my winning it at the last moment. Nothing to which I put my hand succeeded, and I got the reputation of being unlucky, until my companions felt it was always safe to bet against me, no matter what the appearances might be. I became discouraged and listless in everything. I gave up the idea of competing for any distinction at the University, comforting myself with the thought that I could not fail in the examination for the ordinary degree. The day before the examination began I fell ill; and when at last I recovered, after a narrow escape from death, I turned my back upon Oxford, and went down alone to visit the old place where I had been born, feeble in health and profoundly disgusted and discouraged. I was twenty-one years of age, master of myself and of my fortune; but so deeply had the long chain of small unlucky circumstances affected me that I thought seriously of shutting myself up from the world to live the life of a hermit and to die as soon as possible. Death seemed the only cheerful possibility in my existence, and my thoughts soon dwelt upon it altogether.

I had never shown any wish to return to my own home since I had been taken away as a little boy, and no one had ever pressed me to do so. The place had been kept in order after a fashion, and did not seem to have suffered during the fifteen years or more of my absence. Nothing earthly could affect those old gray walls that had fought the elements for so many centuries. The garden was more wild than I remembered it; the marble causeways about the pools looked more yellow and damp than of old, and the whole place at first looked smaller. It was not until I had wandered about the house and grounds for many hours that I realized the huge size of the home where I was to live in solitude. Then I began to delight in it, and my resolution to live alone grew stronger.

The people had turned out to welcome me, of course, and I tried to recognize the changed faces of the old gardener and the old housekeeper, and to call them by name. My old nurse I knew at once. She had grown very gray since she heard the coffins fall in the nursery fifteen years before, but her strange eyes were the same, and the look in them woke all my old memories. She went over the house with me.

"And how is the Woman of the Water?" I asked, trying to laugh a little. "Does she still play in the moonlight?"

"She is hungry," answered the Welshwoman, in a low voice.

"Hungry? Then we will feed her." I laughed. But old Judith turned very pale, and looked at me strangely.

"Feed her? Aye—you will feed her well," she muttered, glancing behind her at the ancient housekeeper, who tottered after us with feeble steps through the halls and passages.

I did not think much of her words. She had always talked oddly, as Welshwomen will, and though I was very melancholy I am sure I was not superstitious, and I was certainly not timid. Only, as in a far-off dream, I seemed to see her standing with the light in her hand and muttering, "The heavy one—all of lead," and then leading a little boy through the long corridors to see his father lying dead in a great easy chair before a smouldering fire. So we went over the house, and I chose the rooms where I would live; and the servants I had brought with me ordered and arranged everything, and I had no more trouble. I did not care what they did provided I was left in peace and was not expected to give directions; for I was more listless than ever, owing to the effects of my illness at college.

I dined in solitary state, and the melancholy grandeur of the vast old dining-room pleased me. Then I went to the room I had selected for my study, and sat down in a deep chair, under a bright light, to think, or to let my thoughts meander through labyrinths of their own choosing, utterly indifferent to the course they might take.

The tall windows of the room opened to the level of the ground upon the terrace at the head of the garden. It was in the end of July, and everything was open, for the weather was warm. As I sat alone I heard the unceasing splash of the great fountains, and I fell to thinking of the Woman of the Water. I rose and went out into the still night, and sat down upon a seat on the terrace, between two gigantic Italian flower pots. The air was deliciously soft and sweet with the smell of the flowers, and the garden was more congenial to me than the house. Sad people always like running water and the sound of it at night, though I cannot tell why. I sat and listened in the gloom, for it was dark below, and the pale moon had not yet climbed over the hills in front of me, though all the air above was light with her rising beams.

Slowly the white halo in the eastern sky ascended in an arch

14

above the wooded crests, making the outlines of the mountains more intensely black by contrast, as though the head of some great white saint were rising from behind a screen in a vast cathedral, throwing misty glories from below. I longed to see the moon herself, and I tried to reckon the seconds before she must appear. Then she sprang up quickly, and in a moment more hung round and perfect in the sky. I gazed at her, and then at the floating spray of the tall fountains, and down at the pools, where the water lilies were rocking softly in their sleep on the velvet surface of the moonlit water. Just then a great swan floated out silently into the midst of the basin, and wreathed his long neck, catching the water in his broad bill, and scattering showers of diamonds around him.

Suddenly, as I gazed, something came between me and the light. I looked up instantly. Between me and the round disk of the moon rose a luminous face of a woman, with great strange eyes, and a woman's mouth, full and soft, but not smiling, hooded in black, staring at me as I sat still upon my bench. She was close to me— so close that I could have touched her with my hand. But I was transfixed and helpless. She stood still for a moment, but her expression did not change. Then she passed swiftly away, and my hair stood up on my head, while the cold breeze from her white dress was wafted to my temples as she moved. The moonlight, shining through the tossing spray of the fountain, made traceries of shadow on the gleaming folds of her garments. In an instant she was gone and I was alone.

I was strangely shaken by the vision, and some time passed before I could rise to my feet, for I was still weak from my illness, and the sight I had seen would have startled anyone. I did not reason with myself, for I was certain that I had looked on the unearthly, and no argument could have destroyed that belief. At last I got up and stood unsteadily, gazing in the direction in which I thought the face had gone; but there was nothing to be seen—nothing but the broad paths, the tall, dark evergreen hedges, the tossing water of the fountains and the smooth pool below. I fell back upon the seat and recalled the face I had seen.

Strange to say, now that the first impression had passed, there was nothing startling in the recollection; on the contrary, I felt that I was fascinated by the face, and would give anything to see it again. I could retrace the beautiful straight features, the long dark eyes, and the wonderful mouth most exactly in my mind, and when I had reconstructed every detail from memory I knew that the whole was beautiful, and that I should love a woman with such a face.

"I wonder whether she is the Woman of the Water!" I said to myself. Then rising once more, I wandered down the garden, descending one short flight of steps after another from terrace to terrace by the edge of the marble basins, through the shadow and through the moonlight; and I crossed the water by the rustic bridge above the artificial grotto, and climbed slowly up again to the highest terrace by the other side. The air seemed sweeter, and I was very calm, so that I think I smiled to myself as I walked, as though a new happiness had come to me. The woman's face seemed always before me, and the thought of it gave me an unwonted thrill of pleasure, unlike anything I had ever felt before.

I turned as I reached the house, and looked back upon the scene. It had certainly changed in the short hour since I had come out, and my mood had changed with it. Just like my luck, I thought, to fall in love with a ghost! But in old times I would have sighed, and gone to bed more sad than ever, at such a melancholy conclusion. Tonight I felt happy, almost for the first time in my life. The gloomy old study seemed cheerful when I went in. The old pictures on the walls smiled at me, and I sat down in my deep chair with a new and delightful sensation that I was not alone. The idea of having seen a ghost, and of feeling much the better for it, was so absurd that I laughed softly, as I took up one of the books I had brought with me and began to read.

That impression did not wear off. I slept peacefully, and in the morning I threw open my windows to the summer air and looked down at the garden, at the stretches of green and at the colored flower- beds, at the circling swallows and at the bright water.

"A man might make a paradise of this place," I exclaimed. "A man and a woman together!"

From that day the old castle no longer seemed gloomy, and I think I ceased to be sad; for some time, too, I began to take an interest in the place, and to try and make it more alive. I avoided my old Welsh nurse, lest she should damp my humor with some dismal prophecy, and recall my old self by bringing back memories of my dismal childhood. But what I thought of most was the ghostly figure I had seen in the garden that first night after my arrival. I went out every evening and wandered through the walks and paths; but, try as I might, I did not see my vision again. At last, after many days, the memory grew more faint, and my old moody nature gradually overcame the temporary sense of lightness I had experienced. The summer turned to autumn, and I grew restless. It began to rain. The dampness pervaded the gardens, and the outer halls smelled musty, like tombs; the gray sky oppressed me intolerably. I left the place as it was and went abroad, determined to try anything which might possibly make a second break in the monotonous melancholy from which I suffered.

2

Most people would be struck by the utter insignificance of the small events which, after the death of my parents, influenced my life and made me unhappy. The gruesome forebodings of a Welsh nurse, which chanced to be realized by an odd coincidence of events, should not seem enough to change the nature of a child and to direct the bent of his character in after years. The little disappointments of schoolboy life, and the somewhat less childish ones of an uneventful and undistinguished academic career, should not have sufficed to turn me out at one-and-twenty years of age a melancholic, listless idler. Some weakness of my own character may have contributed to the result, but in a greater degree it was due to my having a reputation for bad luck.

However, I will not try to analyze the causes of my state, for I should satisfy nobody, least of all myself. Still less will I attempt to explain why I felt a temporary revival of my spirits after my adventure in the garden. It is certain that I was in love with the face I had seen, and that I longed to see it again; that I gave up all hope of a second visitation, grew more sad than ever, packed up my traps, and finally went abroad. But in my dreams I went back to my home, and it always appeared to me sunny and bright, as it had looked on that summer's morning after I had seen the woman by the fountain.

I went to Paris. I went farther, and wandered about Germany. I tried to amuse myself, and I failed miserably. With the aimless whims of an idle and useless man come all sorts of suggestions for good resolutions. One day I made up my mind that I would go and bury myself in a German university for a time, and live simply like a poor student. I started with the intention of going to Leipzig, determined to stay there until some event should direct my life or change my humour, or make an end of me altogether. The express train stopped at some station of which I did not know the name. It was dusk on a winter's afternoon, and I peered through the thick glass from my seat.

Suddenly another train came gliding in from the opposite direction, and stopped alongside of ours. I looked at the carriage which chanced to be abreast of mine, and idly read the black letters painted on a white board swinging from the brass handrail: BERLIN—COLOGNE—PARIS. Then I looked up at the window above. I started violently, and the cold perspiration broke out upon my forehead. In the dim light, not six feet from where I sat, I saw the face of a woman, the face I loved, the straight, fine features, the strange eyes, the wonderful mouth, the pale skin. Her head-dress was a dark veil which seemed to be tied about her head and passed over the shoulders under her chin.

As I threw down the window and knelt on the cushioned seat, leaning far out to get a better view, a long whistle screamed through the station, followed by a quick series of dull, clanking sounds; then there was a slight jerk, and my train moved on. Luckily the window was narrow, being the one over the seat, beside the door, or I believe I would have jumped out of it then and there. In an instant the speed increased, and I was being carried swiftly away in the opposite direction from the thing I loved.

For a quarter of an hour I lay back in my place, stunned by the suddenness of the apparition. At last one of the two other passengers, a large and gorgeous captain of the White Konigsberg Cuirassiers, civilly but firmly suggested that I might shut my window, as the evening was cold. I did so, with an apology, and relapsed into silence. The train ran swiftly on for a long time, and it was already beginning to slacken speed before entering another station, when I roused myself and made a sudden resolution. As the carriage stopped before the brilliantly lighted platform, I seized my belongings, saluted my fellow-passengers, and got out, determined to take the first express back to Paris.

This time the circumstances of the vision had been so natural that it did not strike me that there was anything unreal about the face, or about the woman to whom it belonged. I did not try to explain to myself how the face, and the woman, could be travelling by a fast train from Berlin to Paris on a winter's afternoon, when both were in my mind indelibly associated with the moonlight and the fountains in my own English home. I certainly would not have admitted that I had been mistaken in the dusk, attributing to what I had seen a resemblance to my former vision which did not really exist.

There was not the slightest doubt in my mind, and I was positively sure that I had again seen the face I loved. I did not hesitate, and in a few hours I was on my way back to Paris. I could not help reflecting on my ill luck. Wandering as I had been for many months, it might as easily have chanced that I should be travelling in the same train with that woman, instead of going the other way. But my luck was destined to turn for a time.

I searched Paris for several days. I dined at the principal hotels; I went to the theatres; I rode in the Bois de Boulogne in the morning, and picked up an acquaintance, whom I forced to drive with me in the afternoon. I went to mass at the Madeleine, and I attended the services at the English Church. I hung about the Louvre and Notre Dame. I went to Versailles. I spent hours in parading the Rue de Rivoli, in the neighbourhood of Meurice's corner, where foreigners pass and repass from morning till night. At last I received an invitation to a reception at the English Embassy. I went, and I found what I had sought so long.

There she was, sitting by an old lady in gray satin and diamonds, who had a wrinkled but kindly face and keen gray eyes that seemed to take in everything they saw, with very little inclination to give much in return. But I did not notice the chaperon. I saw only the face that had haunted me for months, and in the excitement of the moment I walked quickly toward the pair, forgetting such a trifle as the necessity for an introduction.

She was far more beautiful than I had thought, but I never doubted that it was she herself and no other. Vision or no vision before, this was the reality, and I knew it. Twice her hair had been covered, now at last I saw it, and the added beauty of its magnificence glorified the whole woman. It was rich hair, fine and abundant, golden, with deep ruddy tints in it like red bronze spun fine. There was no ornament in it, not a rose, not a thread of gold, and I felt that it needed nothing to enhance its splendour; nothing but her pale face, her dark strange eyes, and her heavy eyebrows. I could see that she was slender too, but strong withal, as she sat there quietly gazing at the moving scene in the midst of the brilliant lights and the hum of perpetual conversation.

I recollected the detail of introduction in time, and turned aside to look for my host. I found him at last. I begged him to present me to the two ladies, pointing them out to him at the same time.

"Yes—uh—by all means—uh," replied his Excellency with a pleasant smile. He evidently had no idea of my name, which was not to be wondered at.

"I am Lord Cairngorm," I observed.

"Oh—by all means," answered the Ambassador with the same

hospitable smile. "Yes—uh—the fact is, I must try and find out who they are; such lots of people, you know."

"Oh, if you will present me, I will try and find out for you," said I, laughing.

"Ah, yes—so kind of you—come along," said my host. We threaded the crowd, and in a few minutes we stood before the two ladies.

"'Lowmintrduce L'd Cairngorm," he said; then, adding quickly to me, "Come and dine tomorrow, won't you?" he glided away with his pleasant smile and disappeared in the crowd.

I sat down beside the beautiful girl, conscious that the eyes of the *duenna* were upon me.

"I think we have been very near meeting before," I remarked, by way of opening the conversation.

My companion turned her eyes full upon me with an air of inquiry.

She evidently did not recall my face, if she had ever seen me.

"Really—I cannot remember," she observed, in a low and musical voice. "When?"

"In the first place, you came down from Berlin by the express ten days ago. I was going the other way, and our carriages stopped opposite each other. I saw you at the window."

"Yes—we came that way, but I do not remember—" She hesitated.

"Secondly," I continued, "I was sitting alone in my garden last summer—near the end of July—do you remember? You must have wandered in there through the park; you came up to the house and looked at me—"

"Was that you?" she asked, in evident surprise. Then she broke into a laugh. "I told everybody I had seen a ghost; there had never been any Cairngorms in the place since the memory of man. We left the next day, and never heard that you had come there; indeed, I did not know the castle belonged to you."

"Where were you staying?" I asked.

"Where? Why, with my aunt, where I always stay. She is your

neighbour, since it *is* you."

"I—beg your pardon—but then—is your aunt Lady Blue-bell? I did not quite catch—"

"Don't be afraid. She is amazingly deaf. Yes. She is the relict of my beloved uncle, the sixteenth or seventeenth Baron Bluebell—I forget exactly how many of them there have been. And I—do you know who I am?" She laughed, well knowing that I did not.

"No," I answered frankly. "I have not the least idea. I asked to be introduced because I recognized you. Perhaps—perhaps you are a Miss Bluebell?"

"Considering that you are a neighbour, I will tell you who I am," she answered. "No; I am of the tribe of Bluebells, but my name is Lammas, and I have been given to understand that I was christened Margaret. Being a floral family, they call me Daisy. A dreadful American man once told me that my aunt was a Bluebell and that I was a Harebell—with two l's and an e—because my hair is so thick. I warn you, so that you may avoid making such a bad pun."

"Do I look like a man who makes puns?" I asked, being very conscious of my melancholy face and sad looks.

Miss Lammas eyed me critically.

"No; you have a mournful temperament. I think I can trust you," she answered. "Do you think you could communicate to my aunt the fact that you are a Cairngorm and a neighbour? I am sure she would like to know."

I leaned toward the old lady, inflating my lungs for a yell. But Miss Lammas stopped me.

"That is not of the slightest use," she remarked. "You can write it on a bit of paper. She is utterly deaf."

"I have a pencil," I answered; "but I have no paper. Would my cuff do, do you think?"

"Oh, yes!" replied Miss Lammas, with alacrity; "men often do that."

I wrote on my cuff: "Miss Lammas wishes me to explain that I am your neighbour, Cairngorm." Then I held out my arm before the old lady's nose. She seemed perfectly accustomed to the proceeding, put up her glasses, read the words, smiled, nodded, and addressed me in the unearthly voice peculiar to people who hear nothing.

"I knew your grandfather very well," she said. Then she smiled and nodded to me again, and to her niece, and relapsed into silence.

"It is all right," remarked Miss Lammas. "Aunt Bluebell knows she is deaf, and does not say much, like the parrot. You see, she knew your grandfather. How odd that we should be neighbours! Why have we never met before?"

"If you had told me you knew my grandfather when you appeared in the garden, I should not have been in the least surprised," I answered rather irrelevantly. "I really thought you were the ghost of the old fountain. How in the world did you come there at that hour?"

"We were a large party and we went out for a walk. Then we thought we should like to see what your park was like in the moonlight, and so we trespassed. I got separated from the rest, and came upon you by accident, just as I was admiring the extremely ghostly look of your house, and wondering whether anybody would ever come and live there again. It looks like the castle of Macbeth, or a scene from the opera. Do you know anybody here?"

"Hardly a soul! Do you?"

"No. Aunt Bluebell said it was our duty to come. It is easy for her to go out; she does not bear the burden of the conversation."

"I am sorry you find it a burden," said I. "Shall I go away?"

Miss Lammas looked at me with a sudden gravity in her beautiful eyes, and there was a sort of hesitation about the lines of her full, soft mouth.

"No," she said at last, quite simply, "don't go away. We may like each other, if you stay a little longer—and we ought to, because we are neighbours in the country."

I suppose I ought to have thought Miss Lammas a very odd

girl. There is, indeed, a sort of freemasonry between people who discover that they live near each other and that they ought to have known each other before. But there was a sort of unexpected frankness and simplicity in the girl's amusing manner which would have struck anyone else as being singular, to say the least of it. To me, however, it all seemed natural enough. I had dreamed of her face too long not to be utterly happy when I met her at last and could talk to her as much as I pleased. To me, the man of ill luck in everything, the whole meeting seemed too good to be true.

I felt again that strange sensation of lightness which I had experienced after I had seen her face in the garden. The great rooms seemed brighter, life seemed worth living; my sluggish, melancholy blood ran faster, and filled me with a new sense of strength. I said to myself that without this woman I was but an imperfect being, but that with her I could accomplish everything to which I should set my hand. Like the great Doctor, when he thought he had cheated Mephistopheles at last, I could have cried aloud to the fleeting moment, *Verweile doch, du bist so schon!*

"Are you always gay?" I asked, suddenly. "How happy you must be!"

"The days would sometimes seem very long if I were gloomy," she answered, thoughtfully. "Yes, I think I find life very pleasant, and I tell it so."

"How can you 'tell life' anything?" I inquired. "If I could catch my life and talk to it, I would abuse it prodigiously, I assure you."

"I dare say. You have a melancholy temper. You ought to live out-of-doors, dig potatoes, make hay, shoot, hunt, tumble into ditches, and come home muddy and hungry for dinner. It would be much better for you than moping in your rook tower and hating everything."

"It is rather lonely down there," I murmured, apologetically, feeling that Miss Lammas was quite right.

"Then marry, and quarrel with your wife," she laughed. "Anything is better than being alone."

"I am a very peaceable person. I never quarrel with anybody. You can try it. You will find it quite impossible."

"Will you let me try?" she asked, still smiling.

"By all means—especially if it is to be only a preliminary canter," I answered, rashly.

"What do you mean?" she inquired, turning quickly upon me.

"Oh—nothing. You might try my paces with a view to quarrelling in the future. I cannot imagine how you are going to do it. You will have to resort to immediate and direct abuse."

"No. I will only say that if you do not like your life, it is your own fault. How can a man of your age talk of being melancholy, or of the hollowness of existence? Are you consumptive? Are you subject to hereditary insanity? Are you deaf, like Aunt Bluebell? Are you poor, like—lots of people? Have you been crossed in love? Have you lost the world for a woman, or any particular woman for the sake of the world? Are you feeble-minded, a cripple, an outcast? Are you—repulsively ugly?" She laughed again. "Is there any reason in the world why you should not enjoy all you have got in life?"

"No. There is no reason whatever, except that I am dreadfully unlucky, especially in small things."

"Then try big things, just for a change," suggested Miss Lammas. "Try and get married, for instance, and see how it turns out."

"If it turned out badly it would be rather serious."

"Not half so serious as it is to abuse everything unreasonably. If abuse is your particular talent, abuse something that ought to be abused. Abuse the Conservatives—or the Liberals—it does not matter which, since they are always abusing each other. Make yourself felt by other people. You will like it, if they don't. It will make a man of you. Fill your mouth with pebbles, and howl at the sea, if you cannot do anything else. It did Demosthenes no end of good, you know. You will have the satisfaction of imitating a great man."

"Really, Miss Lammas, I think the list of innocent exercises you propose—"

"Very well—if you don't care for that sort of thing, care for some other sort of thing. Care for something, or hate something. Don't be idle. Life is short, and though art may be long, plenty of noise answers nearly as well."

"I do care for something—I mean, somebody," I said.

"A woman? Then marry her. Don't hesitate."

"I do not know whether she would marry me," I replied. "I have never asked her."

"Then ask her at once," answered Miss Lammas. "I shall die happy if I feel I have persuaded a melancholy fellow creature to rouse himself to action. Ask her, by all means, and see what she says. If she does not accept you at once, she may take you the next time. Meanwhile, you will have entered for the race. If you lose, there are the 'All-aged Trial Stakes,' and the 'Consolation Race.'"

"And plenty of selling races into the bargain. Shall I take you at your word, Miss Lammas?"

"I hope you will," she answered.

"Since you yourself advise me, I will. Miss Lammas, will you do me the honour to marry me?"

For the first time in my life the blood rushed to my head and my sight swam. I cannot tell why I said it. It would be useless to try to explain the extraordinary fascination the girl exercised over me, or the still more extraordinary feeling of intimacy with her which had grown in me during that half hour. Lonely, sad, unlucky as I had been all my life, I was certainly not timid, nor even shy. But to propose to marry a woman after half an hour's acquaintance was a piece of madness of which I never believed myself capable, and of which I should never be capable again, could I be placed in the same situation. It was as though my whole being had been changed in a moment by magic—by the white magic of her nature brought into contact with mine. The blood sank back to my heart, and a moment later I found myself staring at her with anxious eyes. To my amazement she was as calm as ever, but her beautiful mouth smiled, and there was a mischievous light in her dark-brown eyes.

"Fairly caught," she answered. "For an individual who pretends to be listless and sad you are not lacking in humour. I had really not the least idea what you were going to say. Wouldn't it be singularly awkward for you if I had said 'Yes'? I never saw anybody begin to practice so sharply what was preached to him—with so very little loss of time!"

"You probably never met a man who had dreamed of you for seven months before being introduced."

"No, I never did," she answered gayly. "It smacks of the romantic. Perhaps you are a romantic character, after all. I should think you were if I believed you. Very well; you have taken my advice, entered for a Stranger's Race and lost it. Try the All-aged Trial Stakes. You have another cuff, and a pencil. Propose to Aunt Bluebell; she would dance with astonishment, and she might recover her hearing."

3

That was how I first asked Margaret Lammas to be my wife, and I will agree with anyone who says I behaved very foolishly. But I have not repented of it, and I never shall. I have long ago understood that I was out of my mind that evening, but I think my temporary insanity on that occasion has had the effect of making me a saner man ever since. Her manner turned my head, for it was so different from what I had expected. To hear this lovely creature, who, in my imagination, was a heroine of romance, if not of tragedy, talking familiarly and laughing readily was more than my equanimity could bear, and I lost my head as well as my heart. But when I went back to England in the spring, I went to make certain arrangements at the Castle—certain changes and improvements which would be absolutely necessary. I had won the race for which I had entered myself so rashly, and we were to be married in June.

Whether the change was due to the orders I had left with the gardener and the rest of the servants, or to my own state of mind, I cannot tell. At all events, the old place did not look the same to me when I opened my window on the morning after my arrival. There were the gray walls below me and the gray turrets flanking the huge building; there were the fountains, the marble causeways, the smooth basins, the tall box hedges, the water lilies and the swans, just as of old. But there was something else there, too—something in the air, in the water, and in the greenness that I did not recognize—a light over everything by which everything was transfigured. The clock in the tower struck seven, and the strokes of the ancient bell sounded like a wedding chime.

The air sang with the thrilling treble of the song-birds, with the silvery music of the plashing water and the softer harmony of the leaves stirred by the fresh morning wind. There was a smell of new-mown hay from the distant meadows, and of blooming roses from the beds below, wafted up together to my window. I stood in the pure sunshine and drank the air and all the sounds and the odours that were in it; and I looked down at my garden and said: "It is Paradise, after all." I think the men of old were right when they called heaven a garden, and Eden a garden inhabited by one man and one woman, the Earthly Paradise.

I turned away, wondering what had become of the gloomy memories I had always associated with my home. I tried to recall the impression of my nurse's horrible prophecy before the death of my parents—an impression which hitherto had been vivid enough. I tried to remember my old self, my dejection, my listlessness, my bad luck, my petty disappointments. I endeavoured to force myself to think as I used to think, if only to satisfy myself that I had not lost my individuality. But I succeeded in none of these efforts. I was a different man, a changed being, incapable of sorrow, of ill luck, or of sadness.

My life had been a dream, not evil, but infinitely gloomy and hopeless. It was now a reality, full of hope, gladness, and all manner of good. My home had been like a tomb; today it was Paradise. My heart had been as though it had not existed; today it beat with strength and youth and the certainty of realized happiness. I revelled in the beauty of the world, and called loveliness out of the future to enjoy it before time should bring it to me, as a traveller in the plains looks up to the mountains, and already tastes the cool air through the dust of the road.

Here, I thought, we will live and live for years. There we will sit by the fountain toward evening and in the deep moonlight. Down those paths we will wander together. On those benches we will rest and talk. Among those eastern hills we will ride through the soft twilight, and in the old house we will tell tales on winter nights, when the logs burn high, and the holly berries are red, and the old clock tolls out the dying year.

On these old steps, in these dark passages and stately rooms, there will one day be the sound of little pattering feet, and laughing child voices will ring up to the vaults of the ancient hall. Those tiny footsteps shall not be slow and sad as mine were, nor shall the childish words be spoken in an awed whisper. No gloomy Welshwoman shall people the dusky corners with weird horrors, nor utter horrid prophecies of death and ghastly things. All shall be young, and fresh, and joyful, and happy, and we will turn the old luck again, and forget that there was ever any sadness.

So I thought, as I looked out of my window that morning and for many mornings after that, and every day it all seemed more real than ever before, and much nearer. But the old nurse looked at me askance, and muttered odd sayings about the Woman of the Water. I cared little what she said, for I was far too happy.

At last the time came near for the wedding. Lady Bluebell and all the tribe of Bluebells, as Margaret called them, were at Bluebell Grange, for we had determined to be married in the country, and to come straight to the Castle afterwards. We cared little for travelling, and not at all for a crowded ceremony at St. George's in Hanover Square, with all the tiresome formalities afterwards. I used to ride over to the Grange every day, and very often Margaret would come with her aunt and some of her cousins to the Castle. I was suspicious of my own taste, and was only too glad to let her have her way about the alterations and improvements in our home.

We were to be married on the thirtieth of July, and on the evening of the twenty-eighth Margaret drove over with some of the Bluebell party. In the long summer twilight we all went out into the garden. Naturally enough, Margaret and I were left to ourselves, and we wandered down by the marble basins.

"It is an odd coincidence," I said; "it was on this very night last year that I first saw you."

"Considering that it is the month of July," answered Margaret with a laugh, "and that we have been here almost every day, I don't think the coincidence is so extraordinary, after all."

"No, dear," said I, "I suppose not. I don't know why it struck me. We shall very likely be here a year from today, and a year from that. The odd thing, when I think of it, is that you should be here at all. But my luck has turned. I ought not to think anything odd that happens now that I have you. It is all sure to be good."

"A slight change in your ideas since that remarkable perform-ance of yours in Paris," said Margaret. "Do you know, I thought you were the most extraordinary man I had ever met."

"I thought you were the most charming woman I had ever seen. I naturally did not want to lose any time in frivolities. I took you at your word, I followed your advice, I asked you to marry me, and this is the delightful result—what's the matter?"

Margaret had started suddenly, and her hand tightened on my arm. An old woman was coming up the path, and was close to us before we saw her, for the moon had risen, and was shining full in our faces. The woman turned out to be my old nurse.

"It's only Judith, dear—don't be frightened," I said. Then I spoke to the Welshwoman: "What are you about, Judith? Have you been feeding the Woman of the Water?"

"Aye—when the clock strikes, Willie—my Lord, I mean," muttered the old creature, drawing aside to let us pass, and fix-ing her strange eyes on Margaret's face.

"What does she mean?" asked Margaret, when we had gone by.

"Nothing, darling. The old thing is mildly crazy, but she is a good soul."

We went on in silence for a few moments, and came to the rustic bridge just above the artificial grotto through which the water ran out into the park, dark and swift in its narrow channel. We stopped, and leaned on the wooden rail. The moon was now behind us, and shone full upon the long *vista* of basins and on the huge walls and towers of the Castle above.

"How proud you ought to be of such a grand old place!" said Margaret, softly.

"It is yours now, darling," I answered. "You have as good a right to love it as I—but I only love it because you are to live in it, dear."

Her hand stole out and lay on mine, and we were both silent. Just then the clock began to strike far off in the tower. I counted— eight—nine—ten—eleven—I looked at my watch—twelve—thirteen—I laughed. The bell went on striking.

"The old clock has gone crazy, like Judith," I exclaimed. Still it went on, note after note ringing out monotonously through the still air. We leaned over the rail, instinctively looking in the direction whence the sound came. On and on it went. I counted nearly a hundred, out of sheer curiosity, for I understood that something had broken and that the thing was running itself down.

Suddenly there was a crack as of breaking wood, a cry and a heavy splash, and I was alone, clinging to the broken end of the rail of the rustic bridge.

I do not think I hesitated while my pulse beat twice. I sprang clear of the bridge into the black rushing water, dived to the bottom, came up again with empty hands, turned and swam downward through the grotto in the thick darkness, plunging and diving at every stroke, striking my head and hands against jagged stones and sharp corners, clutching at last something in my fingers and dragging it up with all my might. I spoke, I cried aloud, but there was no answer. I was alone in the pitchy darkness with my burden, and the house was five hundred yards away. Struggling still, I felt the ground beneath my feet, I saw a ray of

31

moonlight—the grotto widened, and the deep water became a broad and shallow brook as I stumbled over the stones and at last laid Margaret's body on the bank in the park beyond.

"Aye, Willie, as the clock struck!" said the voice of Judith, the Welsh nurse, as she bent down and looked at the white face. The old woman must have turned back and followed us, seen the accident, and slipped out by the lower gate of the garden. "Aye," she groaned, "you have fed the Woman of the Water this night, Willie, while the clock was striking."

I scarcely heard her as I knelt beside the lifeless body of the woman I loved, chafing the wet white temples and gazing wildly into the wide-staring eyes. I remember only the first returning look of consciousness, the first heaving breath, the first movement of those dear hands stretching out toward me.

That is not much of a story, you say. It is the story of my life. That is all. It does not pretend to be anything else. Old Judith says my luck turned on that summer's night when I was struggling in the water to save all that was worth living for. A month later there was a stone bridge above the grotto, and Margaret and I stood on it and looked up at the moonlit castle, as we had done once before, and as we have done many times since. For all those things happened ten years ago last summer, and this is the tenth Christmas Eve we have spent together by the roaring logs in the old hall, talking of old times; and every year there are more old times to talk of. There are curly-headed boys, too, with red-gold hair and dark-brown eyes like their mother's, and a little Margaret, with solemn black eyes like mine. Why could not she look like her mother, too, as well as the rest of them?

The world is very bright at this glorious Christmas time, and perhaps there is little use in calling up the sadness of long ago, unless it be to make the jolly firelight seem more cheerful, the good wife's face look gladder, and to give the children's laughter a merrier ring, by contrast with all that is gone. Perhaps, too, some sad-faced, listless, melancholy youth, who feels that the world is very hollow, and that life is like a perpetual funeral service, just as I used to feel myself, may take courage from my example, and having found the woman of his heart, ask her to marry him after half an hour's acquaintance. But, on the whole, I would not advise any man to marry, for the simple reason that no man will ever find a wife like mine, and being obliged to go farther, he will necessarily fare worse. My wife has done miracles, but I will not assert that any other woman is able to follow her example.

Margaret always said that the old place was beautiful, and that I ought to be proud of it. I dare say she is right. She has even more imagination than I. But I have a good answer and a plain one, which is this,—that all the beauty of the castle comes from her. She has breathed upon it all, as the children blow upon the cold glass window panes in winter; and as their warm breath crystallizes into landscapes from fairyland, full of exquisite shapes and traceries upon the blank surface, so her spirit has transformed every gray stone of the old towers, every ancient tree and hedge in the gardens, every thought in my once melancholy self. All that was old is young, and all that was sad is glad, and I am the gladdest of all. Whatever heaven may be, there is no earthly paradise without woman, nor is there anywhere a place so desolate, so dreary, so unutterably miserable that a woman cannot make it seem heaven to the man she loves and who loves her.

I hear certain cynics laugh, and cry that all that has been said before. Do not laugh, my good cynic. You are too small a man to laugh at such a great thing as love. Prayers have been said before now by many, and perhaps you say yours, too. I do not think they lose anything by being repeated, nor you by repeating them. You say that the world is bitter, and full of the Waters of Bitterness. Love, and so live that you may be loved—the world will turn sweet for you, and you shall rest like me by the Waters of Paradise.

The Captain's Bride

By Laurence Alma Tadema

So Christmas is near, and you ask me to keep it with you, little cousin. May I thank you, and stay at home! I shall keep Christmas with my folk. I know what you are saying; yes, they are dead, yet in thought I can be with them, and short is the bridge of hours that parts mo from them now. I, too, have reached the winter of my life; the year and I are of an age. What though the blossoms of May bore no fruit? I had my spring; blighted and dark, summer was summer still; and the autumn leaves fell thick at the door of the bare gamer. Now Christmas comes, and I must feast it; then prepare—like the year—soon to lay down my worn old life in peace, making way for a glad, new soul; perhaps a soul that shall be part of yours. Who knows, but God? Child, you are young and I am old, yet we are closely linked; the love that has come to change your life has brought you very near to me, for love knows neither youth nor age. I remember that I promised once—it was the day you first spoke to me of James —to tell you my tale; and I have a mind to do so now. I will keep Christmas with my folk.

My father was made Vicar of Longparish the year that I was born, and the year following my mother died; so father's sister, Aunt Sophia, came to us then, and tended both for many a year. My early recollections are of the simplest, for we lived a plain life among poor and toiling people, whose lives, if possible, were plainer still than ours. I never set foot on an unfamiliar road, and all the faces I ever saw had looked upon me in my cradle. I was a lonely child, and, not being troublesome, was reputed good; there is no better substitute for virtue in the world than absence of vice.

My worst fault in Aunt Sophia's eyes was apparently an early fancy that I had for playing with flowers, wrapping their stalks in scraps of stuff and pretending they were little girls; for I remember that when she came upon me in the garden one day, keeping a rose-bud school, and found that the plucked blossoms were her own—that I had, moreover, tied round their waists the worsteds that should have decked my sampler—she not merely threw my flower-children straight into the river, but whipped me for the only time in my life. My taste in playmates was altogether singular: we lived by the church, and I was accustomed to seek the graves of the children who had died at my age, visiting them daily. I firmly believed that because I loved them they would ask God to make me good; and I hardly care to say how long I cherished the ample faith.

This natural capacity for self-amusement was cultivated by Aunt Sophia, whose aim in life did not go beyond the fulfilment of her household and neighbourly duties; as regarded me; she satisfied her conscience by scolding me mildly on occasions, teaching me my alphabet, my catechism, and the use of the needle, and washing my face whenever I crossed her path. For the rest, I was suffered to live my selfish little life in perfect freedom. Father spoiled me, and took it for granted that I was as I should be. He was a hard-worked man, I his relaxation; and it probably never entered his head that he might have as good a hand as Aunt Sophia in my upraising. He saw in me a plaything, not a miniature woman whose small but eager spirit was beginning to peer with semi-conscious eyes into the book of life.

So I grew up an untrimmed weed, useless and wayward. I had early made up my mind that if—to be good—a woman must be forever teaching Betsy, stitching or dusting, wielding a rolling-pin or a flat-iron, I should not even aspire to any high degree of moral excellence; therefore I displayed only just as much industry as was needful for the securing of my character, and consequently of my freedom. I was not happy, because my neglected mind was clogged with the doubts of years, and because I loved no fellow-creature above myself; but the cause of my discontent was as yet unknown to me, for I had not felt the emptiness of my heart.

When I was sixteen Aunt Sophia fell ill, and this event brought to light the unsuspected deficiencies of my education. She was bedridden for many weeks, during which the vicarage was in a state of anarchy; for I was totally incapable of doing anything that had to be done, save that—in spite of inexperience—I nursed my poor aunt with a tenderness that won me her deep affection. When convalescent she was able to assist me by her counsel; but she never grew strong, and died in the spring, leaving me to mourn her loss and the wasted years of our estrangement. She could, I know, never have satisfied my deeper cravings, for she was accustomed to knead her daily bread in perfect unconsciousness that life held anything more intricate than dough; yet, had she lived, the first years of my womanhood had been less difficult. Father was very kind to me, and put up so patiently with my shortcomings that my zeal grew great.

My eighteenth birthday found me a good housewife, and a sober, thoughtful little woman; nor was that all, for I had meantime earned the good-will of our neighbours and—more precious still—my father's confidence and heart-whole affection. How I in my turn cherished him I cannot say; sincerely, I did not think there was room in me for any other love. He would often tease me by speaking of the future, whereupon I invariably assured him that I should never marry; and, indeed, I did something toward keeping my word in refusing the hand of a certain wealthy young mill-owner, William Carter by name, to whom I afterward owed a most unreasonable grudge for having attempted to draw me from father's side. But in the summer of that year came a change.

At the farther end of our valley there lived a dear woman to whom we were much attached. Miss Dell lived alone, the orphan brothers she had reared having left her to follow their own paths; and we heard one day that Arthur, her youngest and dearest, had been killed in action. So I went, the next afternoon, to bring her our sorrow. I found her on the doorstep, and beside her a young man, a stranger. He stepped aside to let me pass; and Miss Dell, having kissed me, turned to him with moist eyes.

"Goodbye, Captain Charvel," said she. "God bless you for your kindness to my poor boy!"

"Goodbye" he replied, smiling; "but it's for a very short while, Miss Dell; I shall pass here next month, when I leave my mother."

"Thank you," she said; "then it shall not be 'goodbye.'"

The young man bowed and went; but, as luck would have it, he turned to look back over the hedge; and there was I, tiptoe on the doorstep like a fool, looking over the hedge at him. I blushed for this all the way home; and at supper that night, when father taxed me for my silence, I discovered that I was still thinking of the young man. However, when I saw the prosy daylight flooding my prosy little room next morning, I was rather inclined to laugh at my momentary foolishness.

About four weeks later I determined to visit Miss Dell again, and was so long over my simple toilet that if anyone had seen me they must have laughed. I should even have gone in my best bonnet, had I not found myself creeping downstairs like a thief to avoid the inquisitive eye of Betsy; whereupon I was so ashamed that I went back and laid aside my finery. Miss Dell was alone, and we sat down to tea together, I being in the worst of humours; for it was now clear to me that I had hoped to see Captain Charvel, and that I was bitterly disappointed. I remember it all well. The sun was hot, but Miss Dell had no taste for fresh air, so she let the burning rays pour through her speckless panes into the stuffy little parlour, on to the wintry carpet and multitudinous beaded chairs, the faded walls studded with pictures, and the myriad china figures, crystals, and sea-shells that swarmed on table, bracket, ledge, and sill.

Miss Dell was serving me a second cup when the bell rang, and I upset my chair, so swiftly did I run to the window.

"Miss Dell," cried I, conscious of a sudden pallor, "it's a gentleman; I think it's the one who came last month." And, before I could look indifferent, my hand was in his.

At the end of an hour Captain Charvel's features were still unknown to me, for I had not the courage to look him in the face; but the carpet at his feet, the chair he sat on, his chain, his waistcoat, and above all his hands, are still indelible in my mind's eye; while the sound of his voice sank into me. And I stayed above an hour.

Although addressing both, Captain Charvel had at first faced me rather than Miss Dell, and I suspected—nay, I was convinced—that he tried his utmost to make me raise my eyes. In all else I was obedient: I laughed when he laughed; if he shifted his chair, I found myself turning; but higher than his collar I would not look. So he presently stood up, and, sitting opposite Miss Dell, who was working in the window, gave his whole attention to her tapestry. The consequence was that I lifted my head and looked at his handsome profile, clearly cut against the sunny pane; I looked again and again, each time more lengthily, and at last, when my heart was in my gaze, what must he do but turn suddenly with a bright smile that made my blood rush, and so fix his clear blue eyes on me that I could not set mine free, but, conquered, sat there impotent with quivering lip, till he had drawn my very soul away. Then I rose abruptly, and, bending over the mantelshelf, let a scalding tear of shame fall into the lap of a china shepherdess. It was so long before I recovered, that I had not the courage to turn round again until Miss Dell called me to admire her work, after which I took leave and went with all imaginable awkwardness. I had not reached the gate when Captain Charvel came after me.

"Miss Nobel," said he, "you have left your mittens; at least, one."

I received the relic with a violent blush, for I knew I had dropped both, and could only suppose that he had kept the other.

"Goodbye," said I, and would have fled, but he held my hand.

"We shall not meet for a year," said he; "will you remember me then?"

"Of course," I stammered, "I never forget anybody."

"Very well," he replied, "I shall come back."

I looked up for an instant, but I saw nothing; and we parted.

To all outward appearance, the months that followed differed in no way from the preceding, yet, to me, the whole world bore a new aspect. I never slept but Captain Charvel was my last thought, never began a day without blessing him. My secret was not hard to keep, for at nineteen the heart is buoyant, and hope a constant guest; it was only at times that the high tide of my love rose and bore down the barriers of patience, and then it was as much as I could do not to confess all. That father and I should live our lives face to face, he ignoring, I concealing, the first object of my existence, caused me remorse and pain. But instinct told me that this surrender of my being to one I had twice met would be incomprehensible to father; and I shrank from exposing to light treatment—even at the hands of one so dear—the most vital portion of my heart.

As for Miss Dell, the windows of her mind resembled ground glass: let in what light one would, she was incapable of discerning anything. I often went to see her, and would sometimes make bold to ask if she had heard from Captain Charvel; she never had heard, and indeed I soon found that she knew nothing about him, beyond the fact that he had been her brother's best friend, and had twice visited her in accordance with a promise made to his dead comrade. Once, however, she found mention of him in an old letter of Arthur Dell's, in which he said that Charvel was more petted by the women, wherever they went, than any man in the regiment. I did not much relish this news.

Another time she told me that his name was William, and although I had hitherto hated the name, I now canonized it, making myself forget that it also belonged to the irrepressible admirer whose obstinate attentions continued to vex me. It must have been about this time, by the way, that the young man took to sending me weekly nosegays, I was too fond of flowers to destroy them, yet I did not wish him to see them about when he called, so I kept them in gallipots in the attic.

One night father felt a pain in his side, and, being as nervous as most men, began to fear that his heart was diseased; which, thank Heaven, was not the case. However, he was fidgety for some time, and my future loneliness, should he be taken from me, troubled him considerably. Therefore, as we sat by the fire after supper one March evening, he said suddenly:

"Pussy, how old are you!"

"Not twenty yet, father."

"That's none too young to marry," answered he. "I should like to see you married, Pussy;" and he backed his desire by many good reasons, even speaking well of William Garter. I listened patiently, then—

"Father," said I, "I couldn't marry him," and my head sank. "I don't think I shall ever marry."

"Tut, tut," said he, "that nonsense, that's childish, that's carrying your love for me too far, my pet. You see, Pussy, fathers can't live forever. I value this love above all things, Mary, but believe me, you're mistaken. You can find room for another in your heart, my dear child; yes, and for more to follow."

"Words cannot express the prickings of my conscience. I just fell on my knees beside him and burst into tears.

"Father," I cried, "dear, dearest father, I do love you, but I have been very deceitful I know there's room for two, you and another—and—he's there already, father!"

No answer. I pressed his hand, no return; and when I ventured to look at him, he was sitting as stiff as pride, with the eyes of a judge and the mouth of a martyr. Presently he rose, and walked round the table.

"I'm surprised," said he, "I'm surprised; don't speak to me."

So I sat still, and had completely dried my tears, when he came and stood behind me.

"I never could understand women," said he, dryly. "If you love him—and I'm bound to believe you—why don't you have him?"

"Why don't I have him? Why, father, he may have forgotten me, for all I know!"

Father stared and I stared, then I began to laugh, for I saw he was thinking of Will Carter; so, mustering my courage, I drew him to a chair, and told him what I could about Captain Charvel.

"My dear child," said he, when I had finished, "I'm sorry for you. You've shown yourself less prudent than I thought; but rest assured the young man's forgotten you by now, so there's an end of it."

"Yes," I sighed, "I suppose he has forgotten me! But that makes no difference."

"How makes no difference? My dear Mary, I can't answer you; you're not serious. It's impossible that a good, sensible young woman like you can make herself believe she cares as much for a strange man she knows nothing about, as for the father she has known all her life. Do you mean to say that you would leave me for that soldier, that white-washed ne'er-do-well?"

"Of course, father," said I, in a peace-making tone, "I should never leave you altogether."

"Still, you would leave me, and for him? That's enough. My dear Mary, you surprise me. You allow yourself to openly love a man you've twice met, to take possession of him, to place him above me. I can only say that to my mind you are neither wise nor modest No, certainly not modest. If I believed you, I should be truly grieved."

"What!" I cried. "Do you doubt my word? I tell you that Captain Charvel is not only the best and handsomest man God ever made, but that I love him with all my soul, and that unless I marry him I shall die as I am!" Whereupon I bounced out of the room.

The following day, father and I were chilly; we spoke of the weather and of our neighbours, but never an intimate word; and a longer evening I never spent, although we went to bed at nine o'clock for very dullness.

So at breakfast next morning I put out his favourite jam, and decked the table with his favourite flowers, and gave the warmest return pride would allow to his bleak kiss; but when we had half done, and yet no word, my heart sank. Suddenly father pushed his cup toward me.

"Pussy," said he, breaking the silence with a cheerfulness that startled me, "that tea was nice. I'll have some more;" and he began, "All in the Downs the fleet was moored."

I did not often sing at meals, still I joined in as best I could, until my voice broke in the very middle of "sweet William." And thus our quarrel ended; nor did we mention Captain Charvel again.

One Sunday, early in June, I was waiting for father in the churchyard after service, while he spoke to a parishioner; and although accustomed to his being thus detained weekly, by the time I had watched the last loiterer go in to dinner, I was weary, and fell to pacing up and down. And chancing to look up as I approached the road, I saw a man leaning over the hedge with his eyes fixed upon me. For an instant I did not know him, then I found myself trembling; it was Captain Charvel.

"Oh," said I, "it's you."

"Yes," he replied, "and a little before my time, Miss Nobel. It is not quite a year since we parted."

I said, "Oh, isn't it?" but he must have known that this was no news to me. Although agitated past all control, I did not think to say good-day and retire; foolishly heroic, I stood before him, and looked at my feet while he looked at me. Presently he asked—

"How is Miss Dell!"

"I don't know," said I, "aren't you staying there?"

"No," he replied, "I'm at the 'Cock and Bull.' I haven't come to see Miss Bell."

I almost think I should have fled if father had not that instant arrived. He glanced at me critically, then turned to the captain, and they exchanged salutations with evident mutual interest.

"Father," I mumbled, "it's a friend of Miss Dell's—Cap— Captain Charvel."

"Sir," said dear father, pompously, "I'm delighted to meet you.

If you are staying at Longparish, we shall hope to see you at the vicarage. Pussy, won't you ask Captain Charvel to tea?"

"Oh, yes," said I; but here followed an alarming pause, to which Captain Charvel put an end by accepting with alacrity the invitation he had not received.

They were happy days that followed. If I suffered some misery, it was only of the kind bestowed by an all-wise Providence on those who have much joy, lest they should forget Heaven. Captain Charvel came daily at father's request, and this in itself was bliss; but, as day followed day and yet he scarcely spoke to me, I grew uneasy. Father's vigilance was as great as any woman's; he never left us alone for two minutes together, and but for this I should almost have thought he did not know that—in my estimation—Captain Charvel was not as most men. He spoke of him ever as of one hitherto a stranger, and indeed went so far as to ask my pardon once for having spoiled our pleasant solitary life by his constant company, assuring me that the conversation of so intelligent a young man was beneficial to him. However, in spite of doubt and silence, I could not help feeling that Captain Charvel cared for me a little; nor could I meet his eyes without being conscious of some exchange between us; how greatly to his gain, Heaven only knew.

And three weeks passed. One afternoon, having left Captain Charvel and father together, I went to visit a sick woman down the valley; and while I sat by her bedside, reading, one of her children ran to me in great haste: someone was waiting for me downstairs, would I come? So I slipped on my bonnet and ran out with my cape in my hand. It was Captain Charvel.

"Is anything the matter?" cried I, when we got into the road; "father isn't ill, is he? What does he want me for?"

The captain smiled.

"I don't know," said he, "I daresay your father does want you, but I'm not aware of the fact. It is I that want you."

I turned giddy, and my fingers shook so that I could not fasten my cape; seeing which, Captain Charvel stood still and hooked it for me. I was wretched, for he took ever so much longer about it than need have been, and he must have felt how I trembled.

"Miss Nobel," said he, on the road, "I'm afraid you don't like me."

"Yes, I do," was my reply, "I always like people."

"You must be very happy, then. I like but few."

"Isn't that rather selfish!" I ventured to remark.

"Of course it is, but I can't help being selfish; I've been lonely nearly all my life."

"Oh," said I, feeling that I must say something quickly, "I did not know that men minded being lonely."

He slackened speed a little.

"Have you never felt," said he, "that your life was incomplete?"

"Yes," I whispered, "often."

"Well, so have I. Remember, Miss Nobel, that men and women are each but one half of a perfect whole, needing the other for their own completeness. A single life is but a fragment."

"Oh, I don't see that," I answered, hurriedly, "I think I could live alone quite well. I should very much like to live alone and be a schoolmistress."

"No," said Captain Charvel, "you would not."

"You don't know," I replied; "it would only need a little courage, ambition, and self-reliance."

"Well and good; but you forget that a woman's courage, ambition, and reliance usually end in being transplanted. Woman's virtues seldom blossom in their own soil, and the man who has her heart has all; for him she is brave, for him aspiring, and her trust is placed in him."

"Perhaps," said I; but I knew he was right, and wondered where he had learned this truth. Presently I noticed that we were going out of our way.

"Don't you think," I timidly suggested, "that we had best keep to the road! It's getting late."

"It won't be dark for another hour," said Captain Charvel positively; "you're not afraid, are you? With me?"

"No," I replied, "I'm not afraid," which was not strictly truthful, considering how I feared him, "but father, he mayn't like my being out so late."

"Very well," said he, "I'm sorry you don't like being with me; we'll go back." Which we did, to my inconceivable disappointment. I walked as slowly as possible, hoping he might repent; and at last (I really could not help it) I said—

"Captain Charvel! Perhaps father wouldn't mind."

He turned on his heel that instant.

"Of course he won't mind," said he. "Your father would trust you anywhere with me. Your father likes me very much, Miss Nobel; he would be very hardhearted if he didn't, don't you think?"

I tried to laugh because I thought I must; then I said: "I don't see why."

"You don't see why? I think I've done my best to make him like me." And I began to feel sorry we had come the long way, after all. It must have been soon after this that I stepped into a ditch and twisted my ankle; slightly, to be sure, yet enough to make me limp.

"I think you'd better take my arm," said Captain Charvel. I had not the strength to refuse, but I gave him the veriest tips of my fingers.

"Why, this won't support you," laughed he; laying hold of my hand, he drew it well through his arm, and kept it there with firm but gentle pressure.

I was so much alarmed that I just pretended not to notice what he did, but at every step I felt my face glow redder, and it seemed an eternity that passed. Suddenly he let me go, and I stumbled with a strange sense of loss; but in an instant his arm was round my waist.

There was no ignoring this; if Captain Charvel had been William Carter I could not have struggled more frantically for freedom, and the consequence was that he folded me in both his arms and held me to him, quenching me utterly, so that when he presently bade me lift my head I had not the power to disobey. And if any part of my immortal spirit were not his already, I think he took it from me at that moment.

We did not say much going home; but when we reached the field behind the vicarage I asked him to leave me, that I might tell father alone; and, after much protest, he consented, having first extorted from me an avowal that I loved him—which I told him was wasting breath, since I had loved him long before he ever cared for me. Of course, being a man, he denied this.

"You are an angel," said he, "but you must not speak so. If I had not loved you in the beginning, you would never have thought of me again."

I did not tell him that it was just the other way round; I only said that he was very conceited even to think of such things, and we parted as gayly as possible.

Our wedding-day was fixed for the first of September, and the weeks that intervened sped fast. Miss Dell came to stay at the vicarage on purpose to help me with my clothes. Indeed, I should never have got on alone, for although I kept my thimble on all day, it did not follow that Captain Charvel allowed me to use it. I took him to see all the people I knew. I was sinfully proud of him, and thought that every woman in the parish must grow green with jealousy when she set eyes on his beautiful face. It came to my ears one day that many laughed at me, and said one would think from my behaviour that Captain Charvel had walked out of heaven.

But I was not cross; I only thought them rather wicked. I must confess, however, that I was not quite happy; I grudged him every moment of absence; he could not keep away an hour at a stretch but I was in a fever of apprehension; and one day I unfortunately saw him talking to the barmaid of the "Hare and Hounds," a remarkably pretty girl, on whom he was bestowing rather more attention than I found needful. That very afternoon he chanced to ask if there were anything about him that displeased me, vowing that he would instantly reform; and what must I do but beg him not to smile at the barmaid again.

"Mary!" he exclaimed with such solemnity that I flinched,

46

"you're not going to tell me that you're jealous?"

"Of course not," said I, "I'm not at all jealous, William, but I—I can't help wanting all your smiles for the present. I dare say I shall be less fussy when we're married. And oh," I added, hiding my face, "I'm in such mortal fear sometimes lest you should not love me after all, or grow tired of me."

He did not answer, and presently I said, without looking up:

"Did you ever love another, William? I don't expect you to tell me if you'd rather not, but—I wonder."

"My dear Mary," he replied, almost sternly, "what a child you are. Of course, if I had ever loved another as I love you, you could not be Mrs. Charvel. But you surely don't suppose that a man can live twenty-five years without seeing a woman that pleases him?"

"No," said I, mournfully; "I suppose not. I'm not jealous, William."

"But you are," retorted he, "and this is terrible. A woman must be all trust and belief. A jealous woman—"

"But, William, I'm not jealous! Only don't you think you might feel funny if you saw me stand five minutes—it was quite five minutes—talking to—to the hostler? And smiling, too, like I smile at you? Perhaps you wouldn't, but I like to think you would."

"That's different," he replied; "a man must be jealous, a woman may not."

"Oh," cried I, "that's unfair. We poor women, how you treat us!"

"Silly Mary!" said he then; "it is because you are better than we that we expect you to conform to a higher standard. Always yield, always believe; that is how wives keep their husbands. But," added he, smiling suddenly, "you're not going to be a jealous wife! Come what may, you would always forgive me, and that's why I love you. Don't try to say No—you would."

"We'll see," said I, "or rather, we won't, please God. But oh, you are conceited, Captain Charvel!"

I remember that I asked him, later, if he would forgive me,

were there need; and he answered:

"No, by Heaven!" But it was half in jest.

The weeks passed rapidly. Toward the end of August Captain Charvel left Longparish to visit his mother, intending to return on the eve of our marriage. I thought I should be miserable without him, and so I was, in a way. Yet I enjoyed the last quiet days with father in my dear home. The thirty-first of August found all ready, and my wedding-dress spread under a sheet on the spare-room bed. Father and I meant to take a last walk together in the afternoon, but he was called away; so I went out alone into the fields, pondering over the past, and filled with a fluttering joy that nothing could quell. I dared not go far, lest Captain Charvel should arrive in my absence.

I was resting on a stile, my eyes fixed on the church and my thoughts on the future, when, hearing footsteps behind me, I turned and saw a woman cross the meadow. She was apparently a little older than I, young and fair, buxom and neat; her shoes were white with dust, and she had probably come from far, but her lilac print dress was scrupulously clean; a large straw hat was hanging down her back; in one hand she carried a bundle, in the other a green umbrella. I can see her still. What struck me most was the stolid determination of her walk. She looked weary but unconquerable, and her honest face bore a smile of radiant joy.

"Miss," said she as she approached, "is that Longparish Church?"

"Yes," I replied. "But you are out breath; there is room for two on the stile."

The girl sat down, and, drawing a white handkerchief from the bundle, wiped her rosy cheeks.

"I'm hot," said she," I've come a good bit of a way."

"Where from?" asked I.

"From Stonyhead."

"From the sea?" I cried; "not today?"

"Bless you, no!" laughed the girl. "It's three days since I started."

"Oh, how dreadful," said I. "I hope you've had plenty to

eat?"

She shook her head and smiled to herself.

"Thank you. It's not in want of food that I am; it's my heart that is hungry for the sight of a face."

There was something inexpressibly tender in the tone of the girl's voice that went to my heart. I begged her to come home with me and rest.

"I'm not tired, Miss," she replied. "You're very good to me. But my sweetheart lives here, and I've come to fetch him."

"Oh," cried I then, beaming with sympathy, "I'm waiting for my sweetheart! I'm going to be married tomorrow, and you must come to the wedding."

The girl looked solemn.

"It is not I," she said, "that know when mine will be."

In the face of my own happiness I could not bear to see another mournful, so I gently touched her brown hand.

"Aren't you happy?" asked I; "aren't you sure of him? I dare say it's no use asking, but I should like to help you if I could. I want everyone in Longparish to be happy tomorrow."

Tears started to her eyes, and I was silent awhile, regretting my words; then I said gently:

"How long is it since you saw him?"

This sympathy seemed to melt the girl; she dropped her bundle and drew nearer.

"Miss," she said, "you are very kind! And since you know what it is to love a man, and since you wish to hear, shall I tell you?"

It was not a long tale. Her name was Susan Wood, and her father had been a coast-guard at Stonyhead. There was a rich family on the cliff, a lonely boy that stole down when he dared, to play with Susan. They were nearly of an age, but she was sturdier than he; and once—they were children then—she wrestled with the waves for his dear life. The boy told his father, who gave the girl a guinea and forbade all future intercourse between them; but still they met almost daily, the lad escaping from his tutor at every opportunity to visit his playmate by the sea, his preserver, the only young creature that brightened his austere young life. And, as year followed year, their love grew to passion. They were no longer children; and the father, seeing a figure scale the wall one night, hastened to the cliff and beheld his son in the arms of the coast-guard's daughter. So the youth was banished. "Susan," cried he at parting, "come what may you are my wife. Always trust, through silence and through ill-report. It may be for years, but keep faith; I am yours only."

He sent her gold and gifts from foreign lands, and letters full of deep affection. When they ceased, the coast-guard thought him dead, but the girl still hoped. His family had left Stonyhead. It was a servant of his mother's, returning home for a while, who told Susan her lover was alive; she had seen letters addressed to him at Longparish.

We were both silent at the close of the tale, then I said—

"Susan, you have been beautifully faithful. I hope he is worthy of you."

The girl laughed.

"He worthy! I worthy, you mean. I'm a common girl, but he loves me, and I'd work my fingers to the marrow for him. Oh, I cannot doubt! I have his word."

I doubted; yet I can say with truth that I was wholly free from presentiment. She spoke of "him," and I understood and respected that, dislike to uttering a lover's name; I was besides—and this must be confessed—too full of my own thoughts for sympathy to descend to inquisitiveness. I rose and kissed the girl.

"Bless you, Susan," said I, "I hope you will be happy. We must be friends." And I asked her once more to take tea with me.

She would not, she must seek him.

"Then I must leave you," said I; "or if you'll come across we can go together. But we must make haste; see! 'tis six o'clock, and Captain Charvel—that's my sweetheart, Susan—may have come."

I was looking toward home; but, hearing no word, turned to my new friend. She was standing just behind me, upright with hanging arms, her gray eyes staring, her flesh colourless. And then I knew.

Speechless we stood before each other, gazing with horror at the wreck of our lives. Her lips quivered.

"The name," she muttered, "the name." And suddenly she seized me by the shoulders. "The name!" she cried; "speak!"

But I uttered no sound, and she let me go. I fell against the hedge; the girl was at my feet.

"Miss," she breathed, "it is not Charvel, not William Charvel, not my Will that I saved from the sea? Say no! I'm a poor girl, his love is all I have. I came to fetch him home."

But still I could not speak. My face was hidden in my hands. I only heard the groaning of the girl, and presently a heavy, fearful thud;—again—again. I looked, and saw her kneeling by the stile, striking her head against the wood.

"What are you doing?" called I; her teeth were clenched, and there was blood upon her face.

"I am killing myself," she said. "God! Christ! Holy angels! I want to die! Kill me, O Lord God! Kill your servant!"

I seized her and kept her down.

"Susan!" I cried, "he is not worth this, he is a devil! We must hold our hearts and live."

But she broke from me with an awful cry, and leaped across the grass to where the river ran.

I know not how long I stayed beside the hedge; it was Miss Dell that roused me, calling my name across the meadow. The sun had set. I crept toward her; for all my deadness I could see the horror in her face, ill masked beneath her smiles.

"Dear," said she, with unwonted tenderness, "come home by the road, Mary, not through the garden, not tonight."

We were already at the wicket; I pushed it open, unclasping her reluctant hands. I can still hear her cry. "Mary! Mary! Oh, for God's sake stop her! Tomorrow is her wedding-day."

Father, and some men I knew, were standing by the river; and on the bank lay Susan, dead, her print dress dinging to her buxom form. They would have drawn me to the house, but I crouched down and peered into the dead girl's face; white and wet, staring without sight, gaping without breath, contorted without anguish.

And suddenly I heard the garden gate swing, footsteps swift and gay upon the path. It was he. I rose and went toward him; folding my arms behind me as if to shun his outstretched hands, I looked boldly, lovelessly, into his smiling eyes. They were all there— father, and Miss Dell, and the men.

"Captain Charvel," said I, aloud, that all might hear, "there is bad news for you. Your wife is dead."

His smile faded, but he only looked at me as one without understanding, and the silence remained unbroken, save for the murmuring of those around.

"If not your wife," said I then, "the woman who should have borne that name." And I pointed to where she lay.

He started almost imperceptibly, and his head fell low; it was dark, but my keen glance saw all; the twitching lip, the glazed, bewildered eye. Suddenly he drew himself up to his full height; standing before me he scanned me well from head to foot, I meeting with cold defiance the high disdainful sorrow of his gaze. Then, turning to the rest—

"Take up the girl," said he, "and bring her to the church."

They obeyed, as if helplessly, and, raising poor Susan in their arms, bore her solemnly across the lawn, between the graves, along the winding path. And Captain Charvel followed.

Father stood motionless; Miss Dell, poor soul, had sunk on to the ground and wept; it seemed that I alone saw all unmoved.

"Come," said I, "let us go too."

My words roused father; he started forward, and hand in hand we followed hastily, reaching the church just as they prepared to enter.

"Stay!" cried he, sternly, "this must not be. There shall be no defiling of God's house."

Captain Charvel turned round proudly.

"Then lay her here," said he, "for the Spirit of the Father is unconfinable, and the whole earth his altar."

There came a pause; kneeling, he clasped the dead girl's hand,

and many knelt with him. Not I; the silent heart in Susan's breast was not more cold than mine.

"I charge you," cried he then, "as many as are here present, in the name of God, to witness this my oath. I swear that from this hour this woman is my wife; nor will I touch another, either in friendship or in love, between this day and the day of my death. Lord! save her! Among the angels let her soul find rest!"

He raised her stiffening fingers to his lips, then rose.

There was no sound but his heavy footfall; slowly he faded into the closing night; and then my dead heart quickened suddenly.

Half blind, half mad, I staggered through the darkness.

"Come back!" I cried. "Come back! you are forgiven."

But he neither turned nor spoke; and when they came to lift me from the ground they thought I never should awaken more.

Such was not the will of Heaven. I lived, and was strong.

"We left Longparish, never to return, and I buried the past in my barren heart, below the reach of words.

I was still young when father left me; and the years rolled on. One day there came a letter telling me that I was possessed of a fortune. I was a gray-haired woman; but the tears I had shed at twenty for him I loved, were not more bitter than those I shed now. Colonel Charvel fell at Cawnpore.

The Spectre of Strathannan

By W. E. Norris

I always rather liked old Lady Strathannan. She was not uni-
versally popular, it is true; I have heard her accused of being
worldly and grasping; many people declared that she had been a
bad mother; and there was a general vague impression that she
had not behaved particularly well to her nephew, Bob Innes. But
when one came to examine into these charges, what did they
amount to? Worldly she may have been: so are a great many other amiable and agreeable persons. Whether she was grasping or
not I really could not say; but if, in her capacity of co-executrix
and trustee under her late husband's will, she was doing her best
to set an encumbered estate free, and to ensure for her only son
the prospect of a handsome fortune when his long minority
should terminate, that, I take it, was no more than her bounden
duty, and ought to go far toward clearing her from the imputa-
tion of being a bad mother.

Is a bad mother one who displays perseverance and ingenuity
in marrying her numerous daughters to men of rank and wealth?
It all depends upon the point of view. Lady Strathannan had succeeded in doing what most ladies in her position endeavour to
do, and what few, in these hard times, can achieve; this, perhaps,
might account for a certain degree of envy and jealousy on the
part of the disappointed ones. As for her daughters, they have
not, to the best of my knowledge and belief, objected to the
husbands selected for them. With regard to Bob Innes, all that
was known for certain was that he had once been engaged in an

informal sort of way to his cousin, Lady Janet, and that the old lady had put a stop to the engagement. Perhaps she disapproved of first-cousin marriages; the disapproval is a plausible and by no means an uncommon one. In any case, Bob—who, though the best fellow in the world, is only a clerk in a government office, and is notoriously straitened as to income—could not reasonably complain, as it seemed to me, when he was sent about his business.

To set against these alleged shortcomings, Lady Strathannan had some attractive qualities. When in London, she entertained a good deal in an unostentatious but agreeable way; the beauty for which her daughters were celebrated must, I imagine, have been inherited from her, for at the age of sixty or thereabouts she was a very handsome and venerable-looking lady, with an abundance of gray hair, which, together with her waxen complexion, gave her a resemblance to an old miniature. Her manners were snare and amiable when she chose; and that she did not always choose to make them so rendered her civility all the more flattering to those who were favoured by it. To me she had always been kind and polite, which seemed to be a proof of disinterestedness, since she must have been perfectly well aware that my means were not such as to make me a conceivable candidate for the hand of the only unmarried member of her family. Therefore, when she was so good as to send me an invitation to spend a week at Strathannan Castle, I wrote and accepted forthwith, although it is not everybody who could induce me to travel into the depths of Scotland in the middle of the winter.

To tell the truth, it was not for the sake of this old woman, agreeable though I had always found her, nor for the sake of Lady Janet, who was also agreeable, but who had never troubled herself to notice my existence particularly, nor for that of any of the people whom I was likely to meet there, that I decided to visit Strathannan. The house is one in which I had always wished very much to stay. That it possessed a ghost was in no way remarkable; all old houses of any respectability possess a ghost. But what made the Strathannan spectre so peculiarly awe-inspiring was that it was said only to manifest itself to those who had some undiscovered crime upon their conscience—an attribute which, I should think, must have made many of the late Lord Strathannan's guests feel exceedingly uncomfortable. The legend connected with it was that it had first revealed itself to a certain disloyal Lord Strathannan, whose feelings were so worked upon by the apparition that he straightway made full confession of his treachery, and requested that he might be put to death, in accordance with his deserts.

His request was complied with (at all events, it seems certain that there was a Lord Strathannan whose head was cut off in the early part of the fourteenth century); and, encouraged by this really striking success, the spectre, it was said, had continued to show itself at intervals to other guilty persons, whether belonging to the family or not, who came within its reach. As an indirect testimony to the integrity of my acquaintances, I am glad to be able to add that not one of them had set eyes upon this gruesome thing, though all professed to have heard it pattering about the corridors, at night. That was nothing when you were used to it, they said; the Innes family were no more perturbed by it than by the inexplicable bursting open of doors every now and again, accepting such manifestations merely as a salutary warning that they had better behave themselves. However, I was cautioned that Lady Strathannan, who was a nervous woman, did not like the subject to be spoken of in her presence.

Bob Innes and I are old friends and old schoolfellows. If we do not meet quite as often as we once did, that is because our respective avocations do not happen to throw us together. We are very glad to see one another when we do meet, and, as chance would have it, I encountered him at the club on the day previous to that named in my invitation to Strathannan. Bob is a good-looking, good-tempered young fellow, of six or seven and twenty. He has carried about a somewhat gloomy countenance since his disappointment in the matter of Lady Janet; but he has not withdrawn himself from society, where I believe that he is a great favourite; nor is he given to talking about his troubles.

He had never mentioned the affair to me, although I suppose I know him about as well as anybody. When, however, I told him that I was about to spend a few days in the cradle of his race, he became pensive, and for the first time alluded to what I had hitherto imagined that he wished to treat as a forbidden topic.

"You'll see Janet," he said, with a sigh. "Give her my love, will you, old chap?—and tell her that I haven't changed."

"All right," I answered, hesitatingly; for I don't much fancy such commissions. "Do you think I had better give her your love, though?"

"Oh, you needn't unless you like," he returned. "I dare say she will ask you whether you've seen me, that's all. She doesn't need any messages, really. She trusts me just as much as I trust her, and she knows well enough that neither of us will change our minds at this time of day."

"But I thought it was all off," I said; because I divined that he would not be displeased if I questioned him a little.

Bob blew a cloud of smoke, and remained silent for a minute or two before replying.

"It's all off in one sense. The old cat represented to me that we were too poor to marry, which I couldn't deny, and of course I was bound to say that Janet was free, so far as I was concerned; but you can't force a girl to accept her freedom if she don't choose to accept it. I told Janet she might throw me over if she liked; I didn't think it my duty to throw her over. So there it is. I've been perfectly square with the old cat; there's no correspondence, no meeting on the sly—nothing of that sort. Only Janet considers herself engaged to me, and I consider myself engaged to her."

"It seems a poor lookout for both of you," I remarked.

"Very," he replied, laconically.

After a short pause, he resumed: "There's just this to be said, that her father didn't forbid the engagement. He thought there was no reason why we should not marry some day, and, indeed, we might have married if —if he had carried out what he always told me were his intentions. I don't know whether you

57

are aware that he used to allow me three hundred a year—most people seem to be aware of it."

I said I had not heard.

"Well, he did. He said he considered me entitled to that, because my father hadn't had all the money left to him that he expected to get. The fact is, that my grandfather spent every penny he could lay hands on, and didn't leave enough personalty to pay his debts or his legacies either. My uncle managed to get things moderately straight in process of time; he laid by a certain amount every year, and, I believe, paid off some of the mortgages. He was an awfully good old fellow. Of course he wasn't obliged to make me an allowance, but he thought he was, and he used to apologize because he couldn't see his way to increasing it. However, he told me over and over again that I should get ten thousand pounds when he died; so that I was naturally rather astonished and rather disappointed when it turned out that I wasn't even mentioned in his will. It was a very old will, dated the year of his marriage. Nobody disputed the fact of his having made a second one; only, as it wasn't forthcoming—why, I was left out in the cold. My own belief was that that old aunt of mine had made away with it, and I had the bad manners to tell her so."

"Really," said I, "I think that was rather bad manners, and rather bad judgement into the bargain."

"Very likely. At all events she and I are not the best of friends nowadays, as you may imagine. If you want to give her pleasure, you might tell her that I've taken to drink, or play, or some other little vice of that kind. Then she'll repeat it to Janet, who won't believe

her, and so you'll have made your hostess happy, without doing anybody any harm."

I observed that making away with a will was a serious matter, and ventured to add that by all accounts a member of the Innes family who should commit such an offence would be exposed to perils which do not threaten the ordinary felon.

Bob laughed a little uneasily. In these days few people like to confess their faith in anything which does not admit of mathematical demonstration, although, for some reason or other, it seems to be considered less ridiculous to believe in hobgoblins than in a revealed religion.

"Oh," he said, "there's a lot of nonsense talked about the old place. You'll hear footsteps, I dare say. I've heard them myself scores of times—easily explained, no doubt. There is only one room which is supposed to be haunted, and you're not likely to be put into that, or to see anything startling if you are."

He changed the subject at once, and did not allude again to my approaching visit to Strathannan until just before we parted, when he said, rather wistfully: "You might drop me a line from Scotland, if it wasn't too much trouble. I won't ask you to give any message to Janet; perhaps it's better not; but there couldn't be much harm in your just letting me know how she is looking—and that sort of thing."

I was not cruel enough to refuse so modest a request; nor did I deem it incumbent upon me to mention what Bob may already have known, namely, that Lady Janet was, by common report, likely to become betrothed ere long to young Hopley, the eldest son of the rich brewer who had recently been raised to the peerage as Lord Trent. I was sorry for Bob; but it seemed to me that he was slightly unreasonable. When people can't afford to marry, and when there is no prospect of their being able to do so, the lady's relatives are surely justified in breaking off the match. As for the destruction of the late Lord Strathannan's will, everything pointed to the probability that it had been effected by his own hands. He would not be the first old gentleman who has promised to provide for needy collaterals and has thought better of his benevolent intentions, reflecting that charity begins at home.

It was, therefore, by no means as a strong partisan of my friend Bob's that I betook myself to Strathannan Castle; yet I admit that, after I had seen Lady Janet, I felt much more able to sympathize with him. Logically, of course, the fact that she was so pretty and looked so good did not alter the situation; but nobody, thank Heaven I can compel us to be logical, and I suppose it will be allowed that if Lady Janet had been a young woman like the ordinary run of fashionable young women, neither Bob nor anybody else would have incurred an irreparable loss in resigning her. It was as one among a number of fashionable young women that I had hitherto seen her, and I had not noticed anything distinctive about her, except that, like all her family, she had a beautiful complexion. Now, however, having a reason for being interested in her, I observed the wistful expression of her soft brown eyes, and her pleasant voice, and what I fancied was a look of quiet determination about the lower part of her face. I could well imagine her capable of holding her own in a gentle, persistent way.

It was she who received me, on my arrival, in a vast saloon which modern furniture had not availed, to deprive of the somewhat gloomy and forbidding aspect which characterized the whole building. She did not ask any questions about Bob Innes; so that I was not tempted to deliver the message which that luckless individual had authorized me to give or withhold. After a few minutes, Lady Strathannan came in, followed by a number of her guests, among whom I recognized Mr. Hopley, a commonplace, good-humoured-looking youth, of the type commonly described as "cheery," and frequently—perhaps rather too frequently for some people's taste—to be met with in country houses.

One had only to look at him to be convinced that, upon very small provocation, he would arrange a skilful booby-trap over one's bedroom door, and take the first opportunity of playing some humorous trick with one's gun. I had a slight acquaintance with him, but, for the reasons above hinted at, did not encourage familiarity on his part, and I was glad to note that he had been provided with a few kindred spirits upon whom to vent the exuberance of his vitality.

Strathannan Castle looks a large house from the outside, but will not, I believe, accommodate a very large party. About twenty of us sat down to dinner; and my neighbour informed me that we were *au grand complet.*

"I should not be much surprised," she added, rather maliciously, in an undertone, "if they had quartered you in the ghost-room. I suppose you know there *is* a ghost-room?"

I replied that I had been told so, but had understood that the ghost only disturbed the slumbers of the guilty; consequently, I felt no anxiety on my own score. At the same time, I should be glad to know what authority she had for stating that I was to invade its special domain.

"If I tell you," said she, "will you promise not to breathe a word to Lady Strathannan ?" And, on receiving the required pledge, she continued: "Well, my maid heard the housekeeper say to one of the housemaids that she would be obliged to put you in the south wing, because the room which you were to have occupied has been made uninhabitable by a dead rat, but that this was on no account to be mentioned to her ladyship. Are you afraid, Mr. Hervey? Do you believe in ghosts?"

"I am not afraid," I answered, "and I am not at present a believer, though open to conviction by the evidence of my own senses. Novel experiences are always interesting; so I trust that if there is a disembodied spirit about the premises he won't fail to look me up in the course of the night."

Must I confess that, despite these brave words, I did not altogether relish the idea of passing the night in a so-called haunted apartment! Certainly, I do not believe in ghosts. Upon the face of it, nothing can be more childishly ridiculous than to suppose that an immortal soul, after quitting this body, may have no better employment assigned to it than to linger about the scenes of its earthly pilgrimage and scare posterity with undignified gibberings; yet, as everybody knows, theory and practice are two different things, and neither in belief nor in disbelief is poor humanity prone to be consistent. I may sum up my sentiments upon the subject, by saying that I was willing to believe in a ghost when I saw one, but that I was not in the least anxious to see one.

Later in the evening, when I entered the smoking-room,

where I found Hopley and his friends, together with some of my fellow-guests who were of more advanced years, I discovered, somewhat to my disgust, that the surmise of the lady whom I had taken in to dinner was shared by them. No member of the family being present, they were free to question me as to the whereabouts of my room, and, after I had accurately described its position, Hopley slapped his leg and cried:

"By George, then, it's *the* room! I thought as much! I remember old Strathannan telling me exactly where it was, and he said he had never dared to put any friend of his into, it This is grand sport! Now we shall know what the Spectre looks like. Tell you what, Hervey, I'll sit up all night with you, if you like."

"Many thanks," I answered—for this jocularity seemed to me to be rather misplaced—"but, all things considered, I think I should prefer the spectre. There will be a good big jug of cold water at his service when he comes, anyhow."

These last words were spoken with deliberate emphasis; because I did not doubt my young friend's capacity for playing bogey upon occasion, and I trusted that the prospect of a shower-bath on a December night would be found uninviting, even by the most hardened of practical jokers.

But Hopley returned, "If that's meant for me you may set your mind at rest, my dear fellow. I wouldn't venture into your part of the house after other people had gone to bed for any money. I believe most people who see that spectre either drop down dead or go mad; but you've got plenty of pluck, and I dare say you may pull through. You won't find *me* stirring the thing up, though."

"In that case," said I, "I shall probably have a quiet night. But I shall keep the cold water handy, all the same."

I was as good as my word. I placed the water-jug by my bedside, and, as I was not in the least sleepy when I retired to rest, I read a pamphlet about Free Trade until my ideas were agreeably confused. Then I blew out the candle, turned over on the other side, and closed my eyes.

I don't know how many hours after this it was that I awoke

with a start, and with a horrible conviction that I was not alone. Although I was frightened—why should I not admit it? everybody who wakes with a start must be frightened—I thought at once of Hopley, and lay as still as a mouse, waiting to see what would happen. The room was not quite dark, for the embers of the wood fire which had been burning in the old-fashioned grate when I went to sleep diffused a glow, by the light of which I could distinguish a shadowy white form bending over me. That the memory of sundry by-gone peccadilloes flashed across my mind I will not deny; but I had the self-control to abstain from any articulate confession of them. Suddenly the apparition stretched out its arm, flicked away my pillow from under my head, and noiselessly vanished.

Not quite noiselessly, however, for I distinctly heard the click of a closing lock, and that sound dispelled all my fears. A ghost worthy of the name cannot possibly be under any obligation to open or shut doors. I was out of bed in a trice, and grasping my water-jug I rushed out into the long corridor; but never a sign could I discover of Hopley and his boon companions. Retiring at length to my room, somewhat discomfited, I struck a light, and then for the first time my eyes fell upon a door-handle close to the head of my bed. The door to which it belonged was not panelled, but was papered all over, like the rest of the wall; so that my having failed to notice it was not very astonishing. I opened it now without any hesitation, and passing through it, found myself in an untenanted room very like my own, only rather longer.

That it was untenanted I satisfied myself by careful investigation; presumably Hopley, or whoever my nocturnal visitant had been, had escaped through it to the corridor, and was now safe on the other side of the house, whither pursuit was out of the question. There was nothing for it but to go back to bed; so to bed I went, and prepared to finish the night as comfortably as I could without a pillow. It was annoying that I should have failed to drench the fellow, but I derived a good deal of comfort from the conviction that my rest had been disturbed by a being of flesh and blood. Ghosts are immaterial or they are nothing; and I do not believe that a member of the Society for Psychical Research would go so far as to affirm that a ghost is capable of picking up a material object like a pillow and marching off with it under his arm. With my nerves soothed by these reflections, I soon dropped asleep, and was not molested again until my servant came to wake me in the morning.

When I went down to breakfast I noticed that several of the men who had been in the smoking-room on the previous evening regarded me with an eager curiosity, to which I took care that my features should convey no response; but the innocent unconsciousness of Hopley staggered me a little. He looked up as I entered, and nodded to me, but was to all appearance engrossed in conversation with Lady Janet, who was pouring out the tea, and to whom he was making love after the manner of his kind—that is to say, with a frank openness as bewildering in its way as Prince Bismarck's diplomacy. It was difficult to believe that a man who advertised his sentiments so publicly could have serious intentions, yet I was assured in the course of the day that Mr. Hopley was quite in earnest, and, moreover, that Lady Janet fully intended to accept him.

Her demeanour at breakfast did not lead me to share that conviction. She was civil and unembarrassed with her neighbour, but did not seem to be paying much attention to what he said; and after I had taken the vacant place on the other side of her, she honoured me with the greater share of her conversation. Her mother, she told me, was unable to come down, as she was suffering from one of the bad neuralgic headaches to which she was subject.

"Mamma is always having headaches here," Lady Janet said. "I don't think the air of Strathannan suits her; and, indeed, a great many people complain of it at first. I hope it hasn't given you a headache, Mr. Hervey."

Now the truth was that I had rather a headache, owing to my having lain for several hours with my head a great deal too low; but I replied that I thought the air of Strathannan delightful, and that I had slept capitally.

This I said for the benefit of Hopley, who grinned, as if he had suddenly remembered that a different report might have been expected. "Oh, you did, eh! No spectres, then?" he asked.

Lady Janet looked slightly annoyed. There was some laughter, under cover of which I noticed she bent forward and said something in a low voice to Hopley; and I overheard his hasty rejoinder: "Oh, no! it's all right. I didn't mean anything—only chaff, you know."

Some shooting took place during the morning in the coverts near the house; but the results were not magnificent, and were loudly murmured at by Mr. Hopley, who, being the son of a brewer, was naturally accustomed to better things. "The old girl has let the place go down disgracefully," he confided to me, just before luncheon. "Gets her rents paid pretty regularly, I believe; but, dash it all! rents ain't everything, you know."

Lady Strathannan may have deemed it wise—and probably it was wise—to economize in the matter of gamekeepers, but it does not cost much money to have the ice on your lake swept; and as it had been freezing hard for more than a week, we had a capital afternoon's skating. Lady Janet was a skilful and graceful performer. I watched her evolutions with great interest for some time, and was surprised to notice that she kept her eyes pretty steadily on me; for I could not natter myself that this was due to any display of skill or grace on my part. She was closely attended by Hopley, of whom, however, she managed at length to get rid by persuading him to join in a curling match which had been arranged; and the first use that she made of her freedom was to come skimming across the smooth, glassy surface toward the humble writer of these pages.

"Mr. Hervey," said she, when, with an ease which I envied, she had whisked round, and brought herself to a standstill beside me, "I want to ask you a question."

"Delighted to answer any question, Lady Janet," I declared, guessing what it was likely to be.

But my powers of divination proved less accurate than I had

supposed, and it was not the name of Bob Innes that fell from her lips when she opened them again. "I wanted to know," she said, with a little hesitation, "whether—whether you saw anything last night?"

"Since you ask me," replied I, "I did. But it wasn't a ghost. Somebody came into my room in the dead of the night and snatched my pillow from under my head. In all probability it was Mr. Hopley, I was rather startled for the moment, so he made his escape; but I think I may promise to give him a more fitting reception if he turns up again tonight."

Lady Janet did not smile. "I never heard of anything of that kind happening before," said she, gravely; "I don't understand it. "What object could there be in taking your pillow away?"

"The object," I answered, laughing, "was no doubt an amiable wish to frighten me; but it wasn't a conspicuous success, because I heard the door shut; and, without knowing much about ghosts, I will venture to say that they are not in the habit of opening and shutting doors."

"Oh, but indeed they are!" she rejoined; "that is exactly what so often occurs. Of course, though, you would think it all superstitious nonsense, and I am very glad that you are not frightened. It was only this afternoon that I found out where Mrs. Menzies had put you, and I was very angry with her about it. Still, if you really don't mind—"

I assured her that I didn't mind in the least—rather liked it, in fact.

"Then," she said, "would it be asking too much if I begged you not to mention to my mother what room you are in? She would be so displeased if she knew; and—and, to tell you the truth, there isn't another vacant room in the house."

I had only just had time to give the promise requested of me when our interview was interrupted by Hopley, who wanted Lady Janet to come and see what a first-rate hand he was at curling; so that I was unable to make the inquiries about the haunted chamber which I should have liked to make. When all is said and done, we mortals are an uncertain and, to a large extent, irresponsible race. Who will dare to boast that his judgement is superior to the accidents of time, place, and health? For my own part, I would rather not write myself down an ass, but honesty constrains me to avow that I am not quite the same man in the dark as I am in broad daylight. Few things are more utterly absurd and groundless than the fear of ghosts, spectres, and goblins.

One knows exactly how such superstitions arise, one understands that they are inevitable in a low state of civilization; and when one is walking down Pall Mall, or sitting in the club, one can smile at them easily enough. Yet if one be the occupant of a room reputed to be haunted, in a lonely Scotch castle, one's flesh may quite as easily be made to creep by unexplained nocturnal noises. I speak, of course, of my own flesh; but I imagine that there are many other people like me.

The fact is that I slept very badly that night, and that I heard innumerable noises for which I was unable to account—footsteps, whisperings, even subdued sighs or moans. It may have been the wind; it may have been rats or bats or fifty things: all I know is that I spent a very long and very disagreeable night, and that neither spectre nor practical joker appeared to bring my vague disquietude to a climax. When my man came in, in the morning, it occurred to me to tell him of the trick which had been played upon me, and which had not been repeated.

"Williams," said I, "the night before last one of the young gentlemen came into my room and ran away with my pillow. It has been replaced, I see. Do you happen to know where it was discovered?"

Williams, I believe, prides himself upon his impassibility; yet it seemed to me that just the suggestion of a smile flitted across his face as he replied: "Found in Lady Strathannan's room, yesterday morning, sir, I understand."

Really this was a little startling. Lady Strathannan, as I knew, had been bad with neuralgia all day, and had not got up until just before the dinner hour. It was impossible to suppose that she herself had robbed me of my pillow. How in the world, then, had it found its way into her room? I frowned at Williams, to repress any ill-timed merriment on his part, and remarked that jokes of that kind were not only very silly, but in extremely bad taste, to which he replied, "Yes, sir."

Williams, though a good servant, is a most aggravating man. I perceived from his manner that he had something more to say; but I did not choose to question him, because I make it a rule never to encourage any repetition of servants'-hall gossip. After all, the very best answer to a practical joke is *to* take no notice of it until you see your way to reprisals.

The succeeding day was marked by no event worthy of record. Lady Strathannan, recovered from her neuralgia, joined us at breakfast and made herself extremely agreeable to everybody—as, indeed, she usually does. Personally I had no opportunity of talking with her until the evening, when she created an opportunity by leading me to the picture-gallery to show me the famous Guido, which is considered to be one of the chief treasures of Strathannan. That this was a mere pretext she candidly avowed as soon as I had seated myself beside her on the old oak settle which faced the celebrated canvas in question.

"Mr. Hervey," said she, "I brought you here because I am very anxious to have a few words with you about my nephew Robert. I know you are a great friend of his, and most likely he has told you all about his troubles."

She paused for me to make a sign of assent, and continued: "I dare say he has said some disagreeable things to you about me, too; but that is of no consequence. I am sorry that he should think badly of me; but I must do my duty, and I should think that I was acting very wrongly if I allowed his silly half-engagement to dear Janet to go on. At the same time, one cannot but admit that he has some reason to consider himself unlucky. Perhaps you think so."

I replied that, without imputing the smallest blame to anybody, I was disposed to regard that as a simple matter of fact.

"Exactly so; and these family quarrels are so very painful, are they not? That is why I have made up my mind to offer Robert an allowance. I shouldn't feel justified in making it quite as much as he used to receive from his uncle; but I think I could manage two hundred a year. Now, dear Mr. Hervey, will you do me a great favour, and try to arrange this for me ?"

"Of course I can deliver any message that you are pleased to intrust me with, Lady Strathannan," I answered; "but wouldn't it be shorter to write to Bob yourself?"

"Well, no," she said; "because, unfortunately, he is so prejudiced against me that he would be quite sure to refuse by return of post. And then I must tell you that I wish to add a little condition to this offer. I want him to promise me upon his honour that he will give up all thought of marrying Janet, and that he will say as much distinctly to her herself. Then we could be friends again, and I would undertake to find him a nice girl with a little money of her own before long, who would make quite as good a wife for him as Janet or anybody else. Now you know, Mr. Hervey—don't you?—that it really doesn't matter in the least, after a year or two, whether a man has happened to be in love with his wife when he married her or not."

I was unable to divine why she should attribute any such knowledge as this to a bachelor; but she went on to speak in such flattering terms of my well-known tact, and the amiability of my disposition and so forth, that I ended by accepting the mission thrust upon me, though I gave her fair warning that I did not expect to be successful. Bob Innes, I suspected, was incorruptible, and even if he had been open to a bribe, two hundred pounds a year is not a very high price to set upon a man's self-respect. For the obvious meaning of all this was that Lady Janet would not consent to enter the noble family of Hopley until her cousin should not only have set her free but renounced her.

However, I like to get on with people as pleasantly as I can, so I assured my hostess that I would do what in me lay to bring about the reconciliation which she had so much at heart, and forbore to inquire whether she had noticed such a thing in her bedroom on the previous morning as a pillow which did not belong to her. She retired almost immediately after we had re-entered the drawing-room, complaining of a return of her neuralgia, and leaving Lady Janet to entertain the company.

Hopley and his young friends were very jocular about the spectre that night in the smoking-room. Concealment is not very difficult; but to conceal the fact that you have something to conceal is a higher branch of art, and they evidently either knew or suspected that I had not related the whole truth with regard to my experience in the haunted chamber. In any case, I was determined that I would not allow myself to be drawn. I baffled their queries; I submitted imperturbably to their chaff, and I patiently sat them out—one consequence of which was that when at length I reached my bedroom I was dead tired. Ghost or no ghost, I could not go through a second vigil; and I suppose I had not been in bed five minutes before I was sound asleep.

I awoke precisely as I had done on the previous occasion, with a shuddering conviction that something or somebody was near me. As before, the room was not quite dark, there being still a glow from the dying fire, and, as before, that shadowy white figure was bending over me. I don't in the least mind admitting that my heart beat hard and fast; I believe that the motion of anybody's heart would have become accelerated under the circumstances; and I did what I think was quite the best thing to do, in lying perfectly still, and waiting for the apparition—whoever or whatever it might be—to make the next move. But when for the second time a hand—a most distinct, prehensile hand—was stretched forward and plucked at my pillow, common sense on a sudden re-asserted itself. It is contrary to all reason, and beyond the limits of the most credulous assertion, that a ghost can have hands capable of grasping pillows. That dim white figure was Hopley, or, if not Hopley, some other human being with whom I was resolved to deal as he deserved. Unluckily, I had forgotten to place the water-jug beside me; but with a sudden bound I sprang up and stood erect upon the bed.

At the same instant, to my utter amazement, my ghostly visitant collapsed upon the floor, and lay there in a huddled heap, uttering moans of the extremest terror and anguish. I don't know whether my nerves might not have been shaken by this unexpected exhibition, if presently the moans of the prostrate one had not resolved themselves into more or less coherent entreaties, and if I had not recognized, beyond all doubt, the voice of Lady Strathannan.

"Mercy! mercy!" she shrieked. "Oh, I *knew* this would happen to me some day! I ought never to have entered your room! I will do anything you tell me—I will give back the ten thousand pounds—anything! Fool that I was! I was beginning to disbelieve in you! Oh, why, why, why have you appeared to me!"

What a thing it is to have presence of mind! With the rapidity of a flash of lightning, the whole situation became clear to me. Lady Strathannan had robbed her nephew; I was the spectre, and it was my mission to make her disgorge her ill-gotten gains. I threw myself into the part with a readiness for which I do think that I deserve the greatest credit. Many years ago, when I was a boy, I took a few lessons in ventriloquism, and learned, if not to ventriloquize, at least to disguise my voice. It was in hollow accents, which, at such an hour and in such a place, would have struck terror into the stoutest heart, that I uttered the words: "Woman, confess your crime!"

"But not publicly!" she groaned. "Ah, don't make me do that! For my poor children's sake, spare me! It was for my children's sake that I burned the will. It was wrong, I know; but I acted for the best, and—and for Janet's happiness. I shall be sent to prison if I confess, and others will suffer quite as much as I shall. You wouldn't bring such misery upon an innocent family!"

"Yes, I would," I replied; it was rather a colloquial fashion of expressing myself, but she was too much scared to notice that. "Wrong must be set right, and stolen money must be restored."

"It shall be; I promise it—I swear it!" she gasped out eagerly. "The money shall be paid to him as soon as ever I can realize it."

"That is not all," I continued solemnly, after a short pause. "You have defrauded your nephew of more than money, and you must make amends to him. You must consent to his marriage with your daughter."

All this time Lady Strathannan was grovelling on the ground, and, as far as I could see, had her face hidden in her hands. She made no articulate reply; but, listening intently, I heard her mutter between her teeth, "I won't!"

Without an instant's hesitation I responded. "You will not obey?" I asked. "Die, then!" It was rather a bold threat, because, in the first place, I could not kill her, and, in the second, there are a good many people who would prefer death to disgrace. Fortunately, however, it appeared that Lady Strathannan was not one of these.

"No, no!" she shrieked, "I will obey, indeed I will! Only give me time! I acted for the best. I didn't think it was for her happiness to marry that man, and I don't think so now—I can't think so. Still, I will give my consent, if I must."

"You must!" I replied from the pit of my stomach.

Now this was all very satisfactory, so far as it went; but the question was, how on earth was I to conclude the interview! I ought, of course, to have faded slowly away, but it was altogether out of my power to fade away; besides which, I really couldn't trust the old woman. It was essential that I should extort some tangible pledge from her, otherwise courage might return to her with the return of day; and it was exceedingly improbable that I should have a second chance of frightening her out of her wits. It was a ticklish situation, and I fully realized the risk of detection that I was running, but I had to make the best of it.

"Go to your room," quoth I, in sepulchral accents, "take pen and paper and write as follows: 'I, Elizabeth, Countess of Strathannan, hereby acknowledge that I have defrauded my nephew, Robert Innes, of ten thousand pounds, left to him by his uncle in a will which I feloniously destroyed; and, in consideration of his clemency in sparing me public exposure, I engage to pay him the said sum as the marriage-portion of my daughter, Janet Innes, and to welcome him as my son-in-law and the husband of the said Janet.' When you have written and signed this paper, bring it back and leave it here. It will have disappeared in the morning; and, unless you prove false to it, no mortal eye ever will see it." I had a moment of intense anxiety after I had thus delivered myself. It was obvious that no spectre who understood his business would ask for a signed engagement, yet, as I said before, I had to make the best use I could of my opportunity, and I imagine that her ladyship was too much delighted at the prospect held out to her of immunity from public disgrace to cavil at details. She bleated out a lachrymose assent, scrambled to her feet and trotted away, without so much as glancing at me.

Then I had another painful minute—five minutes, indeed, I should think—of suspense. Would she ever come back again? When once she had reached her own room, would she not, like a sensible woman, reflect that no apparition had ever shown itself to her there, and that by the simple expedient of avoiding the spectre's special hunting-grounds, she might hope to avoid all future molestation? It was true that I had received a distinct admission of guilt from her, and that I might hold this over her *in terrorem,* but then there was nothing to prevent her from meeting my assertion with a point-blank denial, nor anything to convince a cold and sceptical world that I had not been the victim of a nightmare.

I don't know when I have felt so thankful in my life as when I heard the pattering of her returning feet in the adjoining room. In she came, bearing a folded paper in her hand, and the instant that she was within my reach, I made a grab at it and secured it. So overjoyed was I at my success, that I really did not notice the circumstance that she had brought a candle with her. But when, instead of a grisly phantom, she found herself confronted with a gentleman of the nineteenth century, apparelled in the customary nocturnal garb of the period, she realized the heartless deception which had been practiced upon her, and protested against it with not unnatural warmth.

"You wretch!" she ejaculated. "You infamous, wicked wretch!"

I am a very modest man by nature. I hopped deftly into bed

and covered myself up, taking care, however, to keep a firm hold upon the paper. "My dear Lady Strathannan," said I, "let us not call one another hard names. After what you have told me, I might say some uncomplimentary things to you; but I won't. I am persuaded that you have repented of your sin, and you have bound yourself down to make reparation for it. More than that no charitable fellow-sinner would wish to exact, and yon may be sure that, so long as you observe the terms of our agreement, neither the strong arm of the law nor the censure of society will fall upon you."

"Of course," she returned sullenly, after a few seconds of consideration, "I am in your power, and I must obey your orders. You have extorted information by a most disgraceful and ungentlemanlike trick; but I suppose you are not likely to feel ashamed of yourself. As a matter of curiosity, though, I should like to hear how you found your way into this room."

"Well, do you know, Lady Strathannan," I returned, "that is the very question that I was thinking of putting to you. How did you find your way into this room? And, without for one moment permitting myself to speak about disgraceful and unlady-like tricks, may I ask what your object is in plucking my pillow from under my head and running off with it? Because, after all, it *is* my pillow for the time being; and, for the time being, this is also my bedroom."

"What!" she cried. "Do you mean to tell me that this is the room they gave you when you arrived?"

"It is, indeed," I answered; "and if you don't believe me, you can look in the wardrobe and the chest of drawers, and you will find all my things there."

"Menzies shall have a month's warning tomorrow," muttered Lady Strathannan.

"I hope you will not punish Mrs. Menzies," I said.

"I believe she was much distressed at having to put me here; but it seems that the room originally destined for me has a leak in the roof, or a dead rat behind the wainscot, or something; and really I think you had better say nothing to her about it, because, if you do, she will want to know how you found out the truth, which, as I need hardly point out to you, might give rise to scandal. And now that I have satisfactorily accounted for my presence, may I once more venture to inquire—"

"Oh, bother!" she interrupted. And then, after a short pause: "Well, if you want to know, I can't sleep without a pile of pillows when I have these neuralgic headaches, and so I sometimes collect them from this room and the next one, which communicates with mine. If Menzies had put you into the next room, all this would have been avoided; but, unfortunately, she did once put an old gentleman in there—who snored, and I told her that such a thing must not occur again. Why didn't you speak when I helped myself to your pillow the first time?"

"To tell you the truth," I replied, "I took you for the family spectre. You returned the compliment tonight, so we may cry quits."

"Mr. Hervey," said Lady Strathannan, changing her manner all of a sudden, and speaking in the dulcet tones which I had always hitherto been accustomed to associate with her, "I see that I was wrong in suspecting you of a deliberate design, and I hope you will overlook anything disagreeable that I may have said in the heat of the moment. Of course, I have treated Robert Innes badly. I won't attempt to justify myself; but, as you so truly say, I have repented, and I am going to make reparation. And now, will you kindly give me back that slip of paper, which you snatched from me?"

"Most certainly I will, Lady Strathannan," answered I. "I will give it back to you on Bob's wedding-day."

And I kept my word. She received the written confession of her fraud one day in the following June, at the conclusion of a largely-attended ceremony in a fashionable London church, and after I had taken care to ascertain that Bob's £10,000 had been duly paid over to him. Everybody said that Lady Strathannan had behaved so nicely about it, and had provided so much more handsomely for her daughter than could have been expected.

Such, I believe, is the view taken by Bob himself, who has

become reconciled with his mother-in-law, and who tells me that she is really not at all a bad old woman in her way. With what feelings her ladyship regards me I do not know, for she is rather clever at concealing her feelings. She is extremely civil to me when we meet, but she has not asked me to stay with her in Scotland again, and it seems highly probable that I shall go down to my grave without having had a second opportunity of finding out whether the celebrated Spectre of Strathannan is a myth or not.

A Mystery of the Campagna
By Von Degen

1

Marcello's voice is pleading with me now, perhaps because after years of separation I have met an old acquaintance who had a part in his strange story. I have a longing to tell it, and have asked Monsieur Sutton to help me. He noted down the circumstances at the time, and he is willing to join his share to mine, that Marcello may be remembered.

One day, it was in spring, he appeared in my little studio among the laurels and green alleys of the Villa Medici. "Come, *mon enfant*" he said, "put up your paints;" and he unceremoniously took my palette out of my hand. "I have a cab waiting outside, and we are going in search of a hermitage." He was already washing my brushes as he spoke, and this softened my heart, for I hate to do it myself. Then he pulled off my velvet jacket and took down my respectable coat from a nail on the wall. I let him dress me like a child. We always did his will, and he knew it, and in a moment we were sitting in the cab, driving through the Via Sistina on our way to the Porta San Giovanni, whither he had directed the coachman to go.

I must tell my story as I can, for though I have been told by my comrades, who cannot know very well, that I can speak good English, writing it is another thing. Monsieur Sutton has asked me to use his tongue, because he has so far forgotten mine that he will not trust himself in it, though he has promised to correct my mistakes, that what I have to tell you may not seem ridiculous, and make people laugh when they read of Marcello. I tell him I wish to write this for my countrymen, not his; but he reminds me that Marcello had many English friends who still live, and that the English do not forget as we do. It is of no use to reason with him, for neither do they yield as we do, and so I have consented to his wish. I think he has a reason which he does not tell me, but let it go. I will translate it all into my own language for my own people. Your English phrases seem to me to be always walking sideways, or trying to look round the corner or stand upon their heads, and they have as many little tails as a kite. I will try not to have recourse to my own language, but he must pardon me if I forget myself. He may be sure I do not do it to offend him. Now that I have explained so much, let me go on.

When we had passed out of the Porta San Giovanni, the coachman drove as slowly as he liked. The pay is more outside the gates, and they always pretend then that their horses are tired, and creep as slowly as possible; but Marcello was never practical. How could he be, I ask you, with an opera in his head? So we crawled along, and he gazed dreamily before him. At last, when we had reached the part where the little villas and vine- yards begin, he began to look about him.

You all know how it is out there; iron gates with rusty names or initials over them, and beyond them straight walks bordered with roses and lavender leading up to a forlorn little casino, with trees and a wilderness behind it sloping down to the Campagna, lonely enough to be murdered in and no one to hear you cry. We stopped at several of these gates and Marcello stood looking in, but none of the places were to his taste. He seemed not to doubt that he might have whatever pleased him, but nothing did so. He would jump out and run to the gate, and return saying, "The shape of those windows would disturb my inspiration," or, "That yellow paint would make me fail my duet in the second act;" and once he liked the air of the house well enough, but there were marigolds growing in the walk, and he hated them. So we drove on and on, until I thought we should find nothing more to reject. At last we came to one which suited him, though it was terribly lonely, and I should have fancied it very *agaçant* to live so far away from the world with nothing but those melancholy olives and green oaks—ilexes, you call them—for company.

"I shall live here and become famous!" he said decidedly, as he pulled the iron rod which rang a great bell inside. We waited, and then he rang again very impatiently and stamped his foot.

"No one lives here, *man vieux!* Come, it is getting late, and it is so damp out here, and you know that the damp for a tenor voice—" He stamped his foot again and interrupted me angrily.

"Why, then, have you got a tenor? You are stupid! a bass would be more sensible; nothing hurts it. But you have not got one, and you call yourself my friend! Go home without me." How could I, so far on foot! "Go and sing your lovesick songs to your lean English misses! They will thank you with a cup of abominable tea, and you will be in Paradise! This is *my* Paradise, and I shall stay until the angel comes to open it!"

He was very cross and unreasonable, and those were just the times when one loved him most, so I waited and enveloped my throat in my pocket-handkerchief and sang a passage or two just to prevent my voice from becoming stiff in that damp air.

"Be still! silence yourself!" he, cried. "I cannot hear if anyone is coming."

Someone came at last, a rough-looking sort of keeper, or *guardiano* as they are called there, who looked at us as though he thought we were mad. One of us certainly was, but it was not I. Marcello spoke pretty good Italian, with a French accent, it is true, but the man understood him, especially as he held his purse in his hand. I heard him say a great many impetuously persuasive things all in a breath, then he slipped a gold piece into the *guardiano's* horny hand, and the two turned toward the house, the man shrugging his shoulders in a resigned sort of way, and Marcello called out to me over his shoulder—

"Go home in the cab, or you will be late for your horrible English party! I am going to stay here tonight." *Ma foi!* I took his permission and left him; for a tenor voice is as tyrannical as a jealous woman. Besides, I was furious, and yet I laughed. His was the artist temperament, and appeared to us by turns absurd, sublime, and intensely irritating; but this last never for long, and we all felt that were we more like him our pictures would be worth more. I had not got as far as the city gate when my temper had cooled, and I began to reproach myself for leaving him in that lonely place with his purse full of money, for he was not poor at all, and tempting the dark *guardiano* to murder him.

Nothing could be easier than to kill him in his sleep and bury him away somewhere under the olive trees or in some old vault of a ruined catacomb, so common on the borders of the Campagna. There were sure to be a hundred such convenient places. I stopped the coachman and told him to turn back, but be shook his head and said something about having to be in the Piazza of St. Peter at eight o'clock. His horse began to go lame, as though he had understood his master and were his accomplice. What could I do? I said to myself that it was fate, and let him take me back to the Villa Medici, where I had to pay him a pretty sum for our crazy expedition, and then he rattled off, the horse not lame at all, leaving me bewildered at this strange afternoon.

I did not sleep well that night, though my tenor song had been applauded, and the English misses had caressed me much. I tried not to think of Marcello, and he did not trouble me much until I went to bed; but then I could not sleep, as I have told you. I fancied him already murdered, and being buried in the darkness by the *guardiano*. I saw the man dragging his body, with the beautiful head thumping against the stones, down dark passages, and at last leaving it all bloody and covered with earth under a black arch in a recess, and coming back to count the gold pieces.

But then again I fell asleep, and dreamed that Marcello was

standing at the gate and stamping his foot; and then I slept no more, but got up as soon as the dawn came, and dressed myself and went to my studio at the end of the laurel walk. I took down my painting-jacket, and remembered how he had pulled it off my shoulders. I took up the brushes he had washed for me; they were only half cleaned after all, and stiff with paint and soap. I felt glad to be angry with him, and *sacré*'d a little, for it made me sure that he was yet alive if I could scold at him. Then I pulled out my study of his head for my picture of Mucius Scaevola holding his hand in the name, and then I forgave him; for who could look upon that face and not love it?

I worked with the fire of friendship in my brush, and did my best to endow the features with the expression of scorn and obstinacy I had seen at the gate. It could not have been more suitable to my subject! Had I seen it for the last time? You will ask me why I did not leave my work and go to see if anything had happened to him, but against this there were several reasons. Our yearly exhibition was not far off and my picture was barely painted in, and my comrades had sworn that it would not be ready. I was expecting a model for the King of the Etruscans; a man who cooked chestnuts in the Piazza Montanara, and who had consented to stoop to sit to me as a great favour; and then, to tell the truth, the morning was beginning to dispel my fancies.

I had a good northern light to work by, with nothing sentimental about it, and I was not fanciful by nature; so when I sat down to my easel I told myself that I had been a fool, and that Marcello was perfectly safe: the smell of the paints helping me to feel practical again. Indeed, I thought every moment that he would come in, tired of his caprice already, and even was preparing and practising a little lecture for him. Someone knocked at my door, and I cried "*Entrez!*" thinking it was he at last; but no, it was Pierre Magnin.

"There is a curious man, a man of the country, who wants you," he said. "He has your address on a dirty piece of paper in Marcello's handwriting, and a letter for you, but he won't give it up. He says he must see 'il Signor Martino.' He'd make a superb model for a murderer! Come and speak to him, and keep him while I get a sketch of his head."

I followed Magnin through the garden, and outside—for the porter had not allowed him to enter—I found the *guardiano* of yesterday. He showed his white teeth, and said "Good day, *signore*," like a Christian; and here in Rome he did not look half so murderous, only a stupid, brown, country fellow. He had a rough peasant-cart waiting, and he had tied up his shaggy horse to a ring in the wall. I held out my hand for the letter and pretended to find it difficult to read, for I saw Magnin standing with his sketch-book in the shadow of the entrance-hall. The note said this—I have it still, and I will copy it. It was written in pencil on a leaf torn from his pocket-book:

> *Mon vieux!* I have passed a good night here, and the man will keep me as long as I like. Nothing will happen to me, except that I shall be divinely quiet, and I have already a famous *motif* in my head. Go to my lodgings and pack up some clothes and all my manuscripts, with plenty of music paper and a few bottles of Bordeaux, and give them to my messenger. Be quick about it!
>
> Fame is preparing to descend upon me! If you care to see me, do not come before eight days. The gate will not be opened if you come sooner. The *guardiano* is my slave, and he has instructions to kill any intruder who in the guise of a friend tries to get in uninvited. He will do it, for he has confessed to me that he has murdered three men already."
>
> (Of course this was a joke. I knew Marcello's way.)
>
> When you come, go to the *poste restante* and fetch my letters. Here is my card to legitimate you. Don't forget pens and a bottle of ink! Your
>
> Marcello.

There was nothing for it but to jump into the cart, tell Magnin, who had finished his sketch, to lock up my studio, and go bumping off to obey these commands. We drove to his lodgings in the Via del Governo Vecchio, and there I made a bundle of all that I could think of; the landlady hindering me by a thousand questions about when the *signore* would return. He had paid for the rooms in advance, so she had no need to be anxious about her rent. When I told her where he was she shook her head, and talked a good deal about the bad air out there, and said "Poor *signorino!*" in a melancholy way, as though he were already buried, and looked mournfully after us from the window when we drove away. She irritated me, and made me feel superstitious. At the corner of the Via del Tritone I jumped down and gave the man a *franc* out of pure sentimentality, and cried after him, "Greet the *signore!*" but he did not hear me, and jogged away stupidly while I was longing to be with him. Marcello was a cross to us sometimes, but we loved him always.

The eight days went by sooner than I had thought they would, and Thursday came, bright and sunny, for my expedition. At one o'clock I descended into the Piazza di Spagna, and made a bargain with a man who had a well-fed horse, remembering how dearly Marcello's want of good sense had cost me a week ago, and we drove off at a good pace to the Vigna Marziali, as I was almost forgetting to say that it was called. My heart was beating, though I did not know why I should feel so much emotion. When we reached the iron gate the *guardiano* answered my ring directly, and I had no sooner set foot in the long flower-walk than I saw Marcello hastening to meet me.

"I knew you would come," he said, drawing my arm within his, and so we walked toward the little gray house, which had a sort of *portico* and several balconies, and a sundial on its front. There were grated windows down to the ground floor, and the place, to my relief, looked safe and habitable. He told me that the man did not sleep there, but in a little hut down toward the Campagna, and that he, Marcello, locked himself in safely every night, which I was also relieved to know.

"What do you get to eat!" said I.

"Oh, I have goat's flesh, and dried beans and *polenta*, with *pecorino* cheese, and there is plenty of black bread and sour wine," he answered smilingly. "You see, I am not starved."

"Do not overwork yourself, *men vieux,*" I said; "you are worth more than your opera ever will be."

"Do I look overworked?" he said, turning his face to me in the broad, outdoor light. He seemed a little offended at my saying that about his opera, and I was foolish to do it.

I examined his face critically, and he looked at me half defiantly. "No, not yet," I answered rather unwillingly, for I could not say that he did; but there was a restless, inward look in his eyes, and an almost imperceptible shadow lay around them. It seemed to me as though the full temples had grown slightly hollow, and a sort of faint mist lay over his beauty, making it seem strange and far off. We were standing before the door, and he pushed it open, the *guardiano* following us with slow, loud-resounding steps.

"Here is my Paradise," said Marcello, and we entered the house, which was like all the others of its kind. A hall, with *stucco bas-reliefs*, and a stairway adorned with antique fragments, gave access to the upper rooms. Marcello ran up the steps lightly, and I heard him lock a door somewhere above and draw out the key, then he came and met me on the landing.

"This," he said, "is my work-room," and he threw open a low door. The key was in the lock, so this room could not be the one I heard him close. "Tell me I shall not write like an angel here!" he cried. I was so dazzled by the flood of bright sunshine after the dusk of the passage, that I blinked like an owl at first, and then I saw a large room, quite bare except for a rough table and chair, the chair covered with manuscript music.

"You are looking for the furniture," he said, laughing; "it is outside. Look here!" and he drew me to a rickety door of worm-eaten wood and coarse greenish glass, and flung it open on to a rusty iron balcony. He was right; the furniture was outside: that is to say, a divine view met my eyes. The Sabine Mountains, the Alban Hills, the broad Campagna, with its mediaeval towers and ruined aqueducts, and the open plain to the sea. All this glowing and yet calm in the sunlight. No wonder he could write there! The balcony ran round the corner of the house, and to the right I looked down upon an alley of ilexes, ending in a grove of tall laurel trees—very old, apparently. There were bits of sculpture and some ancient sarcophagi standing gleaming among them, and even from so high I could hear a little stream of water pouring from an antique mask into a long, rough trough.

I saw the brown *guardiano* digging at his cabbages and onions, and I laughed to think that I could fancy him a murderer! He had a little bag of relics, which dangled to and fro over his sunburned breast, and he looked very innocent when he sat down upon an old column to eat a piece of black bread with an onion which he had just pulled out of the ground, slicing it with a knife not at all like a dagger. But I kept my thoughts to myself, for Marcello would have laughed at them. We were standing together, looking down at the man as he drank from his hands at the running fountain, and Marcello now leaned down over the balcony, and called out a long "*Ohé!*" The lazy *guardiano* looked up, nodded, and then got up slowly from the stone where he had been half-kneeling to reach the jet of water.

"We are going to dine," Marcello explained. "I have been waiting for you." Presently we heard the man's heavy tread upon the stairs, and he entered bearing a strange meal in a basket.

There came to light *pecorino* cheese made from ewe's milk, black bread of the consistency of a stone, a great bowl of salad apparently composed of weeds, and a sausage which filled the room with a strong smell of garlic. Then he disappeared and came back with a dish full of ragged-looking goat's flesh cooked together with a mass of smoking *polenta*, and I am not sure that there was not oil in it.

"I told you I lived well, and now you see!" said Marcello. It was a terrible meal, but I had to eat it, and was glad to have some rough, sour wine to help me, which tasted of earth and roots. When we had finished, I said, "And your opera! How are you getting on?"

"Not a word about that!" he cried. "You see how I have

written!" and he turned over a heap of manuscript; "but do not talk to me about it. I will not lose my ideas in words." This was not like Marcello, who loved to discuss his work, and I looked at him astonished.

"Come," he said, "we will go down into the garden, and you shall tell me about the comrades. What are they doing? Has Magnin found a model for his Clytemnestra?"

I humoured him, as I always did, and we sat upon a stone bench behind the house, looking toward the laurel grove, talking of the pictures and the students. I wanted to walk down the ilex alley, but he stopped me.

"If you are afraid of the damp, don't go down there," he said; "the place is like a vault. Let us stay here and be thankful for this heavenly view."

"Well, let us say here," I answered, resigned as ever. He lit a cigar and offered me one in silence. If he did not care to talk, I could be still too. From time to time he made some indifferent observation, and I answered it in the same tone. It almost seemed to me as though we, the old heart-comrades, had become strangers who had not known each other a week, or as though we had been so long apart that we had grown away from each other. There was something about him which escaped me. Yes, the few days of solitude had indeed put years and a sort of shyness, or rather ceremony, between us! It did not seem natural to me now to clap him on the back, and make the old, harmless jokes at him. He must have felt the constraint, too, for we were like children who had looked forward to a game and did not know what to play at.

At six o'clock I left him. It was not like parting with Marcello. I felt rather as though I should find my old friend in Borne that evening, and here only left a shadowy likeness of him. He accompanied me to the gate, and pressed my hand, and for a moment the true Marcello looked out of his eyes; but we called out no last words to each other as I drove away. I had only said, "Let me know when you want me;" and he had said, "*Merci!*" and all the way back to Rome I felt a chill upon me, his hand had been so cold, and I thought and thought what could be the matter with him.

That evening I spoke out my anxiety to Pierre Magnin, who shook his head and declared that malaria fever must be taking hold of him, and that people often began to show it by being a little odd.

"He must not stay there! We must get him away as soon as possible," I cried.

"We know Marcello, and that nothing can make him stir against his will," said Pierre. "Let him alone, and he will get tired of his whim. It will not kill him to have a touch of malaria, and some evening he will turn up among us merry as ever."

But he did not. I worked hard at my picture and finished it, but for a few touches, and he had not yet appeared. Perhaps it was the extreme application, perhaps the sitting out in that damp place, for I insist upon tracing it to something more material than emotion. Well, whatever it was, I fell ill; more ill than I had ever been in. my life. It was almost twilight when it overtook me, and I remember it distinctly, though I forget what happened afterward, or, rather, I never knew, for I was found by Magnin, quite unconscious, and he has told me that I remained so for some time, and then became delirious, and talked of nothing but Marcello. I have told you. that it was very nearly twilight; but just at the moment when the sun is gone the colours show in their true value. Artiste know this, and I was putting last touches here and .there to my picture, and especially to my head of Mucius Scaevola, or, rather, Marcello.

The rest of the picture came out well enough; but that head, which should have been the principal one, seemed faded and sunk in. The face appeared to grow paler and paler, and to recede from me; a strange veil spread over it, and the eyes seemed to close. I am not easily frightened, and I know what tricks some peculiar methods of colour will play by certain lights, for the moment I spoke of had gone, and the twilight grayness had set in; so I stepped back to look well at it. Just then the lips, which had become almost white, opened a little, and sighed! An illusion, of course. I must have been very ill and quite delirious already, for to my imagination it was a real sigh, or, rather, a sort of exhausted gasp.

Then it was that I fainted, I suppose, and when I came to myself I was in my bed, with Magnin and Monsieur Sutton standing by me, and a Soeur de Charité moving softly about among medicine bottles, and speaking in whispers. I stretched out my hands, and they were thin and yellow, with long, pale nails; and I heard Magnin's voice, which sounded very far away, say, "*Dieu merci!*" And now Monsieur Sutton will tell you what I did not know until long afterward.

Martin Detaille.

2

ROBERT SUTTON'S ACCOUNT OF WHAT HAPPENED
AT THE VIGNA MARZIALI

I am attached to Detaille, and was very glad to be of use to him, but I never fully shared his admiration for Marcello Souvestre, though I appreciated his good points. He was certainly very promising—I must say that. But he was an odd, flighty sort of fellow, not of the kind which we English care to take the trouble to understand. It is my business to write stories, but not having need of such characters I have never particularly studied them. As I say, I was glad to be of use to Detaille, who is a thorough good fellow, and I willingly gave up my work to go and sit by his bedside. Magnin knew that I was a friend of his, and very properly came to me when he found that Detaille's illness was a serious one and likely to last for a long time. I found him perfectly delirious, and raving about Marcello.

"Tell me what the *motif* is! I know it is a *Marche Funèbre!*" And here he would sing a peculiar melody, which, as I have a knack at music, I noted down, it being like nothing I had heard before. The Sister of Charity looked at me with severe eyes; but how could she know that all is grist for our mill, and that observation becomes with as a mechanical habit? Poor Detaille kept repeating this curious melody over and over, and then would stop and seem to be looking at his picture, crying that it was fading away.

"Marcello! Marcello! You are fading too! Let me come to you!" He was as weak as a baby, and could not have moved from his bed unless in the strength of delirium.

"I cannot come!" he went on; "they have tied me down." And here he made as though he were trying to gnaw through a rope at his wrists, and then burst into tears. "Will no one go for me and bring me a word from you? Ah! if I could know that you are alive!"

Magnin looked at me. I knew what he was thinking. He would not leave his comrade, but I must go. I don't mind acknowledging that I did not undertake this unwillingly. To sit by Detaille's bedside and listen to his ravings enervated me, and what Magnin wanted struck me as troublesome but not uninteresting to one of my craft, so I agreed to go. I had heard all about Marcello's strange seclusion from Magnin and Detaille himself, who lamented over it openly in his simple way at supper at the academy, where I was a frequent guest.

I knew that it would be useless to ring at the gate of the Vigna Marziali. Not only should I not be admitted, but I should arouse Marcello's anger and suspicion, for I did not for a moment believe that he was not alive, though I thought it very possible that he was becoming a little crazy, as his countrymen are so easily put off their balance. Now, odd people are oddest late in the day and at evening-time. Their nerves lose the power of resistance then, and the real man gets the better of them. So I determined to try to discover something at night, reflecting also that I should be safer from detection then. I knew his liking for wandering about when he ought to be in his bed, and I did not doubt that I should get a glimpse of him, and that was really, all I needed.

My first step was to take a long walk out of the Porta San Giovanni, and this I did in the early morning, tramping along steadily until I came to an iron gate on the right of the road with "Vigna Marziali" over it; and then I walked straight on, never stopping until I had reached a little bushy lane running down toward the Campagna to the right. It was pebbly, and quite shut in by luxuriant ivy and elder bushes, and it bore deep traces of the last heavy rains. These had evidently been effaced by no footprints, so I concluded that it was little used. Down this path I made my way cautiously, looking behind and before me, from a habit contracted in my lonely wanderings in the Abruzzi. I had a capital revolver with me—an old friend—and I feared no man; but I began to feel a dramatic interest in my undertaking, and determined that it should not be crossed by any disagreeable surprises.

The lane led me further down the plain than I had reckoned upon, for the bushy edge shut out the view; and when I had got to the bottom and faced round, the Vigna Marziali was lying quite far to my left. I saw at a glance that behind the gray casino an alley of ilexes ended in a laurel grove; then there were plantations of kitchen-stuff, with a sort of thatched cabin in their midst, probably that of the gardener. I looked about for a kennel, but saw none, so there was no watchdog. At the end of this primitive kitchen garden was a broad patch of grass, bounded by a fence, which I could take at a spring. Now, I knew my way, but I could not resist tracing it out a little farther. It was well that I did so, for I found just within the fence a sunken stream, rather full at the time, in consequence of the rains, too deep to wade and too broad to jump. It struck me that it would be easy enough to take a board from the fence and lay it over for a bridge. I measured the breadth with my eye, and decided that the board would span it; then I went back as I had come, and returned to find Detaille still raving.

As he could understand nothing, it seemed to me rather a fool's errand to go off in search of comfort for him; but a conscious moment might come, and, moreover, I began to be interested in my undertaking; and so I agreed with Magnin that I should go and take some food and rest and return to the Vigna that night. I told my landlady that I was going into the country and should return the next day, and I went to Nazarri's and laid in a stock of sandwiches and filled my flask with something they called sherry, for, though I was no great wine-drinker, I feared the night-chill.

It was about seven o'clock when I started, and I retraced my morning's steps exactly. As I reached the lane, it occurred to me that it was still too light for me to pass unobserved over the stream, and I made a place for myself under the hedge and lay down, quite screened by the thick curtain of tangled overhanging ivy.

I must have been out of training, and tired by the morning's walk, for I fell asleep. When I awoke it was night; the stars were shining, a dank mist made its way down my throat, and I felt stiff and cold. I took a pull at my flask, finding it nasty stuff, but it warmed me. Then I rang my repeater, which struck a quarter to eleven, got up and shook myself free of the leaves and brambles, and went on down the lane. When I got to the fence I sat down and thought the thing over. What did I expect to discover? What *was* there to discover? Nothing! Nothing but that Marcello was alive; and that was no discovery at all, for I felt sure of it. I was a fool, and had let myself be allured by the mere stage nonsense and mystery of the business, and a mouse would creep out of this mountain of precautions!

Well, at least, I could turn it to account by describing my own absurd behaviour in some story yet to be written, and, as it was not enough for a chapter, I would add to it by further experience. "Come along!" I said to myself. "You're an ass, but it may prove instructive." I raised the top board from the fence noiselessly. There was a stile just there, and the boards were easily moved. I laid down my bridge with some difficulty and stepped carefully across, and made my way to the laurel grove as quickly and noiselessly as possible.

There all was thick darkness, and my eyes only grew slowly accustomed to it. After all there was not much to see; some stone seats in a semicircle, and some fragments of columns set upright with antique busts upon them. Then a little to the right a sort of arch, with apparently some steps descending into the ground, probably the entrance to some discovered branch of a catacomb. In the midst of the inclosure, not a very large one, stood a stone table, deeply fixed in the earth. No one was there; of that I felt certain, and I sat down, having now got used to the gloom, and fell to eat my sandwiches, for I was desperately hungry.

Now that I had come so far, was nothing to take place to repay me for my trouble? It suddenly struck me that it was absurd to expect Marcello to come out to meet me and perform any mad antics he might be meditating there before my eyes for my especial satisfaction. Why I had supposed that something would take place in the grove I do not know, except that this seemed a fit place for it. I would go and watch the house, and if I saw a light anywhere I might be sure that he was within. Any fool might have thought of that, but a novelist lays the scene of his drama and expects his characters to slide about in the grooves like puppets. It is only when mine surprise me that I feel they are alive.

When I reached the end of the ilex alley I saw the house before me. There were more cabbages and onions after I had left the trees, and I saw that in this open space I could easily be perceived by any one standing on the balcony above. As I drew back again under the ilexes, a window above, not the one on the balcony, was suddenly lighted up; but the light did not remain long, and presently a gleam shone through the glass oval over the door below.

I had just time to spring behind the thickest trunk near me when the door opened. I took advantage of its creaking to creep up the slanting tree like a cat, and lie out upon a projecting branch.

As I expected, Marcello came out. He was very pale, and moved mechanically like a sleep-walker. I was shocked to see how hollow his face had become, as he held the candle still lighted in his hand, and it cast deep shadows on his sunken cheeks and fixed eyes, which burned wildly and seemed to see nothing. His lips were quite white, and so drawn that I could see his gleaming teeth. Then the candle fell from his hand, and he came slowly and with a curiously regular step on into the darkness of the ilexes, I watching him from above. But I scarcely think he would have noticed me had I been standing in his path. When he had passed, I let myself down and followed him. I had taken off my shoes, and my tread was absolutely noiseless; moreover, I felt sure he would not turn round.

On he went with the same mechanical step until he reached the grove. There I knelt behind an old sarcophagus at the entrance, and waited. What would he do? He stood perfectly still, not looking about him, but as though the clockwork within him had suddenly stopped. I felt that he was becoming psychologically interesting, after all. Suddenly he threw up his arms as men do when they are mortally wounded on the battlefield, and I expected to see him fall at full length. Instead of this, he made a step forward.

I looked in the same direction and saw a woman, who must have concealed herself there while I was waiting before the house, come from out of the gloom, and as she slowly approached and laid her head upon his shoulder, the outstretched arms clasped themselves closely around her, so that her face was hidden upon his neck.

So this was the whole matter, and I had been sent off on a wild-goose chase to spy out a common love-affair! His opera and his seclusion for the sake of work, his tyrannical refusal to see Detaille unless he sent for him—all this was but a mask to a vulgar intrigue which, for reasons best known to himself, could not be indulged in in the city. I was thoroughly angry! If Marcello passed his time mooning about in that damp hole all night, do wonder that he looked so wretchedly ill, and seemed half mad! I knew very well that Marcello was no saint. Why should he be? But I had not taken him for a fool! He had had plenty of romantic episodes, and as he was discreet without being uselessly mysterious no one had ever unduly pried into them, nor should we have done so now.

I said to myself that that mixture of French and Italian blood was at the bottom of it; French flimsiness and light-headedness and Italian love of cunning! I looked back upon all the details of my mysterious expedition. I suppose at the root or my anger lay a certain dramatic disappointment at not finding him lying murdered, and I despised myself for all the trouble I had taken to this ridiculous end: just to see him holding a woman in his arms. I could not see her face, and her figure was enveloped from head to foot in something long and dark; but I could make out that she was tall and slender, and that a pair of white hands gleamed from her drapery. As I was looking intently, for all my indignation, the couple moved on, and still clinging to one another descended the steps. So even the solitude of the lonely laurel grove could not satisfy Marcello's insane love of secrecy!

I kept still awhile; then I stole to where they had disappeared, and listened; but all was silent, and I cautiously struck a match and peered down. I could see the steps for a short distance below me, and then the darkness seemed to rise and swallow them. It must be a catacomb, as I had imagined, or an old Roman bath, perhaps, which Marcello had made comfortable enough, no doubt, and as likely as not they were having a nice little cold supper there. My empty stomach told me that I could have forgiven him even then could I have shared it. I was in truth frightfully hungry as well as angry, and sat down on one of the stone benches to finish my sandwiches.

The thought of waiting to see this love-sick pair return to upper earth never for a moment occurred to me. I had found out the whole thing, and a great humbug it was! Now I wanted to get back to Rome before my temper had cooled, and to tell Magnin on what a fool's errand he had sent me. If he liked to quarrel with me, all the better!

All the way home I composed cutting French speeches, but they suddenly cooled and petrified like a gust of lava from a volcano when I discovered that the gate was closed. I had never thought of getting a pass, and Magnin ought to have warned me. Another grievance against the fellow! I enjoyed my resentment, and it kept me warm as I patrolled up and down. There are houses, and even small eating-shops, outside the gate, but no light was visible, and I did not care to attract attention by pounding at the doors in the middle of the night; so I crept behind a bit of wall. I was getting used to hiding by this time, and made myself as comfortable as I could with my ulster, took another pull at my flask, and waited.

At last the gate was opened and I slipped through, trying not to look as though I had been out all night like a bandit. The guard looked at me narrowly, evidently wondering at my lack of luggage. Had I had a knapsack I might have been taken for some innocently mad English tourist indulging in the mistaken pleasure of trudging in from Frascati or Albano; but a man in an ulster, with his hands in his pockets, sauntering in at the gate of the city at break of day as though returning from a stroll, naturally puzzled the officials, who looked after me and shrugged their shoulders.

Luckily I found an early cab in the Piazza of the Lateran, for I was dead-beat, and was soon at my lodgings in the Via della Croce, where my landlady let me in very speedily. Then at last I had the comfort of throwing off my clothes, all damp with the night dew, and turning in. My wrath had cooled to a certain point, and I did not fear to lower its temperature too greatly by yielding to an overwhelming desire for sleep. An hour or two could make no great difference to Magnin—let him fancy me still hanging about the Vigna Marziali! Sleep I must have, no matter what he thought. I slept long, and was awakened at last by my landlady, Sora Nanna, standing over me, and saying, "There is a *signore* who wants you."

"It is I, Magnin!" said a voice behind her. "I could not wait for you to come!" He looked haggard with anxiety and watching.

"Detaille is raving still," he went on, "only worse than before. Speak, for Heaven's sake! Why don't you tell me something?" And he shook me by the arm as though he thought I was still asleep.

"Have you nothing to say? You must have seen something! Did you see Marcello?"

"Oh! yes, I saw him."

"Well?"

"Well, he was very comfortable—quite alive. He had a woman's arms around him."

I heard my door violently slammed to, a ferocious "*Sacré gamin!*" and then steps springing down the stairs. I felt perfectly happy at having made such an impression, and turned and resumed my broken sleep with almost a kindly feeling toward Magnin, who was at that moment probably tearing up the Spanish Scalinata two steps at a time, and making himself horribly hot. It could not help Detaille, poor fellow! He could not understand my news. When I had slept long enough I got up, refreshed myself with a bath and something to eat, and went off to see Detaille. It was not his fault that I had been made a fool of, so I felt sorry for him.

I found him raving just as I had left him the day before, only worse, as Magnin said. He persisted in continually crying, "Marcello, take care! no one can save you!" in hoarse, weak tones, but with the regularity of a knell, keeping up a peculiar movement with his feet, as though he were weary with a long road, but must press forward to his goal. Then he would stop and break into childish sobs.

"My feet are so sore," he murmured, piteously, "and I am so tired! But I will come! They are following me, but I am strong!" Then a violent struggle with his invisible pursuers, in which he would break off into that singing of his, alternating with the warning cry.

The singing voice was quite another from the speaking one. He went on and on, repeating the singular air which he had himself called a Funeral March, and which had become intensely disagreeable to me. If it was one indeed, it surely was intended for no Christian burial. As he sang, the tears kept trickling down his cheeks, and Magnin sat wiping them away as tenderly as a woman. Between his song he would clasp his hands, feebly enough, for he was very weak when the delirium did not make him violent, and cry in heart-rending tones, "Marcello, I shall never see you again! Why did you leave us?" At last, when he stopped for a moment, Magnin left his side, beckoning the Sister to take it, and drew me into the other room, closing the door behind him.

"Now tell me exactly how you saw Marcello," said he; so I related my whole absurd experience—forgetting, however, my personal irritation, for he looked too wretched and worn for anybody to be angry with him. He made me repeat several times my description of Marcello's face and manner as he had come out of the house. That seemed to make more impression upon him than the love business.

"Sick people have strange intuitions," he said, gravely; "and I persist in thinking that Marcello is very ill and in danger. *Tenez!*" And here he broke off, went to the door, and called "*Ma soeur!*" under his breath. She understood, and after having drawn the bedclothes straight, and once more dried the trickling tears, she came noiselessly to where we stood, the wet handkerchief still in her hand. She was a singularly tall and strong-looking woman, with piercing black eyes and a self-controlled manner. Strange to say, she bore the adopted name of Claudius, instead of a more feminine one.

"*Ma soeur,*" said Magnin, "at what o'clock was it that he sprang out of bed and we had to hold him for so long?"

"Half-past eleven and a few minutes," she answered promptly. Then he turned to me.

"At what time did Marcello come out into the garden ?"

"Well, it might have been half-past eleven," I answered, unwillingly. "I should say that three quarters of an hour might possibly have passed since I rang my repeater. Mind you, I won't swear it!" I hate to have people try to prove mysterious coincidences, and this was just what they were attempting.

"Are you sure of the hour, *ma soeur?*" I asked, a little tartly. She looked at me calmly with her great, black eyes, and said:

"I heard the Trinità de' Monti strike the half-hour just before it happened."

"Be so good as to tell Monsieur Sutton exactly what took

place," said Magnin.

"One moment, *monsieur*," and she went swiftly and softly to Detaille, raised him on her strong arm, and held a glass to his lips, from which he drank mechanically. Then she came and stood where she could watch him through the open door.

"He hears nothing," she said, as she hung the handkerchief to dry over a chair; and then she went on. "It was half-past eleven, and my patient had been very uneasy—that is to say, more so even than before. It might have been four or five minutes after the clock had finished striking that he became suddenly quite still and then began to tremble all over, so that the bed shook with him." She spoke admirable English, as many of the Sisters do, so I need not translate, but will give her own words.

"He went on trembling until I thought he was going to have a fit, and told Monsieur Magnin to be ready to go for the doctor, when just then the trembling stopped, he became perfectly stiff, his hair stood up upon his head, and his eyes seemed coming out of their sockets, though he could see nothing, for I passed the candle before them. All at once he sprang out of his bed and rushed to the door. I did not know he was so strong. Before he got there I had him in my arms, for he has become very light, and I carried him back to bed again, though he was straggling like a child. Monsieur Magnin came in from the next room just as he was trying to get up again, and we held him down until it was past, but he screamed Monsieur Souvestre's name for a long time after that. Afterward he was very cold and exhausted, of course, and I gave him some beef-tea, though it was not the hour for it."

"I think you had better tell the Sister all about it," said Magnin, turning to me. "It is best that the nurse should know everything."

"Very well," said I; "though I do not think ifs much in her line." she answered me herself: "Everything which concerns our patients is our business. Nothing shocks us." Thereupon she sat down and thrust her hands into her long sleeves, prepared to listen. I repeated the whole affair as I had done to Magnin. She never took her brilliant eyes from off my face, and listened as coolly as though she had been a doctor hearing an account of a difficult case, though to me it seemed almost sacrilege to be describing the behaviour of a love-stricken youth to a Sister of Charity.

"What do you say to that, *ma soeur?*" asked Magnin, when I had done.

"I say nothing, *monsieur.* It is sufficient that I know it;" and she withdrew her hands from her sleeves, took up the handkerchief, which was dry by this time, and returned quietly to her place at the bedside.

"I wonder if I have shocked her, after all?" I said to Magnin.

"Oh, no," he answered. "They see many things, and a *soeur* is as abstract as a confessor; they do not allow themselves any personal feelings. I have seen Soeur Claudius listen perfectly unmoved to the most abominable ravings, only crossing herself beneath her cape at the most hideous blasphemies. It was last summer when poor Justin Revol died. You were not here." Magnin put his hand to his forehead.

"You are looking ill yourself," I said. "Go and try to sleep, and I will stay."

"Very well," he answered; "but I cannot rest unless you promise to remember everything he says, that I may hear it when I wake;" and he threw himself down upon the hard sofa like a sack, and was asleep in a moment; and I, who had felt so angry with him but a few hours ago, put a cushion under his head and made him comfortable.

I sat down in the next room and listened to Detaille's monotonous ravings, while Soeur Claudius read in her book of prayers. It was getting dusk, and several of the academicians stole in and stood over the sick man and shook their heads. They looked around for Magnin, but I pointed to the other room with my finger on my lips, and they nodded and went away on tiptoe.

It required no effort of memory to repeat Detaille's words to Magnin when he woke, for they were always the same. We had another Sister that night, and as Soeur Claudius was not to return till the next day at midday, I offered to share the watch with Magnin, who was getting very nervous and exhausted, and who seemed to think that some such attack might be expected as had occurred the night before. The new Sister was a gentle, delicate-looking little woman, with tears in her soft brown eyes as she bent over the sick man, and crossed herself from time to time, grasping the crucifix which hung from the beads at her waist. Nevertheless she was calm and useful, and as punctual as Soeur Claudius herself in giving the medicines.

The doctor had come in the evening, and prescribed a change in these. He would not say what he thought of his patient, but only declared that it was necessary to wait for a crisis. Magnin sent for some supper, and we sat over it together in silence, neither of us hungry. He kept looking at his watch.

"If the same thing happens tonight, he will die!" said he, and laid his head on his arms.

"He will die in a most foolish cause, then," I said, angrily, for I thought he was going to cry, as those Frenchmen have a way of doing, and I wanted to irritate him by way of a tonic; so I went on—

"It would be dying for a *vaurien* who is making an ass of himself in a ridiculous business which will be over in a week! Souvestre may get as much fever as he likes! only don't ask me to come and nurse him."

"It is not the fever," said he slowly, "it is a horrible nameless dread that I have; I suppose it is listening to Detaille that makes me nervous. Hark!" he added, "it strikes eleven. We must watch!"

"If you really expect another attack you had better warn the Sister," I said; so he told her in a few words what might happen.

"Very well, *monsieur*," she answered, and sat down quietly near the bed, Magnin at the pillow, and I near him. No sound was to be heard but Detaille's ceaseless lament.

And now, before I tell you more, I must stop to entreat you to believe me. It will be almost impossible for you to do so, I know, for I have laughed myself at such tales, and no assurances would have made me credit them. But I, Robert Sutton, swear that this thing happened. More I cannot do. It is the truth.

We had been watching Detaille intently. He was lying with closed eyes, and had been very restless. Suddenly he became quite still, and then began to tremble, exactly as Soeur Claudius had described. It was a curious, uniform trembling, apparently in every fibre, and his iron bedstead shook as though strong hands were at its head and foot. Then came the absolute rigidity she had also described, and I do not exaggerate when I say that not only did his short-cropped hair seem to stand erect, but that it literally did so. A lamp cast the shadow of his profile against the wall to the left of his bed, and as I looked at the immovable outline which seemed painted on the wall, I saw the hair slowly rise until the line where it joined the forehead was quite a different one—abrupt instead of a smooth sweep. His eyes opened wide and were frightfully fixed, then as frightfully strained, but they certainly did not see us.

We waited breathlessly for what might follow. The little Sister was standing close to him, her lips pressed together and a little pale, but very calm. "Do not be frightened, *ma soeur*," whispered Magnin; and she answered in a business-like tone, "No, *monsieur*," and drew still nearer to her patient, and took his hands, which were stiff as those of a corpse, between her own to warm them. I laid mine upon his heart; it was beating so imperceptibly that I almost thought it had stopped, and as I leaned my face to his lips I could feel no breath issue from them. It seemed as though the rigor would last forever.

Suddenly, without any transition, he hurled himself with enormous force, and literally at one bound, almost into the middle of the room, scattering us aside like leaves in the wind. I was upon him in a moment, grappling with him with all my strength, to prevent him from reaching the door. Magnin had been thrown backward against the table, and I heard the medicine bottles crash with his fall. He had flung back his hand to save himself, and rushed to help me with the blood dropping from a cut in his wrist. The little Sister sprang to us. Detaille had thrown her violently back upon her knees, and now, with a nurse's instinct, she tried to throw a shawl over his bare breast. We four must have made a strange group!

Four? *We were five!* Marcello Souvestre stood before us, just within the door! We all saw him, for he was there. His bloodless face was turned toward us unmoved; his hands hung by his side as white as his face; only his eyes had life in them; they were fixed on Detaille.

"Thank God, you have come at last!" I cried. "Don't stand there like a fool! Help us, can't you?" But he never moved. I was furiously angry, and, leaving my hold, sprang upon him to drag him forward. My outstretched hands struck hard against the door, and I felt a thing like a spider's web envelop me. It seemed to draw itself over my mouth and eyes, and to blind and choke me, and then to flutter and tear and float from me.

Marcello was gone!

Detaille had slipped from Magnin's hold, and lay in a heap upon the floor, as though his limbs were broken. The Sister was trembling violently as she knelt over him and tried to raise his head. We gazed at one another, stooped and lifted him in our arms, and carried him back to his bed, while Soeur Marie quietly collected the broken phials.

"You saw it, *ma soeur!*" I heard Magnin whisper hoarsely.

"Yes, *monsieur!*" she only answered, in a trembling voice, holding on to her crucifix. Then she said, in a professional tone:

"Will *monsieur* let me bind up his wrist?" And though her fingers trembled and his hand was shaking, the bandage was an irreproachable one.

Magnin went into the next room, and I heard him throw himself heavily into a chair. Detaille seemed to be sleeping. His breath came regularly; his eyes were closed with a look of peace about the lids, his hands lying in a natural way upon the quilt. He had not moved since we laid him there. I went softly to where Magnin was sitting in the dark. He did not move, but only said, "Marcello is dead!

"He is either dead or dying," I answered, "and we must go to him."

"Yes," Magnin whispered, "we must go to him, but we shall not reach him."

"We will go as soon as it is light," I said, and then we were still again.

When the morning came at last he went and found a comrade to take his place, and only said to Soeur Marie, "It is not necessary to speak of this night;" and at her quiet "You are right, *monsieur*," we felt that we could trust her. Detaille was still sleeping. Was this the crisis the doctor had expected? Perhaps; but sorely not in such fearful form. I insisted upon my companion having some breakfast before we started, and I breakfasted myself, but I cannot say I tasted what passed between my lips.

We engaged a closed carriage, for we did not know what we might bring home with us, though neither of us spoke out his thoughts. It was early morning still when we reached the Vigna Marziali, and we had not exchanged a word all the way. I rang at the bell, while the coachman looked on curiously. It was answered promptly by the *guardiano*, of whom Detaille has already told you.

"Where is the *signore?*" I asked through the gate. "*Chi lo sa?*" he answered. "He is here, of course; he has not left the Vigna. Shall I call him?"

"*Call him?*" I knew that no mortal voice could reach Marcello now, but I tried to fancy he was still alive.

"No," I said. "Let us in. We want to surprise him; he will be pleased."

The man hesitated, but he finally opened the gate, and we entered, leaving the carriage to wait outside. We went straight to the house; the door at the back was wide open. There had been a gale in the night, and it had torn some leaves and bits of twigs from the trees and blown them into the entrance-hall. They lay scattered across the threshold, and were evidence that the door had remained open ever since they had fallen. The *guardiano* left us, probably to escape Marcello's anger at having let us in, and we went up the stairs unhindered, Magnin foremost, for he knew the house better than I, from Detaille's description. He had told him about the corner room with the balcony, and we pretended that Marcello might be there, absorbed betimes in his work, but we did not call him.

He was not there. His papers were strewn over the table as though he had been writing, but the inkstand was dry and full of dust; he could not have used it for days. We went silently into the other chambers. Perhaps he was still asleep? But, no! We found his bed untouched, so he could not have lain in it that night The rooms were all unlocked but one, and this closed door made our hearts beat. Marcello could scarcely be there, however, for there was no key in the lock; I saw the daylight shining through the key-hole. We called his name, but there came no answer. We knocked loudly, still no sign from within; so I put my shoulder to the door, which wad old and cracked in several places, and succeeded in bursting it open.

Nothing was there but a sculptor's modelling-stand, with something upon it covered with a white cloth, and the model-ling-tools on the floor. At the sight of the cloth, still damp, we drew a deep breath. It could not have hung there for many hours, certainly not for twenty-four. We did not raise it "He would be vexed," said Magnin, and I nodded, for it is accounted almost a crime in the artist's world to unveil a sculptor's work behind his back. We expressed no surprise at the fact of his modelling; a ban seemed to lie upon our tongues. The cloth hung tightly to the object beneath it, and showed us the outline of a woman's head and rounded bust, and so veiled we left her. There was a little winding stair leading out of the passage, and we climbed it, to find ourselves in a sort of belvedere, commanding a superb view. It was a small, open terrace, on the roof of the house, and we saw at a glance that no one was there.

We had now been all over the casino, which was small and simply built, being evidently intended only for short summer use. As we stood leaning over the balustrade we could look down into the garden. No one was there but the *guardiano,* lying among his cabbages with his arms behind his head, half asleep. The laurel grove had been in my mind from the beginning, only it had seemed more natural to go to the house first. Now we descended the stairs silently and directed our steps thither.

As we approached it, the *guardicmo* came toward us lazily.

"Have you seen the *signore?*" he asked, and his stupidly placid face showed me that he, at least, had no hand in his disappearance.

"No, not yet," I answered, "but we shall come across him somewhere, no doubt. Perhaps he has gone to take a walk, and we will wait for him. What is this?" I went on, trying to seem careless. We were standing now by the little arch, of which you know.,

"This?" said he; "I have never been down there, but they say it is something old. Do the *signori* want to see it? I will fetch a lantern."

I nodded, and he went off to his cabin. I had a couple of candles in my pocket, for I had intended to explore the place, should we not find Marcello. It was there that he had disappeared that night, and my thoughts had been busy with it; but I kept my candles concealed, reflecting that they would give our search an air of premeditation which would excite curiosity.

"When did you see the *signore* last!" I asked, when he had returned with the lantern.

"I brought him his supper yesterday evening."

"At what o'clock?"

"It was the *Ave Maria, signore,*" he replied. "He always sups then."

It would be useless to put any further questions. He was evidently utterly unobserving, and would lie to please us.

"Let me go first," said Magnin, taking the lantern. We set our feet upon the steps; a cold air seemed to fill our lungs and yet to choke us, and a thick darkness lay beneath. The steps, as I could see by the light of my candle, were modern, as well as the vaulting above them. A tablet was let into the wall, and in spite of my excitement I paused to read it, perhaps because I was glad to delay whatever awaited us below. It ran thus:

"*Questo antico sepolcro Romano scopri il Conte Marziali nell' anno 1853, e piamente conservòo.*" In plain English:

"Count Marziali discovered this ancient Roman sepulchre in the year 1853, and piously preserved it."

I read it more quickly than it has taken time to write here, and hurried after Magnin, whose footsteps sounded faintly below me. As I hastened, a draught of cold air extinguished my candle, and I was trying to make my way down by feeling along the wall, which was horribly dark and clammy, when my heart stood still at a cry from far beneath me—a cry of horror!

"Where are you?" I shouted; but Magnin was calling my name, and could not hear me. "I am here. I am in the dark!"

I was making haste as fast as I could, but there were several turnings.

"I have found him!" came up from below.

"Alive?" I shouted. No answer.

One last short flight brought me face to face with the gleam of the lantern. It came from a low doorway, and within stood Magnin, peering into the darkness. I knew by his face, as he held the light high above him, that our fears were realized.

Yes, Marcello was there. He was lying stretched upon the floor, staring at the ceiling, dead, and already stiff, as I could see at a glance. We stood over him saying not a word, then I knelt down and felt of him, for mere form's sake, and said, as though I had not known it before, "He has been dead for some hours."

"Since yesterday evening," said Magnin, in a horror-stricken voice, yet with a certain satisfaction in it, as though to say, "You see, I was right"

Marcello was lying with his head slightly thrown back, no contortions in his handsome features; rather the look of a person who has quietly died of exhaustion—who has slipped unconsciously from life to death. His collar was thrown open and a part of his breast, of a ghastly white, was visible. Just over the heart was a small spot.

"Give me the lantern," I whispered, as I stooped over it. It was a very little spot, of a faint purplish-brown, and must have changed colour within the night.

I examined it intently, and should say that the blood had been sucked to the surface, and then a small prick or incision made. The slight subcutaneous effusion led me to this conclusion. One tiny drop of coagulated blood closed the almost imperceptible wound. I probed it with the end of one of Magnin's matches. It was scarcely more than skin-deep, so it could not be the stab of a stiletto, however slender, or the track of a bullet. Still, it was strange, and with one impulse we turned to see if no one were concealed there, or if there were no second exit. It would be madness to suppose that the murderer, if there was one, would remain by his victim. Had Marcello been making love to a pretty *contadina*, and was this some jealous lover's vengeance! But it was not a stab. Had one drop of poison in the little wound done this deadly work!

We peered about the place, and I saw that Magnin's eyes were blinded by tears and his face as pale as that upturned one on the floor, whose lids I had vainly tried to close. The chamber was low, and beautifully ornamented with *stucco bas-reliefs*, in the manner of the well-known one not far from there upon the same road. Winged genii, griffins, and arabesques, modelled with marvellous lightness, covered the walls and ceiling. There was no other door than the one we had entered by. In the centre stood a marble sarcophagus, with the usual subjects sculptured upon it, on the one side Hercules conducting a veiled figure, on the other a dance of nymphs and fauns. A space in the middle contained the following inscription, deeply cut in the stone, and still partially filled with red pigment:

D. M.

VESPERTILIAE·THC·AIMATOПΩTIΔOC·

Q · FLAVIVS · VIX · IPSE · SOSPES ·

MON · POSVIT.

"What is this?" whispered Magnin. It was only a pickaxe and a long crowbar, such as the country people use in hewing out their blocks of "*tufa*," and his foot had struck against them. Who could have brought them here? They must belong to the *guardiano* above, but he said that he had never come here, and I believed him, knowing the Italian horror of darkness and lonely places; but what had Marcello wanted with them? It did not occur to us that archaeological curiosity could have led him to attempt to open the sarcophagus, the lid of which had evidently never been raised, thus justifying the expression, "piously preserved."

As I rose from examining the tools my eyes fell upon the line of mortar where the cover joined to the stone below, and I noticed that some of it had been removed, perhaps with the pickaxe which lay at my feet. I tried it with my nails and found that it was very crumbly. Without a word I took the tool in my hand, Magnin instinctively following my movements with the lantern. What impelled us I do not know. I had myself no thought, only an irresistible desire to see what was within. I saw that much of the mortar had been broken away, and lay in small fragments upon the ground, which I had not noticed before. It did not take long to complete the work. I snatched the lantern from Magnin's hand and set it upon the ground, where it shone full upon Marcello's dead face, and by its light I found a little break between the two masses of stone and managed to insert the end of my crowbar, driving it in with a blow of the pickaxe. The stone chipped and then cracked a little. Magnin was shivering.

"What are you going to do!" he said, looking around at where Marcello lay.

"Help me!" I cried, and we two bore with all our might upon the crowbar. I am a strong man, and I felt a sort of blind fury as the stone refused to yield. What if the bar should snap? With another blow I drove it in still further, then using it as a lever, we weighed upon it with our outstretched arms until every muscle was at its highest tension. The stone moved a little, and, almost fainting, we stopped to rest.

From the ceiling hung the rusty remnant of an iron chain which must once have held a lamp. To this, by scrambling upon the sarcophagus, I contrived to make fast the lantern.

"Now!" said I, and we heaved again at the lid. It rose, and we alternately heaved and pushed until it lost its balance and fell with a thundering crash upon the other side; such a crash that the walls seemed to shake, and I was for a moment utterly deafened, while little pieces of *stucco* rained upon us from the ceiling. When we had paused to recover from the shock we leaned over the sarcophagus and looked in.

The light shone full upon it, and we saw—how is it possible to tell? We saw lying there, amid folds of mouldering rags, the body of a woman, perfect as in life, with faintly rosy face, soft crimson lips, and a breast of living pearl, which seemed to heave as though stirred by some delicious dream. The rotten stuff swathed about her was in ghastly contrast to this lovely form, fresh as the morning! Her hands lay stretched at her side, the pink palms were turned a little outward, her eyes were closed as peacefully as those of a sleeping child, and her long hair, which shone red-golden in the dim light from above, was wound around her head in numberless finely plaited tresses, beneath which little locks escaped in rings upon her brow. I could have sworn that the blue veins on that divinely perfect bosom held living blood!

We were absolutely paralyzed, and Magnin leaned gasping over the edge as pale as death, paler by far than this living, almost smiling face to which his eyes were glued. I do not doubt that I was as pale as he at this inexplicable vision. As I looked, the red lips seemed to grow redder. They *were* redder! The little pearly teeth showed between them. I had not seen them before, and now a clear ruby drop trickled down to her rounded chin and from there slipped sideways and fell upon her neck. Horror-struck I gazed upon the living corpse, till *my* eyes could not bear the sight any longer.

As I looked away my glance fell once more upon the mysterious inscription, half Latin, half Greek, and the awful meaning of the words flashed upon me suddenly as I read them this second time. "To Vespertilia"— that was in Latin, and even the Latin name of the woman suggested a thing of evil flitting in the dusk. But the full horror of the nature of that thing had been veiled to Roman eyes under the Greek τῆς αἱματοποτ¿ λιν, "The blood-drinker, the vampire woman." And Flavins—her lover— *vix ipse sospes*, "himself hardly saved" from that deadly embrace, had buried her here, and set a seal upon her sepulchre, trusting to the weight of stone and the strength of clinging mortar to imprison forever the beautiful monster he had loved.

"Infamous murderess!" I cried, "you have killed Marcello!" and a sudden, vengeful calm came over me.

"Give me the pickaxe," I said to Magnin. I can hear myself saying it still. He picked it up and handed it to me as in a dream; he seemed little better than an idiot, and the beads of sweat were shining on his forehead. I took my knife, and from the long wooden handle of the pickaxe I cut a fine, sharp stake. Then I clambered, scarcely feeling any repugnance, over the side of the sarcophagus, my feet among the folds of Vespertilia's decaying winding-sheet, which crushed like ashes beneath my boot.

I looked for one moment at that white breast, but only to choose the loveliest spot, where the network of azure veins shimmered like veiled turquoises, and then with one blow I drove the pointed stake deep down through the breathing snow and stamped it in with my heel.

An awful shriek, so ringing and horrible that I thought my ears must have burst; but even then I felt neither fear nor horror. There are times when these cannot touch us. I stooped and gazed once again at the face, now undergoing a fearful change— fearful and final!

"Foul vampire!" I said quietly in my concentrated rage. "You will do no more harm now!" And then, without looking back upon her cursed face, I clambered out of the horrible tomb.

We raised Marcello, and slowly carried him up the steep stairs—a difficult task, for the way was narrow and he was so stiff. I noticed that the steps were ancient up to the end of the second flight; above, the modern passage was somewhat broader. When we reached the top, the *guardiano* was lying upon one of the stone benches; he did not mean us to cheat him out of his fee. I gave him a couple of *francs*.

"You see that we have found the *signore*," I tried to say in a natural voice. "He is very weak, and we will carry him to the carriage." I had thrown my handkerchief over Marcello's face, but the man knew as well as I that he was dead. Those stiff feet told their own story, but Italians are timid of being involved in such affairs. They have a childish dread of the police, and he only answered, "Poor *signorino!* He is very ill; it is better to take him to Rome," and kept cautiously clear of us as we went up to the ilex alley with our icy burden, and he did not go to the gate with us, not liking to be observed by the coachman, who was dozing on his box.

With difficulty we got Marcello's corpse into the carriage, the driver turning to look at us suspiciously. I explained we had found our friend very ill, and at the same time slipped a gold piece into his hand, telling him to drive to the Via del Governo Vecchio. He pocketed the money, and whipped his horses into a trot, while we sat supporting the stiff body, which swayed like a broken doll at every pebble in the road. When we reached the Via del Governo Vecchio at last, no one saw us carry him into the house. There was no step before the door, and we drew up so close to it that it was possible to screen our burden from sight. When we had brought him into his room and laid him upon his bed, we noticed that his eyes were closed; from the movement of the carriage, perhaps, though that was scarcely possible.

The landlady behaved very much as I had expected her to do, for, as I told you, I know the Italians. She pretended, too, that the *signore* was very ill, and made a pretence of offering to fetch a doctor, and when I thought it best to tell her that he was dead, declared that it must have happened that very moment, for she had seen him look at us and close his eyes again. She had always told him that he ate too little and that he would be ill. Yes, it was weakness and that bad air out there which had killed him; and then he worked too hard. When she had successfully established this fiction, which we were glad enough to agree to—for neither did we wish for the publicity of an inquest—she ran out and fetched a gossip to come and keep her company.

So died Marcello Souvestre, and so died Vespertilia the blood-drinker at last.

There is not much more to tell. Marcello lay calm and beautiful upon his bed, and the students came and stood silently looking at him, then knelt down for a moment to say a prayer, crossed themselves, and left him forever.

We hastened to the Villa Medici, where Detaille was sleeping, and Sister Claudius watching him with a satisfied look on her strong face. She rose noiselessly at our entrance, and came to us at the threshold. "He will recover," said she, softly. She was right When he awoke and opened his eyes he knew us directly, and Magnin breathed a devout "Thank God!"

"Have I been ill, Magnin?" he asked very feebly.

"You have had a little fever," answered Magnin, promptly; "but it is over now. Here is Monsieur Sutton come to see you."

"Has Marcello been here!" was the next question. Magnin looked at him very steadily.

"No," he only said, letting his face tell the rest.

"Is he dead, then?" Magnin only bowed his head. "Poor friend!" Detaille murmured to himself, then closed his heavy eyes and slept again.

A few days after Marcello's funeral we went to the fatal Vigna Marziali to bring back the objects which had belonged to him. As I laid the manuscript score of the opera carefully together, my eye fell upon a passage which struck me as the identical one which Detaille had so constantly sung in his delirium, and which I had noted down. Strange to say, when I reminded him of it later, it was perfectly new to him, and he declared that Marcello had not let him examine his manuscript. As for the veiled bust in the other room, we left it undisturbed, and to crumble away unseen.

The Witches

By Edmund Gosse

1

At dead of night in Cranley Street,
A silent crowd of yokels meet;
In marshalled line they form, and stand
With candles lighted in their hand;
Then up the lane they turn to go:
Down the calm meads no breezes blow,
The flame scarce wavers to and fro—
The flame to scare the witches.

2

And now, through smoke of flaring dips,
The stars are seen, like ghostly ships,
With all sails set in heaven's dark sea;
And ghostly white from the elder-tree
The clusters hang; but still there flows
No honey from the parched-up rose,
No breath from the honey-suckle blows—
All's blighted by the witches.

3

Through leaden air the young men pass,
Their shoes are dry in the long grass;
No living creature round them stirs,
No weasel squeaks, no fern-owl whirrs;
Through the dull night with might and main—

Each nerve and sinew on the strain—
They bear their candles up the lane
To daunt the midnight witches.

4

But one by one their flames burn blue,
And all but three, then all but two,
By unseen lips at gateways blown,
Go out, till one is left alone;
One trembling flame that seems to shrink
Within its wall of fingers pink,
And now would rise and now would sink,
Sole help against the witches.

5

Still guarding this one light they rise,
Till, darker than the dark blue skies,
A starless mass above them burst—
The windmill upon Coneyhurst;
And through the fern and furze they hear,
With aching nerve of the tingling ear,
A sound that curdles them with fear—
The rustling of the witches.

6

From north, from south, from east, from west,
As by one kindred aim possessed,
Four singing shadows rush together
Toward the old gibbet in the heather;
One passes by the lads and blows
Their sole light vainly as she goes;
The blood within their bodies froze
At the meeting of the witches.

7

Now round the gallows in a ring
They dance, and as they dance, they sing.

But look! for by the saints alive!
They were but four, they now are five;
And mid their shadowy garments gray
A taller, blacker form than they
Now crouches down, now leaps away!
The devil's with the witches!

8

The candle-flame burns low and sick,
And wastes upon the slanted wick;
The lad who holds it's like to die,
With beating heart and palsied eye;
One minute more, one minute more,
And the whole countryside's given o'er
To demons from the night's black shore
And malice-working witches!

9

But still his English heart is stout,
And, seeing the flame is well-nigh out,
With suck'd breath, as one plays the flute,
He darts up to the gibbet's root;
And on the bed that no dew wets
Of moss and whortle-leaves, he sets
His candle-end, and straight forgets
His fear of ghastly witches.

10

In time! in time! with scream and start,
The black descends, the gray depart;
A sulphurous smell invades the brain,
But passes in a whiff of rain.
The morning straight begins to break;
The cocks in Canvil farmstead wake;
The numb world breathes, all for the sake
Of midnight-harrying witches.

11

Now back to town the yokels pass;
Sweet dew falls fresh upon the grass;
From elms within the coppice-pale
Shouts nightingale to nightingale;
The web of stars fades out of sight,
In heavenly odour sinks the night,
The spell is gone, the air is light,
Set free from weight of witches.

12

Nor will they come again this year,
To blast our harvest in the ear,
Or kill our cattle, or, passing by,
Breathe on our babes and make them die;
Men who can dare at night to bring
Clear candle-light to the shameful thing,
And set flame down in the ghastly ring,
Need fear no more from witches.

The Hidden Door

By Vernon Lee

It seemed to Decimus Little that there could be no doubt left. His only wonder was whether anyone else had been near making that discovery. As he sat in a deep window of the big drawing-room, the light of the candles falling yellow upon the shining white arms and shoulders, the shining white expanses of shirt-front, the lustrous silks and lustrous black cloth within doors; the great wave of moor and fell unfurling grayish-green in the pale-blue twilight without; as he sat there alone in the window, he wondered how it would be if any of these creatures assembled for the coming of age of the heir of Hotspur Hall could guess that he knew. His eyes mechanically followed the tall figure of his host, as his broad shoulders and gray beard appeared and reappeared in the crowd; they sought out the yellow ridge of curls of the son and heir, as his head rose and fell while talking to the ladies in the corner.

What if either of them could guess? If old Sir Hugh Hotspur could guess that there was in the world another creature beside himself who knew the position of that secret door; if young Hotspur could guess that there existed close by another man who might, any day, penetrate into that secret chamber to which, at the close of these merry-making days, the youth must be solemnly admitted, to lose, during that fatal hour among unspeakable mysteries, all lightness of heart forever?

Mr. Little was not at all surprised at the fact of having made this extraordinary discovery. Although in no way a conceited man, he was accustomed to think of himself as connected with extraordinary matters, and in some way destined for an extraordinary end. He was one of those men who, without ever having done, or even said, or perhaps even thought, anything especially remarkable, are yet remarkable men. Whenever he came into a room, he felt people's eyes upon him, and knew that they were asking, "Who is that young man?" And still Mr. Decimus Little did not consider himself handsome, nor did anyone else consider him so, to his knowledge. From the matter-of-fact point of view, all one could say was that he was of middle height, more inclined to be fat than thin, with small not irregular features, hair varying between yellow and gray, a slight stoop, a somewhat defective sight, and a preference for clothes of ample cut and of neutral tints.

But then the matter-of-fact eye just missed that something indefinable which constituted the remarkable character of Mr. Little's appearance. As it was with, his person, so likewise was it with his history; there was more significance therein than could easily be defined. A distant relative, on the female side, of the illustrious border house of Hotspur, Mr. Little possessed a modest income and the education of a gentleman. He had never been to school, and had left college without taking his degree. He had begun reading for the law, and left off. He had tried writing for the magazines, but without success. He had at one time inclined to High-Church asceticism and the moralizing of Whitechapel; he had also been addicted to socialism, and spent six months learning to make a chest of drawers in a Birmingham co-operative workshop.

He had begun writing a biography of Ninon de Lenclos, studying singing, and forming a collection of rare medals; and he was now considerably interested in Esoteric Buddhism and the Society for Psychical Research, although he felt by no means prepared to accept the new theosophy, nor to indorse the conclusions concerning thought transference. And finally, and quite lately, Mr. Decimus Little had also been in love, and had become engaged to a cousin of his, a young lady studying at Girton College; but he was not quite sure whether the engagement was absolutely binding on either side, or whether marriage would be certainly conducive to the happiness of both parties.

For Mr. Decimus Little was gradually maturing a theory to the effect of his being a person with a double nature, reflective and idealistic on the one hand, and capable, on the other, of extraordinary impulses of lawlessness; and it is notorious that such persons, and indeed, perhaps, all very complex and out-of-the-common personalities are not very fit for the marriage state. It was consonant with what Mr. Little often lamented as the excessive scepticism of his temper, that he should not have made up his mind about the hidden chamber at Hotspur Hall, and the strange stories concerning it. He had often discussed the matter, which, as he remarked, was a crucial one in all questions of the supernatural He had triumphantly argued with a physiologist at his club that mere delusion could not be a sufficient explanation for so old and diffused a belief, as, indeed, mere delusion could not account for any belief of any kind.

He had argued equally triumphantly with a clergyman in the train against the notion that the occupant of the secret chamber was the Evil One, and had added that the existence of evil spirits offered serious, very serious, difficulties to a thoughtful mind. And Mr. Little, being, as he often remarked, open to arguments and evidence on all points, had elaborated various explanations of the mystery of the hidden chamber, and had even attempted to sound the inhabitants of Hotspur Hall on the subject. But the servants had not understood his polished but rather shadowy Oxford English, or he had not understood their thick Northumbrian, and the members of the family had dropped the subject with a somewhat disconcerting sharpness of manner; and Mr. Little was the last man in the world to rudely invade the secrets of others, by experiments of towels hung out of windows, and such like; indeed, the person capable of such courses would have inspired him with horror.

And by an irony of fate—Mr. Little believed in the irony of fate, and was occasionally ironical himself—it had been given to him, to this sceptical and unobtrusive man, to discover that room hidden in the thickness of the Norman wall, and whose position had baffled so much ingenious, pertinacious, and impertinent inquiry.

There could no longer be any doubt about it; this door, revealed only by its hollow sound and its rusty iron bolt, against which Mr. Little had accidentally leaned that day when the shame of having intruded upon a flirtation (and a flirtation, too, between the heir of Hotspur and the heiress of his hereditary foes the Blenkinsops) had made him rush, like a mad creature, along unknown passages and up the winding staircase of the peel tower—this door, whitewashed to look like stone and hidden just under the highest battlements of Hotspur, could only be that of the mysterious chamber. It had flashed across Mr. Little's mind when first he had leaned, confused and panting, against the wall of the staircase, and the wall had yielded to his pressure and creaked perceptibly; and the certainty had grown with every subsequent examination of the spot, and of the exterior of the castle.

People had hitherto wasted their ingenuity upon seeking a window in Hotspur Hall which should correspond with no ostensible room; accident had revealed to Mr. Little a room which corresponded with no window visible from without. It now seemed so simple that it was impossible to conceive how the secret could so long have been kept The secret chamber was, could be, only in the oldest portion of the castle, in the peel tower, built for the protection of stock and goods from the Scottish raids; and it was, it could be, only under the very roof of the tower, taking air and light through some chimney or trap-door from the battlements above.

There could be no doubt about it; and as Mr. Decimus Little sat in the window-seat of the great drawing-room at Hotspur, with on the one side the crowd of guests brilliant in the yellow candle-light, and the great dark wave of fell and moor rising into the blue twilight on the other, he thought how strange it was that of all these people there was only one, besides the master of

Hotspur, who knew the position of the fatal room: only one besides the heir of Hotspur who might—who knows!—penetrate into its secrets, and that one person should be himself. Strange; and yet, somehow, it did not take him by surprise.

And, after all, what was the secret of that chamber? A monstrous creature, or race of creatures, hidden away by the unrightful heirs? An ancient ancestor, living on by diabolic arts throughout the centuries? A demon, a spectre, some horror nameless because inconceivable to those who had not seen it, or perhaps some almost immaterial evil, some curse lurking in the very atmosphere of the place? It was notorious that the something, whatever it was, made it impossible for a Hotspur ever to marry a Blenkinsop; that the heir of Hotspur was introduced to this mystery on coming of age; and that no Hotspur, after coming of age, had ever been known to smile: those were well authenticated facts; but what mystery or horror upon earth or in hell could be sufficient cause for these well ascertained results, no one had ever discovered. Every explanation was futile and insufficient.

These were the thoughts which went on in Mr. Little's mind throughout that week of coming of age at Hotspur Hall. All day and all night—at least, as much of the night as he could account for—these questions kept going round and round in his mind, presenting now one surface, now another, but ever present and ever active. He walked about, ate his dinner, talked, danced automatically, knowing that he did it all, but as one knows what another person is doing, or what one is reading in a book, without any sense of its being one's self or its being real; nay, with a sense of being removed miles and miles from it all, living in a different time and place, to which this present is as the past and the distant.

The secret chamber—its mystery; the door, the colour of the wall, the shape of the iron bolt, the slant of the corkscrew steps—these were reality in the midst of all this unrealness. And withal a strange longing: to stand again before that door, to handle once more that rusty bolt; a wish like that for some song, or

some beloved presence, the desire for that ineffable consciousness, that overwhelming sense of concentrated life and feeling,
of being there, of realizing the thing. No one, reflected Mr. Little, can know what strange joys are reserved for strange natures;
how certain creatures, too delicate and unreal for the every-
day interests and pleasures of existence to penetrate through the
soul-atmosphere in which they wander, will vibrate, with almost
agonized joy, live their full life on contact with certain mysteries.
Every day Mr. Little would seek that winding staircase in the
peel tower; at first with hesitation and shyness, stealing up almost
ashamed of himself; then secretly and stealthily, but excited, reso-
lute, like a man seeking the woman he loves, bent upon the joy
of his life.

Once a day at first, then twice, than thrice, counting the
hours between the visits, longing to go back as soon as he had
left, as a drunkard longs to drink again when he has just drunk.
He would watch for the moment when the way was clear, steal
along the corridors and up the winding stairs. Then, having
reached close to the top of the staircase, near a trapdoor in the
ceiling which led on to the battlements of the tower, he would
stop, and lean against the shelving turning wall opposite the
door, or sit down on the steps, his eyes fixed on the tower wall,
where a faint line and the rusty little bolt revealed the presence
of the hidden chamber.

What he did it would be hard to say; indeed, he did nothing,
he merely felt. There was nothing at all to see, in the material
sense; and this piece of winding staircase was just like any other
piece of winding staircase in the world: it was not anything ex-
ternal that he wanted, it was that ineffable something within
himself. So at least Mr. Little imagined at first, frequently persuading himself that, to a nature like his, all baser satisfaction of
curiosity was as nothing; telling himself that he did not care what
was inside the room, that he did not even wish to know. Why, if
by the pulling of that bolt he might see and know all, he would
not pull it. And, saying this to himself, by way of proving it, he
laid his fingers gently on the bolt.

And in so doing he discovered the depth of his self-delusion. How different was this emotion when he felt—he actually felt—the bolt begin to slide in his hand, from what he had experienced before, while merely contemplating it! The blood seemed to rush through his veins, he felt almost faint. This was reality, this was possession. The mystery lay there, with the bolt, in the hollow of his hand; at any instant he might . . . . Mr. Little had no intention of drawing the bolt. He never reasoned about it, but he knew that that bolt never must, never should, be drawn by him. But in proportion to this knowledge was the entrancing excitement of feeling that the bolt might be drawn, that he grasped it in his fingers, that a little electric current through some of his nerves, a little twitch in some of his muscles, and the mystery would be disclosed.

It was the last of the seven days' revelry of the coming of age. All the other neighbouring properties of the Hotspurs had been visited in turn; tenants had been made to dine and dance on one lawn after another; innumerable grouse had been massacred on the moors; endless sets of Venetian lanterns had been lighted, had caught fire, and tumbled on to people's heads; Sir Hugh's old port and Johannisberg, and the strange honey-beer, called Morocco, brewed for centuries at Hotspur, had flowed like water, or rather like the rain, which freely fell, but did not quench that northern ardour. There was to be a grand ball that night, and a grand display of fireworks. But Mr. Little's soul was not attuned to merriment, nor were the souls, as he suspected, of Sir Hugh Hotspur and his son. For, according to popular tradition, it was on this last night of the seven days' merry-making that the heir of Hotspur must be introduced into the hidden chamber.

Throughout lunch Mr. Little kept his eyes on the face of his host and his host's son. What might be passing in their mind? Was it hidden terror or a dare-devil desperation at the thought of what the night must bring? But neither Sir Hugh nor young Harry showed the slightest emotion; their faces, it seemed to Mr. Little, were imperturbable like stone.

Mr. Little waited till the family and guests were safely assembled on the tennis-lawn, then hastened along the corridor and up the steps of the peel tower. The afternoon, after all the rain, was hot and steamy, clearly foreboding a storm; and as Mr. Little groped his way up the tower steps, he felt his heart moving slackly and irregularly, and a clamminess spread over his face and hands; he had to stop several times in order to take breath. As usual, he seated himself on the topmost step, holding his knees with his arms, and looking at the piece of wall opposite, which concealed the mysterious door.

Mr. Little sat there a long time, while the tower stairs grew darker and darker, the faint line betraying the door grew invisible, and even the bolt was lost in the general darkness. Tonight—the thought, nay, almost the sentence in which it was framed, went on like a bell in Mr. Little's mind—tonight they would creep up those stairs, they would stand before that door. Sir Hugh's hand would be upon that bolt: he saw it all so plainly, he felt every tingle and shudder that would pass through their bodies.

Mr. Little rose and gently grasped the bolt; how easily it would move! Sir Hugh would not require the smallest effort. Or would it be young Harry Hotspur? No; it would doubtless be Sir Hugh. He would pause like that a moment, his hand on the bolt, whispering a few words of encouragement, perhaps a prayer. No; he would be silent. He would hold the bolt, little guessing how recently another hand had been upon it, little dreaming that, but a few hours before another member of the family of Hotspur (for Mr. Little always regarded himself in that light) had had it in his power to . . .

The thought remained unfinished in Mr. Little's mind. With a cry he fell all of a heap upon the steps, a blinding light in his eyes, a deafening roar in his ears. He had opened the secret door.

He came slowly to his senses, and with life there returned an overwhelming, vague sense of horror. What he had done he did not know; but he knew he had done something terrible. He slid, it seemed to him that he almost trickled—for his limbs had turned to water—down the stairs. He ran, and yet seemed to be dragging himself, along the corridors and out of one of the many ivy-grown doorways of the old border castle. To the left hand of the gate, at a little distance, was the tennis-court; a long beam of sun, yellow among the storm-clouds, fell upon the grass, burnishing it into metallic green, and making the white, red, yellow, and blue of the players' dresses stand out like coloured enamel.

Some of them shouted to him, among others young Harry Hotspur; but Mr. Little rushed on, heedless of their shouts, scaling the banks of grass, breaking through the hedges, scrambling up hillside after hillside, until he had got to the top of the fells, where the short grayish-green grass began to be variegated with brown patches of bog and lilac and black patches of heather, and cut in all directions by the low walls of loose black stones. He stopped and looked back. But he started off again, as he saw in the distance below, among the ashes and poplars of the narrow valley which furrowed those treeless undulations of moorland, the chimney-stacks of Hotspur Hall, the battlements of the square, black peel tower, reddened by the low light.

On he went, slower, indeed, but still onward, until every vestige of Hotspur and of every other human habitation was out of sight, and the chain of fells had closed round him, billow upon billow, under the fading light. On he went, looking neither to the right nor to the left, save when he was startled by the bubbling of a brook, spurting from the brown moor bog on to the stony road; or by the bleating of the sheep who wandered, vague white specks, upon the grayish grass of the hillside. The clouds accumulated in gray masses, with an ominous yellow clearing in their midst, and across the fells there came the sound of distant thunder. Presently a few heavy drops began to fall; but Mr. Little did not heed them, but went quickly on, among the bleating of the sheep and the cry of the curlews, along the desolate road across the fells; rain-drop succeeding rain-drop, till the hill-tops were enveloped in a sheet of rain.

But Mr. Little did not turn back. He was dazed, vacant, quite unconscious of all save one thing: he had opened the hidden door at Hotspur Hall.

At length the road made a turn, began to descend, and in a dip of the fells some light shone forth in the darkness and the mist. Mr. Little started, and very nearly ran back: he had thought for a moment that these must be the lights of Hotspur: but a second's reflection told him that Hotspur must lie far behind, and presently, among the blinding rain which fell in cold sheets, he found himself among some low black cottages. In the window of one of them was a light, and over the door, in the darkness, swung an inn sign. He knocked, and entered the inn kitchen, a trickle of water following him wherever he went, and, in the tone and with the look of a sleep-walker, said something about having been overtaken by a storm during a walk on the moors, and wanting a night's shelter. The innkeeper and his wife were evidently too pastoral-minded to reflect that gentlemen do not usually walk on the fells without a hat, and in blue silk socks and patent-leather shoes; and they heaped up the fire, by the side of which Mr. Little collapsed into an armchair, indifferent to the charms of bacon and beer and hot griddle-cakes.

He tried to settle his ideas. Of what had passed he knew but this much for certain, that he had opened the secret door.

The following morning Mr. Little summoned up his courage, and, after a great argument with himself, turned his steps toward Hotspur Hull. The day was fresh and blowy; a delicate blue haze hung over the hills, out of which, larger and larger, emerged a brilliant blue sky. In the valley the towers of Hotspur and its tall chimneys rose among the trees. Soon Mr. Little could see the bright patches of geranium on the lawn. All this, he argued with himself, must have been a delusion, a result of over-psychological study and a thunder-storm upon a nervous and poetical temperament. He tried to remember what he had read about delusions in Carpenter's *Mental Physiology*, and about that supposed robbery, or burglary, which Shelley believed himself to have witnessed.

Mr. Little couldn't remember the details, but he was pleased it should have been Shelley. He felt quite foolish and almost happy as he passed through the rose garden, among the strawberry nets, and in at the by-entrance of Hotspur. He walked straight into the dining-room, where he knew the family was assembled at breakfast, jauntily, and one hand in his pocket. "Why, Little, where the deuce have you spent the night?" cried Sir Hugh Hotspur; and the question was echoed in various forms by the rest of the company.

"Why, Little, have you been in the horse-pond?" cried young Harry, pointing to his guest's clothes, which, drenched the previous night, did indeed suggest some such immersion. Mr. Little did not answer; he felt himself grow cold and pale, and grasped a chair-back. In making this rude remark, the heir of Hotspur had burst into a peal of laughter.

Mr. Little understood; they had found the mysterious chamber empty, its horror fled; he had really opened that door; the heir of Hotspur could still laugh. He explained automatically how he had been caught by a storm on the fells, and been obliged to pass the night at a wayside inn; but the whole time, while he pretended to be eating his breakfast, his brain was on fire with a thought—

"Where had it gone—it, the something which he had let loose?"

That night Mr. Little slept, or rather, as our ancestors more correctly expressed it, lay, at Hotspur. For the word sleep was but a mockery. There was a second storm, and all night the wind howled in the trees, the drops fell from the eaves, and the room was illumined by fitful gleams of lightning. It seemed to Mr. Little that the evil spirit, or whatever else it might be, which had once been safely locked up in the hidden chamber, was now loose in the house. On reflection he could not doubt it: when he had fallen senseless on the stairs, something had passed out of the door; he had heard and felt the wind of its passage. It had issued from the room; it must now be somewhere else, at loose, free to wreak its will with every flash of lightning. Mr. Little expected that the solid masonry of Hotspur would catch fire and burn like a match; with every crash of thunder he expected that the great peel tower would come rattling on to the roof.

He realized for the first time the tales of the companions of Ulysses opening the bag of the winds; of the Arabian fisherman breaking Solomon's seal on the flask which held the *djinn*; they no longer struck him as in the least ridiculous, these stories. He too had done alike. For, after all, was it not possible that there existed in Nature forces, beings, unknown to our ordinary every-day life? Did not all modern investigations point in that direction, and was it not possible, then, that by the mercy of Providence such a force or being, fatal to our weak humanity, might have been permitted to be inclosed within four walls— one family, or rather, one unhappy member of one family, being sacrificed for the good of mankind, and facing this terror alone, that the rest of his kind might not look upon that ineffable mystery?

And now he, in the lawlessness of his scepticism, had stepped in and opened that sacred door. . . . He understood now why he had often felt that he was destined to commit some terrible crime. Mr. Little sat up in bed, and as the lightning fitfully lit up the antique furniture of his room, he began mechanically to mutter some prayers of his childhood, and some Latin *formulae* of exorcism which he had learned at the time of his offering to do the article *Incubus* for the *Encyclopaedia Britannica*. What should he do? Confess to Sir Hugh Hotspur? or to Sir Hugh's son? He felt terrified at the mere notion; but he understood that his terror was no mere vulgar fear of being reprimanded for a gross breach of hospitality and honour—that it was due to the sense that, having this terrible secret, he had no right to ruin therewith the lives of innocent men. The Hotspurs would know but too soon!

Meanwhile Mr. Little felt an imperative need to confess what he had done, to ask advice and assistance. He wished for once that he had been able to go over to Rome that time that Monsignor Tassel had tried to convert him, instead of being deterred by the oleographs in Monsignor Tassel's chapel. What would he not give to kneel down in a confessional, and pour out the horrible secret through the perforated brass plate!

All of a sudden he jumped out of bed, struck a light, and dragged his portmanteau into the middle of the room. He had remembered Esmé St. John, and the fact that Esmé St. John, his former chum at Oxford, was working in the slums of Newcastle, not three hours hence. How could he ever, in the lawless hardness of his heart, have thought Esmé ridiculous, have actually tried to reason him out of his High Church asceticism? This was indeed the just retribution, the fall of the proud, that he should now seek shelter and peace in Earners spiritual arms, and bring to the man, nay, rather to the saint, at whom he had once scoffed, a story which, he would himself have once ridiculed as the most childish piece of superstition.

The mere thought of that act of humiliation did him good; and the terrors of the night seemed to diminish as Mr. Little stooped over his portmanteau and folded his clothes with neat but feverish hands. As soon as it was light, he stole out of the house, walked to the neighbouring village, knocked up the half-idiotic girl who had charge of the post-office, and sent off a sixpenny telegram telling the Reverend Esmé St. John that he would join him at Newcastle that afternoon.

Mr. Little was rather surprised, and in truth rather dashed, when he met his old friend. He had spent the hours in the train framing his confession: a terrible tale to tell, yet which he felt a sudden disappointment at being prevented from telling. Prevented he did feel. He found the Reverend Esmé St. John making a round among his parishioners; they had told him so at Mr. St. John's chapel, and he had realized vividly the whole scene; Esmé, emaciated, hollow-voiced, fresh from some death-bed, leaving the rest of his flock to follow the call of this pale creature, in whom he would scarcely recognize an old friend, and the very touch of whose hand would tell him that things more terrible than death were at stake. But it was otherwise.

After wandering about various black and grimy slums under the thick black Newcastle sky, and up various precipitous alleys and flights of steps strewed with egg-shells and herring-heads,

Mr. Little found his old friend in a back yard sheltered by the crumbling red roof of "The Musician's Rest" inn (where the first bars of *Auld Lang Syne* swung over the door). By his side was a fat, tattered, but extremely jovial red-haired woman washing in a tub, and opposite, an unkempt ragamuffin with his hands in his pockets, singing at the top of his little voice a comic song in Northumbrian dialect Mr. Esmé St John was leaning against the doorway, laughing with all his might; he was fat, bald, had a red face, and a very humorous eye—in fact, did not resemble in the least the hollow-cheeked, flashing-eyed young fanatic of ten years before. He stretched out his broad hand to Mr. Little, and said: "Do listen to this song, it's about the Board School man— it's really too delicious, and the little chap sings it quite nicely!"

Mr. Little listened, not understanding a word, and thinking how little this man, laughing over a foolish song sung by a street-boy, guessed the terrible confession he was about to receive.

When the song was finished, the Reverend Esmé St John took Little's arm, and began to overwhelm him with futile questions while leading him down the steep streets of Old Newcastle, until they got to the door of a large and gorgeous eating-house.

"You must be hungry," said Mr. St. John. "I've ordered dinner here for a treat, because my old housekeeper, although an excellent creature, does not rise above mutton chops and boiled potatoes, and one should do honour to an old friend."

Mr. Little shook his head. "I am not hungry," he answered, while his friend unfolded his napkin opposite him. He felt inclined to say, grimly, "When a man has let loose a mysterious unknown terror that has been locked up in Hotspur Hall for centuries, he doesn't feel inclined for roast mutton and Bass's beer."

But the place, the tables, plates, napkins, the smell of cooking, stopped him, and he felt stopped also by the face—the jovial, red face—of his old friend. This was not the Esmé to whom he had longed to unbosom himself. And he felt very irritated.

Mr. Little's irritation began to subside when he followed his friend to his lodgings.

"You asked for a bed, in your telegram," said the Reverend Esmé St. John, as they left the eating-rooms, "and I have had a bed put in a spare room of mine, just to show my hospitable intentions. But I shan't be the least bit offended if you prefer to go to the hotel, my dear fellow. You see, I think a clergyman, trying to reclaim the people of these slums, ought to live among his flock, and no better than they. But there is no reason why anyone also should live in this crazy old barrack."

They walked, in the twilight, along some precipitous streets, lined with tinkers' dens and old-clothes shops, under the high-level bridge, over whose colossal span the square old castle stood out black against the sky.

Mr. Little crept through a battered wooden gateway, and picked his way among the puddles, the fallen beams, and the refuse heaps of a court-yard. A light appeared at a window.

"Here we are," said Esmé, and they followed an old, witch-like woman, herself following a thin, black cat, up some crazy, wooden stairs, and into a suite of low, large rooms. Mr. St. John held up a lantern. The room in which they stood was utterly dismantled, the very wainscoting torn out, the ceiling gaping in rent lath and plaster. In a corner stood a bed, a crazy chest of drawers, and washing apparatus, a table, and chair; and in the next room, where the old woman's light had preceded them, was a similar bed, a shelf of books, a large black cross nailed to the wall, and a wooden step for kneeling.

"That's my room," said the clergyman. "You may have it if you prefer. But here's a fireplace in this one, so you'd better keep it."

So saying, Mr. St. John applied a match to the fagots, and the gaunt apartment was flooded with a red light

"I must make some arrowroot for an old woman of mine," said the clergyman, producing a tin can and saucepan. "May I make it on your fire?"

Mr. Little watched him in silence, then suddenly said: "Esmé, I thought at first you were changed from old days, but I see you are still a saint. Alas! I fear it is I who have changed but too sadly;" and he sighed.

"You are growing too fat," answered Mr. St. John good-humouredly, but quite missing the fact that this was the exordium of a confession. Then, to Mr. Little's annoyance, he asked him leave to carry the arrowroot to his old woman, who lived in a lane hard by. Mr. Little remained seated by the fire, while the housekeeper (since she must be dignified by such a title) unpacked his portmanteau. Yes, indeed, this was the man to whom he could make his confession, and this was the place—this dismantled, tumble-down old mansion, tenanted now only by a few poor bargees' families and by countless generations of rats. And Mr. Little put another piece of coal on, in preparation of the nightly conference he was about to have.

Presently Mr. St. John returned.

"Esmé," said Mr. Little, putting his hand on his friend's sleeve, "I wish to speak to you."

"About what?" asked Mr. St. John. "It's very late to begin talking."

"About myself," answered Mr. Little, gravely.

"Do you want anything else? Would you like some brandy and water, or another pillow? You may have mine—or an additional blanket?" asked his friend.

Mr. Little shook his head. "I have all I want in the way of material comforts."

"In that case," replied the clergyman, "I shall leave you at once. If, as you imply, you want spiritual comforts, you must wait till tomorrow, for I am perfectly worn out, and have to be up tomorrow at half-past four. I've been nursing a man from the chemical works these five nights. Goodnight!" and, taking his candle, Mr. St. John walked into his room, leaving his friend greatly disconcerted by this want of sympathy.

The following day Mr. Little accompanied his friend on one of his rounds. After visiting a number of squalid places, where Mr. Little would certainly have thought about measles and smallpox had he not been thinking about the mystery of Hotspur Hall, they returned to the row of houses, once fashionable mansions, with their fronts on the river, among which loomed, next to the black and crumbling former Town Hall, the shell of a family mansion in which they were lodged.

"This was once the fashionable part of Newcastle," said Mr. St. John. "An old lady of ninety once told me she could remember the time when this street used to be crowded with coaches and footmen and link boys of a winter's night. I want to show you my mission-room; I'm very proud of it."

They entered a black passage, close to an inexpressibly shabby public-house, and ascended a wide stone staircase, unswept for ages, as was attested by the cabbage-stalks and herring-heads which lay about in various stages of decomposition. On the first landing a rope was stretched, and a line of clothes, or rather rags, drying after the wash-tub, formed a picturesque screen before several open doors, whence issued squealing of babies, grind of sewing machines, and various unsavoury odours. Mr. St. John unlocked a door and admitted his friend into a large hall, gracefully decorated with pastoral *stucco* mouldings, but filled with church seats, and whose raised extremity, suggestive of the dais for an orchestra, was occupied by an altar duly appointed according to ritualistic notions. The place smelt considerably of stale tobacco and damp straw.

"These were the former assembly rooms," explained Mr. St. John; "and this, which is now my little chapel for the lowest scum of Newcastle slums, was once the ball-room. What would those ladies in hoops and powder think of the change, I wonder?"

Mr. Little saw his opportunity.

"This place must be haunted," he said. "By-the-way, Esmé, what are your views on the subject of ghosts and the supernatural? I should be very interested to know."

Mr. St. John had locked the door behind them.

"Never mention the word ghost before me," he exclaimed; it drives me perfectly wild to see all the tomfooling that has been going on of late about apparitions, haunted houses, secret chambers, and all that blasphemous rubbish. It is really a retribution of Heaven to see you agnostic wiseacres taking up such contemptible twaddle. I'm very sorry to hear that you have been in correspondence with those people, Little."

"But—" objected Mr. Little.

"No buts for me!" cried the Reverend Esmé St. John, hotly; "I cannot conceive how any man of education and character can fiddle-faddle about idiotic superstitions which it is the duty of every Christian and every gentleman to pluck out of the minds of the vulgar."

It was clear that this was not the moment to begin a confession about the mysterious room at Hotspur.

"How surprised he will be," thought Mr. Little (and a vague sense of satisfaction mingled with the horror of the thought), "when he hears that I, even I, the sceptical, antinomian Little, have come in contact with mysteries more strange and awful than any ever examined into by any society for psychical research."

Despite his old friend's want of sympathy, Mr. Decimus Little continued to lodge with the Reverend Esmé St. John, in the grimy and crumbling old mansion by the Tyneside, following him about on his various errands of mercy. "A man situated like me," Mr. Little had said to himself, "a great sinner (if you like the pious formula of former ages), a character predestined to evil (if you prefer the more modern phraseology of determinism), does well to live in the shadow of a truly good man: his saintliness is a bulwark against evil spirits; or, at all events, the sight of perfect serenity and purity of mind must calm a deeply troubled spirit." Indeed, he more than once began to make this remark, in terms even more subtle, to his friend; but Mr. St. John, whether from fear of Mr. Little's dialectic power, which might shake some of his most cherished beliefs, or from some other reason, invariably turned a deaf ear to all such beginnings of confession.

But either the serenity of the ritualistic philanthropist was inadequate to calm a brain so over-excited or the evil spirits let loose by Mr. Little made short work of the bulwarks of Esmé's saintliness. The thought of that opened door began to haunt him like a nightmare: the effort at guessing what had been liberated when that door was opened wore out his energies. Was it a monster—a poor, loathsome, half-human thing, hiding, perhaps lying starving at this moment, in some corner of the castle: a thing without mind, or speech, or shape, but endowed with monstrous strength, starting forth in the night and throttling the unrightful owner or his young children with stupid glee?

Or, more horrible almost, forcing by its presence that honourable and kindly old man into crime; tempting him, with the fear lest this hideousness should become known to the world, into spilling the blood of what seemed but a loathly reptile, but might be his third cousin, or his great-uncle? Mr. Little buried his face in his pillow at the thought. But it might be worse still—in that room might have been inclosed some ghastly mediaeval plague, some crumbling long-dead corpse, whose every particle was ready to take wing and spread forgotten diseases over the country. Or was it something less tangible, less conceivable—a ghost, a demon, some fearful supernatural evil?

Every morning, when his tea was set down by the housekeeper upon the rickety table in his dismantled bedroom, Mr. Little would unfold, with trembling fingers, the local newspaper, half expecting that his eye would fall upon a notice headed "Hotspur Hall." And there were moments when he could scarce resist the impulse of rushing to the station, and buying a ticket for the village nearest Hotspur.

But a stop was put to such fears about a week after his arrival at Newcastle; alas! only to be succeeded by fears much more terrible. Returning home one day he saw a letter on his table; a presentiment told him it was about *that*. Yet he shook all over when he saw the address on the back of the envelope, "Hotspur Hall, Northumberland." He sank on to a chair, and was for some time unable to open the letter. It was from Sir Hugh—Sir Hugh writing to the guest, the cousin who had betrayed all the sacred laws of hospitality, to inform him of all the horrors in which his act had involved an innocent, honourable, and happy household.

Mr. Little groaned, and held the letter unopened. Then suddenly he opened it, tore it open madly. It ran as follows:

My dear Little:—I have been too busy of late to let you know that Edwardes discovered in your room here, two days after your sudden departure from Hotspur, a whole outfit which you had apparently forgotten. It consists of a shirt, a pair of check breeches, two white ties, a coloured silk handkerchief, a sponge, and a razor-strap. Let us know where you wish all this to be sent. I write to relieve your mind on the subject, as you have doubtless missed these valuables. Lady Hotspur and Harry unite in hoping that you are enjoying yourself, and that we may see you soon again.

Yours, sincerely,

Hugh North Hotspur.

P. S.—I may tell you—but in strict confidence—a piece of news that will doubtless give you pleasure. Our Hal is engaged since the day before yesterday to the Honourable Cynthia Blenkinsop, whom you admired the evening of the Yeomanry ball. The wedding is for next May.

What did this mean? They did not suspect him, that was clear; and nothing terrible had occurred, that was clear also. What then? Was it possible that .... But Mr. Little's eyes rested on the postscript. Harry Hotspur engaged to the Honourable Cynthia Blenkinsop: a marriage between the two hereditary enemies, whose enmity dated from the time of Chevy Chase! And there returned to his mind the ancient Northumbrian prophecy (he could not quite pronounce it in the original), that as long as the fell is green and the moor is purple, as long as deer haunt the woods (they don't, thought Mr. Little) and the seamew the rocks, as long as the secret door at the Hall remains closed, so long will never a Hotspur wed a Blenkinsop.

The secret door had been opened, they knew it, and with its opening the curse had been removed from the family. The heir might laugh, though he had come of age (he had laughed at Mr.

Little's wet clothes, if you remember); he might marry a Miss Blenkinsop; the door had been opened, and he had opened it!

Mr. Little jumped up from his chair and rushed to his friend's door.

"Esmé," he cried, "we'll dine at the *Kafe*" (that being the local pronunciation of the word *Café*) "tonight; and here's a sovereign for the poor woman who broke her leg. ... Harry Hotspur is going——" But he stopped himself, and when the clergyman opened the door, astounded at these high spirits, and asking why this sudden launching into festivities and lavish charities, he could only answer, "Only a letter I've had from Sir Hugh Hotspur. It seems—it seems I left quite a lot of things behind; a pair of check trowsers among others. Quite valuable, you know—quite valuable!"

But Mr. Little's happiness—nay, self-congratulation—came to a speedy end. That night, as he lay awake, owing, to the unwonted luxury of coffee after dinner, a thought struck him. If the—the thing, the mystery, the whatever it was, had been liberated from the secret chamber, as was proved beyond doubt, not only by his consciousness of having opened the door, but by the news in Sir Hugh's letter; and if, at the same time, it had not manifested itself to the inhabitants of the Hall, as was likewise clearly the case from the cheerful tone in which the master of Hotspur wrote, why, then what had become of it? Mr. Little, who believed in the indestructibility of force, could not have imagined it to have come to an end; and, if still existing, it must be somewhere.

At this moment a sound—a moan, which made his blood run cold—issued from the darkness of the room. Mr. Little struck a light. The bare, dismantled room, with its unwainscoted walls and torn lath ceiling, was empty, and its bareness admitted of no hiding-place anywhere.

"It is the wind in the chimney!" he said to himself, and extinguished his candle.

But the ghastly moan, this time ending in a sort of gurgling laugh, was repeated, and with it a horrible thought flashed across

Mr. Little's mind: What if that mysterious something should attach itself to the man who had disturbed its long seclusion—if the Terror of Hotspur Hall should have fastened upon the rash creature who had let it loose!

And again there issued from the darkness of that dismantled room the moan, the gurgling laugh. In what shape would it reveal itself? Mr. Little, in the course of his studies, had read M. Maury's *Magie au Moyen Age*; a similar work by the Rev. Baring Gould; the valuable *Essay on Superstition in the Middle Ages*, by Dr. Schindler, Royal Prussian Sanitary Councillor and Man-midwife at Greiffenberg; he had also once bought the works of Theophrastus Bombastes of Hohenheim, called *Paracelsus*, but found them too boring to read. So that his mind was well stocked with alternatives among which a mediaeval mystery could select.

His suspicions were one day aroused by a strange-looking man, dark and grimy, who got on to the Tyne steamer one evening at Wallsend, kept his hat over his face and his eyes fixed upon Mr. Little, and then dodged him up and down Newcastle to the very door of his house. "Who are you?" suddenly exclaimed Mr. Little, stopping short and facing him. He half expected the man to unmask—that is, to take off his hat, and, displaying the face of a corpse, to answer, like the mysterious stranger in Calderon's play, "I am thyself." But the man muttered something about its being very hard on a fellow; that since Mr. St. John had been good to the wife, he ought also to be good to the husband; that he had never touched a drop of liquor till after his marriage with that woman—he hadn't, etc. Mr. Little turned away in disgust. On another occasion, his suspicions were awakened by a large black dog, which insisted upon following him, and oven walked into his room, but he proved to have his master's address on his collar, and was consequently sent home next morning.

One day, again, as Mr. Little was leaning out of the lattice window, looking at the red roofs of Gateshead, the solitary black church on the green mound, surrounded by cinder-heaps and chemical refuse, above the Tyne, his eyes fell upon the gray mass of water which rolled slowly below him; and it seemed to him as if, suddenly, in the curl of a heavy-laden wave, he had seen—a face, upturned eyes staring at him. "Pooh!" said Esmé St. John, whom slumming had made slightly cynical, "it's only some wretched creature who's drowned himself. They'll take him up at the next dead-house."

But Mr. Little shook his head: those eyes had looked at him.

Mr. Little had wondered whether he would be haunted: he soon began to be so, or very nearly. He scarcely ventured to enter his room alone, lest he should find waiting for him, he knew not what; or to approach his own bed, lest, on raising the sheet, he should find it already horribly occupied. Every knock made him start; and it was only by an effort that he could induce himself to cry "Come in!" to the old woman who brought him his hot water.

But the day was serene compared with the night. He would lie awake for hours listening to the sullen lapping of the Tyne under the windows, to the scurrying of the rats round the walls, the creaking of broken woodwork in the wind, the rattling of the incessant trains over the high-level bridge close by: lie awake breathless, feeling a presence in the room, but never daring to open his eyes; feeling it coming nearer and nearer, and at the same time expanding, filling the place, choking him, yet never daring to look; until the horrible consciousness would die away as it had come, and there remain only the sickening terror it had brought, and the speculations, while listening to the strokes of the Gateshead clock, as to what the terror might be. Yet, was it something visible, definable, or was it merely a vague curse?

"Esmé," said Mr. Little one day, "do you consider—do you consider—that a man who knows his life to be under a curse; well, suppose something like insanity, you know: but not that—nothing really hereditary, merely a personal thing, a curse, a something making life quite unbearable to him and everyone else—do you think that such a man would have a right to marry?"

Mr. St. John looked at him long and fixedly. "Such a man, in my humble opinion, ought to have a good course of iron, or phosphorus, or, best of all, of whipping, to take down his conceit; and he certainly oughtn't to get married, unless he knew for certain that the lady would administer some such treatment to him."

"You have grown very coarse, Esmé!" exclaimed Mr. Little, "I admit that you do a great deal of good to others, but I sometimes question whether a man of refinement by associating wholesale with laundresses and bargees does much good to himself."

"Very likely not," replied the clergyman, dryly. "Happily, some men aren't always thinking all day long whether they are doing good to themselves or not"

"He is right, all the same, he is right," said Mr. Little to himself.

Whatever the coarseness of fibre of Mr. St John, and his lack of all power of sympathy and intuition, there was no denying that he had given expression to a very sound ethical view.

No; a man in the position of Decimus Little must not marry. He must not drag another life into the atmosphere of horror with which, in one second of lawlessness, he had surrounded himself. It was impossible to conceive a happy home with the mysterious horror of Hotspur Hall constantly in the' background. No; he must never marry. But had he not foreseen this answer before putting the question to his friend? Nay, had he not always felt, long before setting his foot in Hotspur Hall, that some dark fate would come between him and happiness; that the joys of wife and children were not for a creature like him, unreal and lawless, marked for some strange and horrible destiny? All this had not been mere silly despondency, or, as his friend Esmé would have thought, morbid self-importance.

He determined to write to his cousin and break off at once. But how convey to this charming, buoyant, and decidedly positivistic and positive young student of Girton a fact so contrary to all her beliefs and tendencies, as that an unknown terror, inclosed for centuries in the secret chamber of a border castle, had suddenly, through his fault, shunted itself upon him? Mr. Little revolved the matter in his mind, and found a melancholy little pleasure in so doing. He determined at last upon merely telling the young lady that this marriage had become impossible, and hinting dimly to her that this was due to no diminution of affection, no want of duty on his part, but to a terrible and mysterious curse *(not insanity, nor consumption*—he would underline that) under which he was labouring, and which forbade his ever sharing a life which meant unspeakable horror.

Mr. Little sat for a long time before his writing-case, resting his chin on his hand, and jotting down half sentences at intervals.

Yes, he could see it all: the surprise and mystification of the dear girl, her tears of rage (he knew she would rage), her feeling of faintness and sickness, her sadden calling upon her bosom friend, Miss Hopper (the student of political economy, with the cropped hair and divided skirts)—he had always disliked Miss Hopper, an unwomanly young person—to shed light upon it. And even Miss Hopper, who, he know, had once said she was surprised her Gwendolen could love any man, and least of all a little, gray-haired muff—even Miss Hopper would have to admit that her friend's unhappy lover was marvellously magnanimous.

And then Gwendolen would write imploringly to know what had happened; nay, rather (he knew her well), she would come herself, arrive at Newcastle, drive to his house, and then there would be a grand explanation. Esmé St. John would be present, that would make everything proper, and Esmé would be so astounded; and Gwendolen would go on her knees to him and he on his knees to Gwendolen, and finally they would bid each other farewell, and Esmé would take her hand, and bid her kiss Decimus, and then lead her away to the nearest sisterhood, where she would immediately proceed to turn hospital nurse for the rest of her days, and wear a lock of Decimus's hair round her neck under a scapular.

Mr. Little covered his eyes with his hands, and began to cry. For the first time since opening that door he felt quite peaceable and pleased with himself.

He was startled by the entrance of Martha, Mr. St. John's old housekeeper.

"I beg your pardon, sir," she said, making a violent effort over a strong northern accent, "but would you mind my dusting a little?"

"Dust away," answered Mr. Little, sadly, implying that he, too, was dust and ashes.

In a room as scantily furnished as was Mr. Little's, the operation of dusting would, one might imagine, be necessarily a brief one; but Martha contrived to prolong it singularly. She was passing the duster for the fourth or fifth time over the lid of Mr. Little's portmanteau, when she suddenly turned round, and said—

"I beg your pardon, sir."

"I did not say anything," answered Mr. Little, gloomily.

"No, sir, no more you did, sir. But I was a-saying, sir, if as I might take the liberty, sir, as I see—but there was no prying, sir, I assure you, for I'm greatly averse to prying into folks' concerns, especially the gentry's, and it was all casual like, as we say. I was a-saying, sir, seeing how you received a letter from Sir Hugh Hotspur the other day; if you would just put in a word for me now as they've got a new butler, for it would indeed be a charity, let alone all the injustice, to get a body back into her rights, and a widow, too, as I've been these fifteen years, and with only a third cousin in the world."

"My good woman," interrupted Mr. Little, "explain yourself. I fail to comprehend a word."

"Well, then, sir," proceeded Martha, resuming the violent efforts to get the better of her Northumbrian accent, "you should know that I was once in a better place than this, as good a place as any of them have, ... for I was laundress at Hotspur Hall, and a better laundress you never seed, sir, nor linen better kept than mine was. And then, as Heaven would have it, on account of the wickedness of men, I lost my place through no fault of mine, but merely all along of that room in the peel tower, the room as is lit from the top and as has no windows, as perhaps, sir, you know."

"Hush!" cried Mr. Little, with a gesture like that of a man fainting, "for mercy's sake, woman ... explain ... that room ... the room on the topmost landing of the peel tower. ..."

"Yes, sir, with a door as is hidden in the wall—secret like."

"You opened that door? You were sent away for opening that door? Answer me—for Heaven's Bake, Martha, answer me!" and Mr. Little clutched the old lady's arm.

"Lor, sir! there was no harm meant. I did not mean to be prying into other folks' concerns, as I always says is best left alone. Although there is such as is always a-prying into everything—"

"You opened that door? Yes, or no ?"

"Well, yes, sir, I did, as I was a-going to tell you, sir," cried Martha, terrified at Mr. Little's face, and trying to extricate her arm from his hand. "I beg your pardon, sir, as you're a-tearing of my sleeve."

Mr. Little let her go.

"That door—the last door in the peel tower, on the left; a door hidden in the wall; the door of a room without a window; a room lit from the battlements above?"

"Yes, sir," answered Martha, beginning to quake all over; "exactly as you says, sir. The topmost door in the peel tower, on the left; a door hidden in the wall. It was all along of opening that, as you says, sir."

"Then, Martha," said Mr. Little, solemnly, sitting upright, and fixing his eyes on the old woman's, "you were sent away from Hotspur Hall for opening that door—the door of the secret chamber!"

"Well, sir, it may be called the secret chamber, for all as I know now, and the butler would have had *me* keep it a secret what I saw there, sure enough—all them bottles of wine as he had hidden away to sell to the 'Blue Bull' at Blenkinsop; but of my time there was no one as had a right to call it a secret room, seeing as it was the room as we used to put the drying lines in o' winter, when it was too damp to dry the clothes out of doors, as maybe it still is, on account of that draught from the skylight in the roof."

"Enough!" cried Mr. Little. "Woman, not one word more!"

Visitors at Hotspur Hall still continue to look for the secret room, to hang out towels from the windows, and pump the

143

servants, all in vain. Young Harry Hotspur was never known to laugh quite as much as that time that Mr. Little appeared at breakfast in the clothes which he had worn that night on the fell; at least, he rarely laughed except when he chanced to see Mr. Little. As to the marriage question, and the difficulty of reconciling it to the prophecy that so long as the fell was green and the moor purple, and the deer haunted the woods and the seamew the rocks, as long as the secret chamber at Hotspur Hall remained undiscovered, so long would never a Hotspur wed a Blenkinsop, it might be interesting to examine into this incongruity in a serious psychological spirit.

Such persons as are destitute of any taste for serious psychology merely answer to any objection of the kind, that the Honourable Cynthia Blenkinsop was possessed not merely of a charming person but of sixty thousand a year; and that a secret chamber inhabited by an unspecified horror, although a very delightful heirloom in an ancient family, is not sufficient capital in these days of ostentatious living and riotous luxury. As regards Mr. Decimus Little, he is at present in Turkey, on a trial trip with his cousin Gwendolen and her mother, which will decide whether or not he shall be married to her next January by the Reverend Esmé St John.

Pot-Hooks and Hangers
By William Archer

We were sitting, Sir Marmaduke and I, at the Café de la Régence, one sultry evening in early summer. We had each a *mazagran* and a cigar. Sir Marmaduke was reading the *Times*, while I looked lazily through a veil of smoke at the stars and the passers-by. In the white front of the Théâtre-Français every window blazed with light. The gas lamps of the Avenue de l'Opéra shone like flakes of gold in contrast with the misty pallor of electricity through which, at the end of the vista, the *façade* of the opera-house could be dimly discerned. The fountain of the Place du Théâtre-Français reflected in shifting gleams the thousand lights around.

In front of the great theatre the red lamps of the orange-stalls, shining on the pyramids of fruit, heightened harmoniously the pale yellow of the prevailing light. The monotonously strident cries of the orange-men and programme sellers, together with the tinkle of the liquorice-water-vendor's bell, mingled in my ears with the dull clap-clap of the cab-horses' hoofs upon the asphalt. All sorts and conditions of men and women filed past on the broad pavement; and, watching them, I amused myself by fancifully recognizing in the more noticeable figures this or that personage of Dumas *fils,* or Daudet, or Zola,—a Monsieur Alphonse or a Duc de Septmonts; a Risler *ainé,* a Delobelle, or a Deschellettes; a Sidonie or a Sapho; a Gervaise, a Lantier, a Zéphyrin, or a Satin.

But there were other types in the shifting scene besides those of the French realists. Every now and then there would pass a personage who had evidently walked straight from the pages of Mr. Howells or Mr. James; and the characters of Mr. Du Maorier (a realist, too, after his kind) brought with them airs from Kensington and blasts from Bayswater. Here, for instance, was an unmistakable Englishman crossing toward us from the Théâtre-Français, whence issued two streams of men eager for a breath of air between the acts.

The Englishman was of tallish figure, middle-aged, correct, commonplace. His short brown whiskers were touched with gray; his upper lip and chin were shaved; his mouth was firm, his nose thin and well cut, his eyes small and unremarkable. His eyebrows were the only striking feature of his face—long, bushy, and overhanging, like those which Darwin developed, it is said, by continual concentration over his microscope. On the whole, I took him for a barrister in good practice, or a well-placed civil servant; and the latter hypothesis, as I afterward found, was correct.

He walked up to the Café de la Régence and looked about for a seat in the open space in front. To get at the only unoccupied table he had to pass Sir Marmaduke, whose outspread *Times* was blocking the way. Sir Marmaduke looked up absently at the intruder, then sprang from his seat, almost knocking over his water-*carafe* in his excitement, and seized the astonished Englishman by the hand.

"Philips!" he cried, "where have you dropped from? How glad I am to see you!"

"Ah, Middleton!" said the other, cordially, "I was thinking of you the other day as I passed by Stresa, on my way over the Simplon."

"We haven't met since that day on Maggiore—how many years ago?" said Sir Marmaduke.

"Eight or nine," put in Mr. Philips, who had meanwhile given the waiter his order.

"No; eleven," replied Sir Marmaduke, after a little thought. "What Horace says is—

"*Eheu fugaces*
Anni labuntur, Postume, Postume!'
"Years glide away, and are lost to me, lost to me!'"

"I needn't ask whether you took my advice," said Philips, looking at him. Your hair is scarcely grizzled."

This enigmatic remark excited my curiosity. Could this friend of Sir Marmaduke's be an agent of the hyacinthine Mrs. Allen, or a traveller in *Balm of Columbia*!

"If I hadn't taken your advice, my dear fellow," said Sir Marmaduke, "I shouldn't be here at this moment."

"You'd be settled in Italy?" said the other, with a curious smile.

"Probably," replied Sir Marmaduke, reflecting his friend's smile, "settled for good."

He now introduced me to Mr. Philips, and we nodded to each other with the studied frigidity of true-born Britons.

"And now tell me," said Sir Marmaduke with interest, "what became of you after we parted that morning. You vanished into thin air. Did you find your hippogriff awaiting you when you landed at Pallanzaf. You must know," he added, turning to me, "that Philips is a necromancer, a Cagliostro, by Jove!"

"I didn't find a hippogriff," said Philips, "but a telegram from the Home Office. I took the first steamer for Arona, and was in London two days later."

"Do you still practice the black art?" asked Sir Marmaduke.

"The black and white art, you mean," said the other, laughing. "Oh, yes, in a small way. But now I must be off—I don't want to miss the last act of *Ruy Blas*, and besides, I'm with some people."

"But look here," said Sir Marmaduke, "you mustn't go and perform your great vanishing trick again, as you did the other time. I've something to return you, you know—with many thanks."

"Oh, that!" said the other. "Well, I shouldn't mind having it again, especially as I don't suppose it has any great sentimental value for you. "Where are you stopping?"

"Meurice's."

"And I at the Continental. Well, when I've seen my people home, I'll stroll along if you like."

"Do," said Sir Marmaduke; "you'll find us in the smoking-room."

"All right," was the reply, "expect me about twelve;" and, after paying for his black coffee, Mr. Philips hurried back to the theatre.

"Who's your mysterious friend ?" I asked Sir Marmaduke; "and what's all this stuff about the black art ?"

"No stuff at all," said Sir Marmaduke with conviction. "That's the most wonderful fellow I ever knew. But for him, my boy, I should now have been married and done for."

"Did he cut you out?" I asked. "He *is* a wonderful fellow!"

"Obvious and gratuitous impertinence!" replied the dear old boy, unruffled.

"*Scusi, sa!*" I said. "Tell me all about it. He doesn't look like a magician."

"By his works you shall know him," my friend answered. "The proof of the magician is in his magic, and I'm a living monument to his occult powers. Have another weed?"

We each lighted a cigar, and, that ceremony over, Sir Marmaduke began:

"Before I settled in Venice, you know, I had a villa for some time on the Lago Maggiore, at Stresa. It was a pretty little *châlet* of a place, a good bit above the level of the lake, with a charming outlook over the Borromean Islands. It suited me down to the ground, and I might have stopped there to this day but for the 'events I am about to narrate,' as the story-tellers have it.

"Another villa, much larger than mine, stood on the slope just above it, a narrow lane separating the two gardens. It had long been unoccupied, much to my satisfaction, for I did not care to be overlooked. At last, one morning, my Italian valet brought me the news that it had been taken, and taken by a lady. The Marchesa Trabelli, he said, was her name, but he had been unable to find out anything more about her, except that she

148

was evidently rich. The furnishings, which soon began to arrive in cart-load upon cart-load, confirmed the latter intelligence. My man brought me glowing reports of the Oriental splendour with which the place was being bedizened. The furniture came, not from Milan, but from Paris, and it was a Parisian decorator who was in charge.

"A few weeks sufficed to transform the house from a barrack to a palace, and the garden from a wilderness to a trim pleasance. Then came the lady herself, accompanied by only two servants, a maid and a steward; the other domestics were engaged in the neighbourhood. She remained a mystery to everyone. She neither belonged to the local nobility nor had any friends among them. Her two French servants either knew nothing of her antecedents, or kept what they knew carefully to themselves. On two points only all reports agreed: she was a genuine Italian, and, so far as beauty was concerned, she might well be not merely a *marchesa* but a princess or a queen.

"On the latter point I was somewhat sceptical, for the beauty which knocks the average Italian all of a heap is apt to be too florid, for my taste! But, by Jove, sir, I was punished for my scepticism! The moment I saw her I knew it was all up with me. She came, I saw, she conquered. She wasn't very young—thirty at least—but her beauty had just reached its maturity without losing a jot of its freshness. She was tall and finely proportioned, black-haired, olive-skinned, red-lipped, oval-faced; and, oh! if you could have seen how her head was set on her shoulders, and with what a lovely motion of her neck she would turn her face majestically toward you, and let her two great eyes blaze upon you—positively blaze—like—like—do you know the way the new Calais *phare* sends shaft on shaft of blinding light sweeping slowly round the farthest horizon!"

This burst of enthusiasm left my old friend out of breath, and he came to a sudden pause, illustrating by a rotund gesture the sweep of the Calais light and of the *marchesa's* eyes.

"You're getting quite Musset-ish," I said:

Avez-vous vu, dans Barcelone,

Une Andalouse au sein bruni,
Pâle comme un beau soir d'automne?
C'est ma maîtresse, ma lionne!
La Marquess d'Amaëgui.

"That's about it," said Sir Marmaduke. "And, now I come to think of it, Musset was her favourite poet. Well, I needn't tell you how we made acquaintance with each other, or how our acquaintance ripened. She was educated and accomplished far beyond the Italian average—spoke English and French almost as well as her mother-tongue, had read much in these three languages, sang with a splendid *contralto* voice, and dressed with studied and sober simplicity. Indeed, she was still in half-mourning for her husband, the departed *marchesa*, at whose death one of the most ancient Neapolitan families became extinct. Since then she had lived with relatives in Paris; but, though her English accent was of the utmost purity, she had never crossed the Channel. Her Parisian friends had left for South America; and, as the climate of Naples did not suit her, not to mention the gloomy associations the place must ever have for her, she had determined to settle in North Italy, and lead a quiet life of study and beneficence.

"To say that I fell in love with her would be to misstate the case. I was forty, she scarcely ten years younger; and there was a self-reliance, not to say self-sufficiency, in her character which put all tenderness out of the question. She was a being to be worshiped, not caressed. Even after she was my affianced wife, our relations were courtly rather than cordial. She was not precisely cold; but she seemed to feel, as I, too, felt, that such beauty as here must go hand in hand with perfect dignity, and that playfulness would as ill beseem her as it would the Agrippina of the Capitol. I felt toward her as toward a unique 'thing of beauty.' Have you never thought, in presence of some supreme work of art—the Sistine Madonna, for example, or the Venus of Milo—that you would like to sell all you had and buy that one thing, even though you should end, like Frankenstein, by becoming a slave to it? "Well, that was something like my feeling toward the Marchesa Lucrezia. I thought her, or rather I knew her, to be one of the loveliest beings ever created; and I had an insane desire to call this phoenix mine, as Faustus longed for—

The face that launched a thousand ships,
And burnt the topless towers of Ilium.

You socialists may say what you like; but, as human nature is constituted, there will always be a peculiar, poignant pleasure in the sense of monopoly. Another thing which determined me to affront what I could not but recognize as the perils of matrimony, was the thought of the long face my confounded cousin would pull when he heard of my marriage; but that was a minor motive. I was in reality under a spell, quite as completely as any of those fellows in the mediaeval ballads."

"Sir Marmaduke Tannhäuser," I put in—

Ich hab in meinem sinne:
fraw Venus, edle fraw so zart
ir seind aine teufelinne.

"'Don't go too fast,' said Sir Marmaduke. "Wait and see."

"Well, the day fixed for our marriage drew near," he continued. "It was to be absolutely private. Lucrezia expressed a horror of festivities, especially at a second marriage; and I chuckled at the idea of springing the news on my friends and relations (including my heir-presumptive) through the first column of the *Times*. Our wedding-tour was to be in the East. Lucrezia dreaded the English climate; and, as Dr. Johnson said of clean linen, 'I myself, sir, have no passion for it,' so we looked forward to living permanently south of the Alps.

"One day I happened to row across to the Isola de' Pescatori on some charitable errand of the *marchesa's*; and there, strolling about in the one narrow street, I met Philips. I had known him intimately at Oxford, but we had lost sight of each other for ten or fifteen years, and we were both glad to meet again. He was stopping, he told me, at Pallanza; so I made him dismiss his *barca,* and promised to put him over to the mainland in my own sailing-boat. There was very little wind, so on the way we had a long talk over old times.

"One fad of his remained implanted in my memory, because I used sometimes to ruffle his otherwise imperturbable temper by chaffing him on the subject. He was a devout believer in the possibility of reading character in handwriting, and used to devote a great deal of time and study to what I then regarded as a mere superstition. I asked him if he still kept up this craze, as I called it, and he answered with a smile, and a shrug, that he did. A sudden idea occurred to me. I found in my pocket a note from the *marchesa*—a mere business letter, concluding with an invitation to dinner, and written, moreover, in Italian, which Philips had just been telling me that he did not understand. She wrote a particularly masculine hand; so, in the hope that he would not discover even the sex of the writer, I tore off the signature—'Lucrezia.' Then I handed it to Philips and asked him for a diagnosis of the writer's character.

"I watched his expression as he examined the writing. At the first glance he raised his eyebrows and compressed his lips with the air of a man who finds himself face to face with an unexpected problem. Then he wrinkled his eyebrows together until they hung forward like a pent-house over his eyes, and peered microscopically into each stroke, curve, and dot of the whole letter. The examination lasted, I am sure, a good five minutes, during which neither of us spoke.

"At last he looked straight up at me, and said,'Are you much interested in this—lady?'

"'Ah, then you know it's a lady,' I replied, a little taken aback.

"'I know more than that,' he said, solemnly; and, as he tapped the paper with his forefinger, he added,'This writing is the writing of a murderess!'

"I let go the helm and sprang forward with a cry, almost capsizing the little boat. She luffed up at once into the wind, and I had to return to my post, else I believe I should have assaulted him.

"'Come, Philips,' I said,'a joke's a joke, but this is carrying the thing a little too far.'

"'If it were a joke,' he said, 'it would be in the worst possible taste; but I am in sober earnest.'

"'You're mad!' I said. 'This tomfoolery of yours has become a monomania. Let me tell you that I am about to marry the lady who wrote that letter.'

"'Then, all I can say is,' he replied—'and remember, I'm in solemn earnest—all I can say is, your life's not worth a twelve-month's purchase.' He again examined the letter carefully, and then said: 'Believe me or not, as you like, this is the handwriting of a murderess. And I can tell you more—the hand that formed these letters has clasped a stiletto—that is her weapon!'"

"'Pooh!' I said, beginning, in spite of myself, to be some-what impressed. 'Do you take me for a child? If she had been a poisoner, I suppose you could have told from her handwriting whether she used antimony or arsenic?'

"'That's as may be,' was his answer. 'What I *do* see in the present case is that the hand which wrote this has used cold iron. Do you know the lady's past history ?'

"'I know she's a widow,' I replied.

"'That's not improbable,' said he.

"'And that her husband was a Neapolitan nobleman,' I con-tinued.

"'Hum!' he said, and proceeded to cross-question me in such a way as to show me, what had really never occurred to me, that I had no one's evidence but her own as to a single fact of her past life. At last, driven into a corner, I exclaimed, impatiently, 'Then what do you propose that I should do? I can't go to her and say, "*marchesa*, a necromancer of my acquaintance assures me that you have assassinated some one—probably the late la-mented *marquese*. Pray, is this true?"'

"'Let me think,' Philips replied. Then, after a pause, while he again looked at the letter, 'Your plan is to take her by surprise. She is evidently of a high-strong, nervous temperament.'

"'There you're wrong,' I interrupted.

"'No, I'm not,' he replied, imperturbably. 'I'll stake my reputation on it, that if you were suddenly to show her this stiletto, she would say or do something that would betray her secret;' and, to my astonishment, he produced from under his coat a little dagger that flashed in the sunlight.

"I burst out laughing. 'You come to Italy armed!' I cried. 'You think we are still in the Middle Ages! That accounts for your absurd interpretation of the handwriting.'

"'Not a bit of it,' he replied. 'I always carry this little bit of steel; it's useful in many ways, and it has associations for me. I'm so far from imagining it particularly necessary in Italy, that I dare say you, who live here, haven't such a thing in your possession.'

"I admitted I hadn't. 'Well, then,' he said, unfastening the sheath which hung at his waistband, concealed by his coat, 'I'll make a sort of wager with you. This is a very pretty little toy, you'll admit—an antique Italian dagger, the haft and sheath of ivory inlaid with gold; and here, you see, is a red amethyst set in the butt of the handle, and another in the point of the sheath. Well, I hand this over to you on condition that you suddenly, and without any warning, produce it and present it to the lady. If there is nothing unusual in her method of accepting it, the knife is hers, and I have lost my wager. If you notice anything odd in her behaviour, come and tell me, and we will inquire into the matter further.'

"'Well, positively,' I said, 'it is a sort of insult to the *marchesa* to consent to any such test But you're right, the dagger is a very beautiful piece of workmanship, and—hang it!—I rather like the idea of making her a handsome present at your expense, especially as I dare say the lesson will do you good, and imprint on you the maxim, "*Put not your trust in pot-hooks.*"'

"'Pot-hooks are sometimes hangers as well,' he replied. To this day I don't know what he meant by the remark, for just then I laid the boat in to the steamboat stage at Pallanza, and he stepped ashore. He gave me the name of his hotel, and I promised to look him up the next day and report. Then I sailed back to Stresa with a fresher breeze, pondering on his curious mania and on his last oracular remark.

154

"That afternoon I presented myself at the Villa Trabelli at my usual hour. I had carefully wrapped up the dagger in white paper, tied it with a pink ribbon, and sealed the packet. I found Lucrezia in a rocking-chair on the veranda, looking superbly beautiful. She wore a black summer dress, I remember, of some gauzy, diaphanous material, closed at the throat and at the wrists with knots of red ribbon; and round the alabaster pillar of her throat were three narrow circlets of blood-red coral.

"'*Marchesa*,' I said, as I kissed her hand, 'I have here a small offering for you—a trifle, but I think unique.'

"She untied the ribbon and broke the seals. 'Some amiable surprise, I do not doubt,' she said, as she unrolled the wrappings; but before she had finished doing so, the dagger slipped out, sheath and all, and fell in her lap.

"The instant she set eyes on it she raised her hands in the air and sprang from her seat with a sort of gurgling, stifled cry. The dagger dropped on the matting at her feet, and for a moment she stared at it, her eyes starting from their sockets, while her complexion turned to livid green. Then she staggered back a few paces, as though making for the *salon,* and sank in a huddled heap on the floor.

"'I did not do it! I did not do it!' she moaned. 'It was she— the viper—the fiend! I was innocent! innocent! innocent!' Her voice failed her, but she continued to moan to herself in broken sentences, writhing the while as though in physical agony.

"I called to her maid, who quickly appeared. 'Your mistress is ill,' I said, and together we raised her from the floor. This brought her in some degree to herself, and when I attempted to help the servant in supporting her into the house, she shrank from me with a gesture of horror, leaned her whole weight on the sturdy Frenchwoman's arm, tottered into the *salon,* and disappeared.

"I was bewildered and benumbed. I picked up the dagger, put it in my pocket, hurried down as fast as I could to the lake, jumped into a skiff, and ordered two rowers to take me at racing speed to Pallanza, where I went straight to Philips's hotel. He was gone!—to Arona and Milan, the porter believed, but after that nothing was known of his destination. From that day until this evening I saw and heard nothing of him. He had left me no address, and I knew of none that would find him. From something he said this evening, I presume he must have been in the Home Office, but he had not mentioned the fact. I rather fancied he was an idle globe-trotter like myself, and trusted to the fates, in this little world of ours, to bring us together again. They have done so, you see, though it has taken them eleven years.

"On returning to Stresa, I inquired at the Villa Trabelli and learned that the *marchesa* was ill and in bed. Next morning I called again, when one of the Italian servants handed me a note, and informed me that the *marchesa* and her maid had departed early that morning, no one knew whither. The note was written in English; I can repeat it word for word:

> I imagined that Sir Marmaduke Middleton was a gentleman; is it the part of a gentleman brutally to wrench and wring the nerves of a much-tried woman? Whatever sins have been laid at my door, I have never tortured a being weaker than myself—a friend, who had done me no wrong. If you have a spark of chivalry left, you will make no attempt to track me, and breathe no word of my secret.—L. T.

"You may imagine that when I read this I felt, as the Yankees say, 'almighty mean.' I breathed no word of her secret, for the very good reason that I knew no word of it to breathe; but by way of a little penance, I have mortified my curiosity and carefully refrained from making any attempt to discover it A month or two later I learned that the Villa Trabelli, with all its furnishings and appurtenances, just as it stood, had been sold to a German banker. I soon sold my own chalet, and set off for a three-years' ramble in China, Japan, California, and so forth. Once, at a small station on the Pacific Railroad, I fancied I caught a glimpse of my enchantress's face. Her train was just moving off in the direction of San Francisco, as mine was starting toward Omaha. I felt a momentary impulse to jump out and take the next train in pursuit; but I resisted it—and here I am!"

Mr. Philips was as good as his word, and arrived at Meurice's shortly before midnight The more I studied his solid, well-built, commonplace features, the less did I believe in his clairvoyance, or whatever occult faculty Sir Marmaduke credited him with. I was curious, consequently, to hear their conversation.

Sir Marmaduke began by telling Mr. Philips the result of his experiment, just as he had related it to me.

He was describing the sudden collapse of the Marchesa Lucrezia, when his hearer interrupted him.

"By Jove!" he said, "I gave her credit for more nerve than that!"

"Then your black and white art can't quite rank among the exact sciences," said Sir Marmaduke. "You can't measure nerve force to a millionth of a grain?"

"The fact is," said Philips, smiling, "I confess I was trifling with you to a certain extent. You used to be so obstinately sceptical of my power of reading character, that I could not resist the temptation to pay you out a bit. Handwriting *is* to a certain extent an index to character, and by long and close study of it I developed an abnormally keen sense for minute resemblances and differences; in short, I made myself an expert. At the Home Office my powers quickly became known, and I was given frequent opportunities for exercising them. Then I began to be called as a witness in courts of law, though the impertinent incredulity with which the evidence of experts is generally regarded made me detest these cases.

"Don't you remember a murder trial fourteen or fifteen years ago, in which an Italian lady (she had been an opera singer) was accused of deliberately stabbing her husband, an Englishman, and a man of great wealth, either from jealousy, or from mere cupidity, or perhaps from both combined? She suspected him of carrying on an intrigue with another woman, and she forged a letter, purporting to be in that woman's handwriting, giving him an assignation, at the dead of night, in some lonely corner of his own park. He fell into the trap, came to the spot, and sat down on a log to await the lady's arrival; whereupon his wife stole up behind him and stabbed him in three places, killing him almost before he could utter a cry. That, at any rate, was the theory of the prosecution; but the whole case turned on bringing home to her the forged letter.

"I was one of the experts called, and I had not the slightest hesitation in identifying the writing of the forged letter with the prisoner's acknowledged hand. The other so-called experts, who were mere charlatans, expressed less confidence; and the result was, that the murderess escaped. The moment you showed me that letter, Middleton, I recognized her handwriting. After the trial, I had secured as a curiosity the little stiletto with which the murder was committed; and in this I at once saw a chance of mystifying you a bit, and saving you from the lady's toils. I thought she would betray herself in some way at sight of the weapon, or, at any rate, would take it as a hint that you either knew, or were on the verge of discovering, her secret; but, from her behaviour during the trial, I thought she would have brazened it out a good deal better than she did. What you tell me amounts to an absolute admission of guilt."

"In the disguise of an assertion of innocence" I could not refrain from putting in. "That dagger would have quite sufficiently painful associations for her, though she were as innocent as the day."

"I believe I've been an even greater brute than I thought," said Sir Marmaduke. "It seems to me, Philips, that, by your own showing, you are the only witness against her."

"It was her own hand that condemned her," said the expert.

"No, that's just what it didn't," said Sir Marmaduke. "In this case pot-hooks were not hangers. But why did she take a bogus title? And why—? And why—? On the whole, Philips, I bear you no grudge for having forbidden the banns."

Vincent Hadding

By A. Mary F. Robinson

1

The last time that Colonel Cathcart went to India, he left his wife and the two girls behind in Rome. It was July weather, very hot and sultry. They, however, were compelled to stay there, for Sophie had fallen ill of the fever. If you knew Sophie Cathcart seven years ago (she is Lady Lyndon now), you will admit that you have seldom seen a sweeter girl. I always preferred her to her cousin, Marian Bassett; but Marian was certainly the general favourite. She had such splendid health and spirits, such a youthful and radiant air, that her admirers forgot to notice the ominous contrast of her black brows with her abundant reddish hair; and a certain chivalrous impatient expression redeemed the prominence of her lower lip. Still I always found something odd, some hint of discord in her charming face. And she looked older than Sophie, although she was fully two years younger. Indeed, she can have scarcely been sixteen that summer when her cousin fell so ill in Rome.

Sophie was a long time getting better; and it was then that Marian became so intimate with Vincent Hadding. Mrs. Cathcart, as she sat in Sophie's room, was sorry for her niece, left to herself the whole day long. I think she encouraged Marian's friendship with Hadding, who was quite forty then; he is growing an elderly man. The Cathcarts had met him in June at one of Mrs. Pennington's Thursdays; and their acquaintance had ripened into intimacy now that they and he were the only English people left in Rome. Hadding had travelled too often in the East to fear the heat of an Italian summer; and he would not leave Rome until he had completed his catalogue of Etruscan monuments. He used to take Marian with him to draw the vases in the Museo Italico.

She had never heard before of Hadding, *Archaeology*, or, indeed, of archaeology at all; but she had read his stories and his *Arabian Letters*, and was prepared to accept any of his theories. She was at the age, you know, when discipleship is the most engrossing and the most natural of pastimes. As for Hadding, I think he was interested in the girl because of her melancholy history. It was quite like his own novels. And he liked to absorb this frank, girlish nature, so different from his own strange and critical character. The reflection that in another month they would be strangers, gave a charm to the intimacy of their intercourse. The whole thing seemed to Hadding an episode, bounded by the soft landscape and melancholy atmosphere of Rome.

But if he found a pleasure in recognizing the evanescence of their friendship, delicate and transitory as a flower, Marian naturally did not guess this state of mind. She was young, romantic, quite fresh, and most confiding. Her mind had never even touched the moods which after all were nearest and dearest to Hadding: production, experiment, the sense of humour, and of destiny. Life to her meant warm affection and devoted impulses . . . affection and devotion, which, half unconsciously, she began to consecrate to Hadding.

2

From Vincent Hadding to Marian Bassett.

Wednesday.

Dear Miss Bassett:—The Etruscan towns are, I fear, impossible this weather; ten miles of the Campagna would soon give your cousin a companion in misfortune. But, if you will let me take you to the Gregorian Museum, I can show you there the yield of one of the finest tombs at Cervetri. I will call tomorrow at five, to await your pleasure. So you have been reading my novels "again" (that is a very flattering adverb), and you wonder where I knew such wonderful men and women. I have certainly had every chance of meeting them in adventurous places; but, as a rule, the more interesting are to be discovered nearer home. The year I spent in Arabia was utterly barren in that kind; but last month I found the Via Nazionale a very happy hunting-ground. I know you are burning to hear what I think of the specimen; but, remember, listeners never hear good of themselves.

Monday.

Dear Miss Bassett:—The little set of drawings is very nicely done; but there are some vases in the Museo Italico which you should study for your collection. . . . No! I am not going to tell you any more about my treasure trove in the Via Nazionale. For one thing, I am not yet quite sure of the value of the specimen. You are angry, but, if you are to be a good archaeologist, you must learn to suspect. Else you will spend your fortune on a priceless collection of Brummagem metal and nineteenth century potsherds. *Eperientia docet!*

Friday.

Marianita de mi Alma:—So, did we really live in Grenada, I should address you. Have you forgiven our fiery quarrel of last night? As for me, I have not yet conceived how to thank you for so new and so stirring an excitement There was a moment—do you know?—when with pleasure I could have dragged you across the stage, like Desdemona, by your long red hair. Imagine the surprise of the cabmen in Piazza di Spagna! I cannot account for the irritable violence which is always excited in me by the display of strong feeling in others; there is a mingling of dislike in it, and a vague fear, and an intense revulsion. There, my dear, is something for your note-book!. . . . I fear I must have seemed unkind and harsh; but I was not really angry

161

with you, dear Miss Bassett. In the end, I was glad of my little battle with you; for I believe that, since you are so fantastically loyal to your cousin Sophie, you will cherish the remembrance of your friend. . . . Well, goodbye. . . . Remember, you must rise early, since your aunt is resolved on the picnic to Frascati; for we ought to be in Rome again before they sing the *Ave Maria*.

Friday.

Thank you, my dear playfellow, for your pleasant behaviour yesterday. I have enjoyed no picnic so much for many a year as our little expedition to Frascati. Your aunt is always charming, and pretty little Sophie flirted less than usual with her Italian retainers. Do not be angry, Marianita. Did I say that I objected to your cousin's flirting? On the contrary, I think it a most legitimate charm in woman; and if I am glad that she did not dazzle us on Monday, it is only because I do not like to see you in the shade. Why is it, I wonder, that we take such pleasure in each other's society, we who are always sparring, we that are so different in age and nature?

Of course, of this question there is only one half that I can answer. But I imagine that I feel for you as a man that has married late in life feels for the stepdaughter he has never known in childhood. There is much in you I do not understand; nothing that does not interest me. You appeal to my paternal instincts. . . . I see you as an eager young soul wrestling at every step with invincible angels; and I long to protect you from too many joints displaced. All this is very sentimental. Are you satisfied to be my quasi stepchild?

Sunday.

So you are ill, poor little Minerva mine, and you tell me that I excite you too much! Perhaps, indeed, I have overworked you, and I am very sorry. . . . Until today I never knew you could spell that sad feminine substantive, Re-

proaches. But if I have excited you, I am very truly sorry.
. . . It is as well, perhaps, that our little holiday friendship
is nearly at an end. You will not have to suffer me much
longer. It will all be as if it had never been, and that is the
best end that we can wish to any pleasure. . . . I send you
Gregorovius, and a pot of rose-leaf jam from Chios. You sit
on a terrace in a muslin veil, and eat a little spoonful of the
roses, and sip a glass of water meanwhile. It is even more
Southern than your water-melons, and Firdusi, not Gregorovius, ought to have gone to you along with it. But I
know you love your Rome as much, almost, as any sweat-
meat. . . . Have I studied your two passions successfully?
Keep quiet, then, *ma belle-fille* (you may drop the hyphen,
if you like); keep quiet and get well for Sunday, when we
ought to visit the Gregoriano. *Ars lunga,* and our time is
short.

3

At this time Mrs. Cathcart began to speak of going home to
England. Sophie was so much stronger that she could travel by
little stages; and every hour's journey would take them further
from the suffocating heat of Rome. Hadding made himself very
useful to the Cathcarts, and wrote lists of books for Marian. In
any difficulty, he said, she could always apply for his advice; but
he did not suggest that she should write him regular letters. For
he dreaded lest this pleasant episode should slip into a commonplace or a sentimental correspondence.

Mrs. Cathcart and Sophie were full of the delights of getting
home again—of cool English air, green leaves, and temperate
summer. Rome appeared to them but a hot and desolate place,
when one lay in a dark room Buffering fever-heats and chills, or
sat, unoccupied and stifling, keeping vigil by the sick. Marian's
Rome was a different city, an ancient and still glorious Elysium.
But she could not waste her time there in forestalling her re-
grets. She was still bright and happy, still alert and vigorous in
the pursuit of archaeology, until the very eve of their departure

came.

Hadding was to call that evening, and to take them all to drink of the magical Trevi water which insures return to Rome. The day passed quickly, in the bustle of departure; and soon the evening came, moonlit and cool. The little party walked to the fountain along the shadowy streets, strange exhalations poisoning the air, evil smells of inhabited places, and whiffs of chill vapour from the marsh beyond the wall, with, over all, a strange sickly perfume of lemon-flowers and oleander.

"Oh," cried Mrs. Cathcart, "how thankful I shall be to take you two dear girls away from this dreadful town!"

Poor Sophie pressed her mother's arm; but Marian and Hadding turned to each other and smiled. They, at least, had known how to make the best of Rome.

They stood by the fountain's edge. "I don't call it pretty," said Mrs. Cathcart.

"It has no need to be pretty," cried Marian, "if it will bring us back to Rome!" She threw in a handful of *centesimi*. Hadding followed suit; and Mrs. Cathcart meditatively let a *soldo* slip between her fingers.

"I am not quite sure," she said, "that I want to come back."

Sophie sat on the fountain's rim, clutching the forgotten pennies in her sallow little hands. She, certainly, had no wish but to get away from Rome at once and for ever. She began to shiver, and Mrs. Cathcart was alarmed. In a moment Hadding had hailed a little two-seated *botta,* and packed the two ladies into it.

"I will walk home with Miss Bassett," he said, "when she has tasted the waters of Trevi."

The cab rumbled off, and Marian sat down where Sophie had been on the stone rim of the basin. She, too, began to feel sad and weary now; for this was the last of Rome, and the last of the happiest summer of her life. She looked round, as if she would fix every line, every streak of light and shadow, in her memory. It was the last of Rome. A strange and painful compression of her heart made it difficult to breathe. It was the last of Rome. The waters of the fountain looked white in the moonlight; the fantastic sculptures of Pietro Bracci stood out lividly against their dusky background. Marian saw her face in the smooth water. It looked drowned and mournful, with wet eyes and swollen features.

"You are not drinking," said Hadding, who was standing up beside her, "and yet, you know, you must come back to Rome."

Marian did not answer. He was still there, and still she was in Rome; and yet, since she must leave them both, she wished it were well over. She was filled with a sick exasperation against herself and against these beloved things; because, though they were present still, she could not be happy with them. She stole a glance at the ugly fountain, at the stooping figure of Hadding, looking more grizzled in the moonlight, and wondered why she should be so miserable to go away.

Hadding stood up still, impatient to be gone. He was not looking at Marian nor at the fountain. He stared vacantly at the hideous *façade* of San Vincenzo. He was wishing he had sent Marian home with her aunt; angry at her evident misery, and at an odd reluctance of his own to let her go. This reluctance made him harden his heart.

But the silence was oppressive—the silence, the moonlight, the flickering shadows, the smell of oleanders, and lemons, and gardenia from the gardens near. Hadding felt he must say something.

"Who would have thought," he began, twisting another cigarette, "who would have thought, that evening when I met you at Mrs. Pennington's in the stupid Via Nazionale, that we should become such good companions? And now we must say good-bye. Life has other duties for either. But I shall always look back toward our little friendship as to one of the happiest episodes in my life."

"An episode?" echoed Marian. These words seemed to her of an outrageous cruelty.

"It seems hard to you, does it," went on Hadding meditatively, "to own that any beautiful thing is transitory? But you would not have us swear an eternal friendship, like two school children, we whose paths and duties lie so far apart? We are like two travellers, each in a different train, who wait opposite each other a few minutes in a railway station. *Puff!* and the trains start, one to the north and one to the south, to the different ends of the earth; but, perhaps, one or both of those travellers may often recall the face he saw in passing, and wish that he had known it better."

Marian said nothing.

"And at least," went on Vincent Hadding, "we have had more profit than that out of our friendship of nine weeks. I possess a pure and lasting memory; and you, I hope, have learned a good deal of archaeology. By the way, in going north you must persuade Mrs. Cathcart to take you to Volterra."

Hadding stopped. There was something strange and uncanny in this long monologue of his, standing in the deserted square filled with the moonlight and the faint plash of falling water, the strong sweet scent of the first autumn flowers faint on the air, and, at his feet, that crouching white figure of a beautiful woman, silent—always silent—but whom he knew to be crying for his sake.

Hadding was seized with the sudden vague timidity of an imaginative man. He dared not stand there longer, in that sweet, faint atmosphere, in that abandoned, ghostly place, with that woman still crying, so decorously silent, by the water's edge. A certain fear of himself, a certain fear of the past, a certain remorse and impatience, possessed him. "Let us go home!" he cried, and taking Marian's arm, he hurried her in silence through the deserted streets of Rome in August, until they reached the house where Mrs. Cathcart lodged. The great Roman staircase was pitch dark, and they climbed with difficulty to the door of the apartment. Hadding rang the bell. Someone within cried *"Svbttof"* but no one came.

It was quite dark. Marian could only see the dimmest outline of Vincent Hadding's figure. He did not speak: he seemed already to be gone away. Then the conviction burst upon her that she would never see him again. They were so close together in the darkness; there was a moment to speak in and be heard, and then they would be separate forever.

"*É sempre chiusa!*" cried Hadding, and rapped at the door with his cane.

There was only another moment now. A cold lassitude and numbness stole over Marian. The hand that she had already stretched out, to shake hands at parting, felt like ice within its little glove. Her voice seemed to perish in her throat—the voice that must say goodbye; the limbs to fail her, that must carry her away forever. And yet, while this terrible paralysis seemed to invade all the centres and arteries of life, at the same moment her will awoke with imperious force. She must do something to prevent this utter separation; she would not let it all come to nothing, all be wasted—that treasure of devotion in her heart. She would keep his friendship; oh, she must keep it! Yet she did not know what she would say, or how she would act to this end. Just then they both heard Menichina's sturdy tramp along the passage.

"At last!" thought Hadding.

"At last!" thought poor Marian, but with how different an intonation. Suddenly, without reflecting, she seized Hadding by the arm.

"I dreamed last night," she whispered very fast, "that you said you would like me to be your friend for always." She broke down, expecting his kind answer. But, though Hadding could not see her, he heard the hysterical pathos in her voice. It revolted him. It seemed to him that he had injured the girl—that if he could leave her now she would recover. There would be no danger for either. And Menichina opened the door.

"That's all folly!" he exclaimed, as he loosened Marian's hand from his coat. "A man and a woman can never be friends. Goodbye! Goodnight!"

4

Menichina was holding open the door; the *signorina* was

167

standing dazed upon the threshold. The little Roman shop-keeper's daughter, who never might go out alone, and seldom, therefore, went out at all, was filled with wonder that an English girl, with golden hair, and freedom, and plenty of money, should look as sad as Marian.

"Perhaps she does not want to marry that old man,"

Menichina fancied; and those keen black eyes fixed on Marian's face recalled the tired girl to a sense of reality.

She went in and said "Goodnight" to Mrs. Cathcart, and kissed Sophie, warm in bed, envying her the safe and comfortable shelter of her mother's love. Then Marian went into her own little room, and packed her trunks for the morrow. She had finished while still it was quite early, and there was nothing left to do. She looked round the emptied room bewildered. No, there was nothing left to do; yet she would rather undo her work, and do it all again, than sit unoccupied. But she was strangely tired; she sat down on the edge of the bed and began to think. Every moment now her cheeks burned hotter, as though a lash had been struck across them. Every moment she felt more strongly wrought to a bitter and a savage sense of humiliation. There was one instant when she would have chosen to watch Hadding drown, and not have helped him; so that the same sun should never shine again upon herself and him. While he was alive she felt disgraced.

In the middle of her passion, quite suddenly, she fell asleep.

It was just beginning to grow light when Marian awoke. She felt tired and shattered, and for one numb, painful second she wondered dimly what had happened. Then she turned on her side and began to cry; all her fierce mortification of last night turned into a melancholy pity for herself. It seemed impossible that any one had ever been so cruel to her, little Marian, whom every one praised and loved. How could he do it! Oh, how could he do it! And she had felt so sure that he had liked her; for, indeed, although he was a great man, and she a little girl, he had always seemed to care to have her with him. Here Marian got up, and pulling one of Hadding's novels out of her trunk, she took it to the window and began to read. It was still so dark that she saw the print with difficulty, but as she read on, half guessing at the dear familiar lines, all the force of her old admiration renewed itself in her heart. He was so great, and she of no account.

"Could I have made him a little happier," said Marian softly to herself, "it would not much matter what became of me."

Marian stood still for a moment, and dropped her book, though the gray light of the morning was every moment growing whiter and clearer. She gazed vaguely out of the window, while a new, faint feeling grew stronger in her mind. The first sunbeam came now across the house-roofs, slanting along the bare little room, and across the white figure of the girl who, with all her bright hair dishevelled, stood barefoot at the open window. Peace, and a delicate glory, seemed to envelop her; it appeared impossible to Marian herself that so little while ago such a vindictive passion had torn her miserable heart. She did not feel unhappy now. A great pity diffused itself sweetly through all her thoughts, melting their anger.

There was no one who had taught him to trust and to believe. Ah, could she have been his friend, and really his friend, he should have known all that a woman can be to a man! She would have been so patient, so faithful, so trusting, so full of sympathy. It was a pity that it had all come to nothing. A strange impersonal compassion touched Marian almost to tears; it was as though she stood by the coffin of a child whom she had never seen. It had all come to an end so soon. It was a pity.

By this time the sun was high. Mrs. Cathcart called to Marian through the door. She must get ready now to go away from Rome. But first of all, still in this strange, exalted mood, she took a sheet of paper and wrote a line upon it. "Goodbye," she wrote, "goodbye, and God bless you! I am not angry anymore."

5

When, next evening, Vincent Hadding received Marian's little note, he gave an irritated little laugh, and lit his cigarette with it Then he repented of this miniature brutality, and it occurred to him that he had not played the kindliest part in their *adieus*. "A woman is sure to have the last word," he cried, still thinking of the note; but his mood had already so far developed that he found himself wondering whether that word need really be the last. If she had offended his discretion the night before, the fault was certainly not entirely Marian's. He had treated her very hardly. She must be more generous than many women of her class; for Hadding inclined to believe that magnanimity ended where respectability began. He recalled Marian's ripe and slender figure, her odd beauty and pathetic eyes; and then he remembered his own words about caring for her as a stepfather. Yes, he would like to have her just so near, if he could be quite sure of having her no nearer.

Hadding was self-contained, independent, fastidious, to the last degree. He could not be content to share his life; it must be all for him. His room must be his own, to bolt against the whole world when he wished it so. He loved to dine when he chose, and wait on no other person's hunger; to go to rest when he was tired, and to rise at a different hour every day; to be free in the smallest no less than in the greatest details of existence. The thought of marriage was abhorrent to him—why should a free man put his feet into the stocks? And yet he was sometimes dull, lonely, bored. He would like to have a friend, a soul of his own to confide in and direct. It would be a pleasure, he thought, to have Marian's girlish letters to answer in the evenings. He was too proud and too suspicious to make many friends among his fellows.

But a woman is an excuse for everything one says to her; one may condescend to her weakness without derogation; and there are moments when tired shoulders are glad of an excuse to stoop. Marian at a distance, Marian fixed in England, seemed to Hadding more desirable than ever she had been in Rome. There could be no danger of love-making so far apart. Hadding did not want to make love, but he wanted a woman to confide in, a soft and sisterly relative who yet would have the sweet novelty of a stranger. And he thought that to Marian also that imaginary correspondence might have been a boon; for Hadding, though an egoist, was not what people mean by a selfish person. He thought of himself first, but he thought a good deal of other people afterward; and it gave him pleasure to think of supporting Marian through the mental trials of an intellectual girlhood. He would be her guide, philosopher, and friend until she married. Somehow, Hadding did not relish this conclusion; it seemed to him a threat of being superseded; it made him no more than a stop-gap, a convenience.

Hadding almost resolved that he would not answer Marian's note, and put his writing things aside again. But that night, as he tossed awake, rebelling against the irritating thrill of a *mandoline* in the street, a sudden memory darted through his mind. Of course, Marian's mother had been mad for years! He had not been thinking of Marian at all, when the *mandolin* had somehow cast this drift of recollection across his sleepless night. But it seemed to settle a good many questions. Of course, the daughter of a mad woman could never marry! A warm tide of commiseration here conquered Hadding's last defences. No, poor child! she could never marry either him or any other man. They were both so he said, predestined to celibacy. He did not question himself as to the exact meaning of this satisfying phrase; but, though his own parents had both been most respectably sane, it seemed convincing to him. They were alike predestined to celibacy; and friendship would be a safe, a natural consolation.

6

A few days after this, Hadding's archaeological researches took him to Florence, where, as it happened, Mrs. Cathcart and her party were staying. Hadding, however, was not certain of this fact. He had not answered Marian's note, and only knew that Mrs. Cathcart and her party were travelling slowly northward. The reason of his journey was Etruscan art. . . . As you know, one of the finest collections in Italy is housed in the Florentine Crocetta Palace. In those days, I remember, it was kept in dust

171

and disorder in the monastery of San Onofrio.

Thither Hadding bent his steps. There was a certain vase in Florence which it was imperative that he should see again. He did not hide from himself that, should he meet Marian Bassett, it would please him to point out to her the beauties of this treasure. He owned that he was curious to see how she would receive him after their abrupt and stormy parting. For Hadding, who feared nothing so greatly as to become the dupe of a momentary passion, analyzed and labelled his motives with a frankness strange to the inarticulate majority of minds.

The weather was violently hot, and Hadding travelled to Florence over night. The next day he spent in the dark and desolate rooms of San Onofrio, which no splendour of heat and light could warm for a moment into radiance. He examined his vase minutely, drew it in detail, and from every point of view. When he had finished he went to his hotel, feeling that he had earned a holiday.

In the cool of the morrow morning he went out. He wondered if Marian were in Florence, as he strolled down Lung Arno toward the Uffizj. He walked slowly through the great galleries and along the bridge, pausing before the pictures that he most admired, conscious of a vague, tingling expectation, and yet scarcely sorry if he had missed her. His affection and interest with regard to Lionardo's unfinished picture (or so, at least, he repeated to himself) were as poignant as his interest in Marian. As he went along the bridge into the Pitti, he did not feel that his time had been wasted; and he would have returned to Rome with only the slightest savour of disappointment.

In that case there would have been no story for me to tell—if so slight a thing as the friction of two lives can be called a story. But as he was looking out of one of the broad windows into the Boboli Gardens, Hadding saw a little group of three women: a middle-aged lady sitting with a pale and pretty girl upon a bench; a tall young beauty, her blonde hair shining under a little black bonnet, stooping, on a bank above them, as if to gather flowers out of the sundried and blossomless grass. Hadding felt an intense desire to go away—not to have seen them—to hurry back to Rome. In another moment he had left the window, and was going out to join them in the garden.

As he went he wondered again, with a certain amused and friendly curiosity, in what manner Marian would receive him. He felt like a grown-up person who has had to mortify a charming child. In another moment his doubts were set at rest in the most flattering fashion.

Marian was showing her cousin a few little withered anemone leaves. "I told you it was here we used to pluck them," Hadding heard her say. And then she saw him coming toward them, and nimbly ran down the bank to meet him, holding out a welcoming hand.

"I am so glad you have come!" she began.

"I came to study at San Onofrio," said Hadding. "I thought you might still be here."

"You are only just in time," went on Marian, "for we are going to Parma tomorrow."

"Tomorrow!" Hadding had not expected that he should feel so much annoyed. "I should have liked to show you San Onofrio."

Marian said nothing, for Mrs. Cathcart and Sophie were volubly catechizing Hadding about their journey, about the more comfortable inns, and which towns in Lombardy were most worthy of a visit. Marian stood and looked on, feeling pleased when Hadding turned to glance at her.

"We must be going now," said Mrs. Cathcart at last. "I don't know how to thank you for all your kindness, Mr. Hadding. We should all be very sorry, I'm sure, if this were to be the end of so pleasant an acquaintance. But perhaps you will be in London in the spring; and you will come to see us then, in Kensington?"

"Thank you," said Hadding. "Yes, perhaps I shall be in England;" then, turning to Marian, he said, "Goodbye! Sometimes, when you are not too busy, will you write to me, perhaps, and tell me about your studies?"

Marian blushed very red, and her under-lip assumed its defiant and voluntary pout. But in a moment the tears were in her eyes.

"If I may," she murmured very softly, with the obedient voice of a child.

7

From Vincent Hadding to Marian Bassett.

January.

My dear Miss Bassett:—I am very glad your Christmas was so merry; mine, also, did not deserve the commiseration that you bestowed upon it. I am glad, however, that you did not know this at the time, or perhaps you would not have written me so long a letter. How did I spend my Christmas? Well, to your ears I fear it will sound very dull, after all First of all I read your letter, and it was the echo of it, no doubt, which made the rest of the day so pleasant. I spent the morning in polishing and arranging some Eastern weapons on my wall. I am very proud of my parlour, which has two large southern windows, with plants on the balcony, and it has pale blue walls and furniture covered in red Faenza cotton.

If you saw it you would never dream it belonged to an old bachelor, because you are not yet a woman of experience. So far, you see, there were no events. In the afternoon I drove to Frascati, to dine with the fat little priest there, with whom, if you remember, we both talked archaeology in July. I spent the night with this worthy old gentleman, and we discussed some recent excavations near Orvieto. If our repast was more modest than yours, you must remember that even you will find your cake too sweet in another twenty years, and reconcile yourself to a crust of bread. After a while you will prefer your crust to any cake, and then you will know that you are growing old—like myself and like Don Eusebio.

January.

So you think it rather wicked on my part to spend Christmas Day with a Roman Catholic. If you knew all the strange company that I have mixed with in my life, I fear, my dear child, that you would be indeed afflicted! Don Eusebio is the best of men—the most orderly and devoted and religious. I have a real affection for him, and he seems to me to belong to a fast perishing race. He was born, before earnestness came into fashion, is tolerant, upright, and gentle. Here is a catalogue of virtues sufficient, surely, for any man's friend.

I wonder if I appear to you as a Jesuit in disguise! To me even a Jesuit occasions no shudder; much bad company has long ago corrupted my opinions. But, seriously, why should you think it right only to associate with persons who reflect your own belief? This is a form of vanity and cowardice unworthy of your courage. To shut one's self into any corner, to imagine life as a triangular affair, sufficient to hold your own opinions and, at most, one or two varying excellences, this is the surest way to blind, to paralyze your faculties. After a little while you will try in vain to stir from your corner; all the rest of the world will have become invisible to you. In order to live well, examine everything; take nothing on trust—not even the faults of your enemies! life is an instrument with many stops, and a good player will use them all.

February.

Why should you wish to know me better, my dear Miss Bassett? And why, above all, should you want to agree with me? Do you not know that a lesson quickly learned is seldom long remembered? As for you, I think, with pleasure, that I scarcely know you at all, and that I am aware of at least half a dozen faults in your character. This seems to me an excellent basis for friendship. I distrust all sudden adorations. There are only two ends possible to such a state of mind, and both of them are sufficiently dismal. In the one case, the worshiper gradually discovers that, after all, his idol is not so divine; be recognizes a certain touch to be common, another grotesque, a third a sheer mistake; while, as for the feet, . . . you know the feet of idols are generally restored!

In the second case, the poor suppliant remains faithful to his worship, but only at the cost of his finer sense, his judgment, his acuteness of perception. He kneels still in a posture of adoration, hiding his eyes in his hand. If he sees no fault in his idol, it is because he is voluntarily blind. I am sure, now, that you will say I am a cynic. But no; there is no firmer believer in friendship than I. Only let us be sane, equal, independent; neither kneeling before vain images nor painfully trying to fuse two separate natures into one. Do what you will, Marianita, one and one is two, and always must be two. If you invariably agreed with me, and if, as you wish, I could see into all the recesses of your heart, why then, I fear, my dear child, I should not greatly care for your friendship, nor think you a refuge from my familiar self.

June.

After all, my dear friend, we are not to see each other this summer, and this will be my second exposure to dust and flies and fever in this dreary midsummer Rome. I sprained my foot badly the other day in the new excavations round the *Forum*. There will be no travelling for me at present. I lie on the sofa with my swollen foot foreshortened before me, and think how last year at this time it was not so dull in Rome. Ah, no! not so dull at all! Do you remember, Marianita? Think of me, then, with a little compassion.

September.

How short your letters are becoming, *Mariana de mi vida!* This time last year, do you remember the sort of letters that you used to write me? You were very anxious then for my advice and my opinion. You studied archaeology like any learned young lady at the New Cambridge College. You read all my books, and used to quote them at every turn. And now (does not your conscience reproach you?) once a month or so you send me a line, to say that you cannot think of anything to tell me. You give me to understand that I am your dearest friend (of course), only you are too busy to remember me. Do you think that today you could tell me the characteristics of the "*Vase François*"? or what was the yield of the great tomb at Cervetri? No, it is of Wagner's music that you write at present, although you know I far prefer the melancholy trill of the frogs in the Campagna. . . . Yet you fill your letters with *Lohengrin*, and *Parzival*, and *Tristan and Isolde*. There is only one thing about your music that I really care to know. . . . Tell me, Marianita, who is your professor!

January.

It is Epiphany tonight. The people are all out in the streets despite the bitter wind. You would like to see them, in their plaited cloaks, blowing the long frail glass trumpets which seem as if they had been stolen from some paradise of Fra Angelico's. A hideous screech from scores of these fragile instruments rends the air. My head aches, and I wish they had all but one trumpet, that I might shatter it. . . . The night is cold and draughty; the wood fire gives out no heat. I wonder why the people outside are so merry? This year, Marianita, you made one little letter serve for Christmas and New Year.

Yet I was more in need of your consolations than before. My old friend, Don Eusebio, is dead, and my little blue *Salotto* seemed lonely, for once, on Christmas Day. I have had also a slight attack of fever. . . . When I was young the fever only stayed in Rome when we were out of it in the summer and the autumn, but now it seems one may catch it in December. Decidedly the world does not improve. Sometimes the nearing prospect of old age looks melancholy to me, and colourless. Sometimes—will you believe it, Marianita?—sometimes I wish that I had married. But I soon recover of this insanity; I am too much a bachelor at heart. What woman would not make a senseless litter of flower-pots and cotton reels in my tidy rooms?

Besides, as you know, I am not naturally placid, although so fervent a votary of peace. The friction of an existence *à deux* would often wear me to that irritable excitability of impulse which once or twice already I have expiated in disgust and remorse. No; decidedly the ideal life for me is to live alone, but to hear every week or two from a kind and happy little friend in London.

March.

This year really and truly I may hope to shake hands with you again. I am to come to England early in May. My opinion is wanted on a Roman villa newly excavated at Brightlingham, in Sussex. I might take you down there, one day, to see it, since, after all, I never showed you your Etruscan cities.

8

Early in May Vincent Hadding arrived in London. It was three years now since he had been in England, and many old ties claimed his consideration. He did not tell Marian that he was in London until he had satisfied all these elder friends; nevertheless it was with a new feeling of curiosity and pleasant impatience that Hadding started at last, one sunny afternoon, to visit her.

He walked down Piccadilly and on past Kensington Gore. It was a brilliant day. The light-green haze of the new-fledged trees in the park, the carriages full of women in delicate spring dresses, the gay spots of then-white and crimson parasols, all these things seemed to Vincent Hadding a fresh and varied symbol of the strange young pleasure at his heart. There was something very elating in this English spring. He walked on, along the crowded road, until at last he reached an old-fashioned terrace of houses which stood back behind some trees, opposite Kensington Gardens. At the door of No. 16 several carriages were ranged. It was Mrs. Cathcart's reception-day.

Hadding walked upstairs after the servant; and as he went he had an odd impression that all this had happened once before. He felt as one feels who revisits a favourite child, out of whose little memory one's presence may have slipped. Hadding now was following the man into the drawing-room, where Marian, in a blue dress, was making tea and talking to half-a-dozen visitors. Suddenly she saw Hadding, and advanced quickly and lightly to meet him. It was like the Boboli Gardens!

The day was warm, and the French windows were wide open. Over the balcony a striped awning had been spread: seats were placed under it among the tall palms and India-rubber plants. Here and there a shaft of sunlight struck into the reddish shade. "Come out here," said Marian, "and we will think we are in Rome!"

Hadding followed her, noticing with surprise her altered bearing, no longer childish but almost imperial. He had always fancied that he should find her just the same—a child of sixteen. She had grown a very beautiful young woman, with a dazzling Venetian air. But the old strange contrast of the brows and hair, the old half-chivalrous, half-defiant look, reconciled Hadding to this new Marian.

He glanced at her, perceiving the difference. He found it difficult to think of anything to say, oppressed by that cold intimacy which surrounds a person with whose mind alone we are familiar. It took him some time to realize that this proud and brilliant creature was his little customary friend. But Marian—who only thought how ill and short and grizzled Hadding looked —Marian was free from any such shyness.

"Have you been to Brightlingham yet?" she began.

"No," he answered. "I start tomorrow."

"Will you take me, as you promised!" laughed Marian. "I should like to go!"

"I cannot take you to Brightlingham, of course," went on Hadding; "but, if you like, when I return we will go to the British Museum. It is as quiet and as dusty there as Rome: Perhaps we shall meet our old selves, meeting there."

"I like our new selves better!" put in Marian, quickly, with a flash of her light-gray eyes.

"Do you?" said Hadding, and wondered what she meant. A sudden gentleness softened Marian's glance.

"If I am happier now," she went on, "it is greatly owing to you, Mr. Hadding. I was such a stupid and ignorant little girl; you taught me and helped me when I was very lonely, and showed me a whole world of things outside myself. I often think how patient you were with all my childishness. And now that I am happy I shall never forget it."

Hadding glanced at her again and said nothing. Her face looked beautiful and earnest. Her hands were loosely clasped and hanging down. He could see that she was trying to beat down those barriers of coldness and shyness which so swiftly hedge us in from the absent. But he noticed, with a sad curiosity, that she spoke of her old self, of the Marian whose memory he loved, as of a faulty creature, long since perished and buried out of sight.

"No, you must not forget me," he said, at last. "We must always continue friends. We must each endeavour to adapt ourself to what has altered in the other."

"Yes," said Marian. There was a sudden flicker of light in her eyes, a hesitation in her voice, a movement in her throat, which showed Hadding that she was about to make some further avowal. Suddenly he remembered that last night in Rome, the dark staircase, and Marian's hand laid suddenly on his arm. She had looked then like this, no doubt, only he had not seen her. She was still, he thought, with a smile, the same impulsive, vehement nature. But he had no blame for her today.

"No," he said, looking kindly at her; "you have not really altered."

At this moment Mrs. Cathcart, who had been in the garden when Hadding first appeared, hurried out on to the balcony, full of welcoming exclamations. Sophie would be so pleased! Sophie would not be in till seven! And Sophie would be so sorry to have missed him! Mr. Hadding must stay and dine. But Hadding could not stay. He promised, however, to become a constant visitor on his return from Sussex.

"We must take up our studies again in earnest," he said to Marian at parting.

"Yes," she answered, "if I have time;" and then, with a glance of radiant and confiding softness, "I want to talk to you about so many things."

Hadding went out, delighted with his visit.

9

Hadding was only three days away from London. When he returned he felt a great desire to go and receive the confidence of Marian, to make her confess her backslidings in archaeology. But his fastidious respect for the conventional determined him to wait for Mrs. Cathcart's Wednesday. As it happened, he had to pass the door; but none the less he preserved his resolution, making a sort of pleasure out of his self-denial, as people do who keep in chock an impulse of which they are afraid. Hadding was a little afraid of his interest in Marian. But this only gave a keener edge to the pleasure of looking up at her window from outside. Behind the trees in the terrace, behind the tall plants in the balcony, he could see a blue dress moving to and fro. He liked to think that he was so close to Marian, and that she did not know it Then he smiled at himself for standing there, like an Italian serenader, and walked quickly on toward town.

In Piccadilly a tall, florid man came up to Hadding with an exclamation of surprise. It was Mr. Pennington, at whose house, if you remember, Hadding had first met Marian in Rome. This expansive and unoccupied person, ever glad of a new channel for hip incessant stream of gossip, turned on his steps and walked a little way with Hadding. When the news of all the Penningtons had been told, and all the current topics dismissed, the two men fell to talking over their mutual friends in Rome.

"You remember those people you met at my house?" said Mr. Pennington at last "Those Indian people— what's their name! He's always away. You knew him in Madras."

"Cathcart?" asked Hadding.

"Yes, Colonel Cathcart: awful martinet, he always seemed to me. Popular man, though: can't think why; say he wins five hundred a year at whist at his club."

"I shouldn't have thought it a reason for popularity," remarked Hadding.

"Nor should I! Nor should I! Just what I always said. His wife, at any rate, doesn't seem to break her heart without him. I always expect that when he comes home she'll try the climate of Madras. Ha, ha!"

"She's a very nice woman," said Hadding. "I scarcely know the colonel." He was getting profoundly bored with the garrulous mild backbiting of his companion.

"Yes, a nice woman, a nice woman," went on Mr. Pennington; "so are the girls—nice girls, both of 'em. By-the-by, one of 'em's going to be married in August."

Hadding said nothing; a mute and bitter suspicion filled his heart.

"Handsome couple," went on the irrepressible Pennington; "sing duets together, and all that sort of thing. Awfully musical, Sir Lewis. I think it was over the piano they made up the match."

"Is it Miss Cathcart?" asked Hadding finally. "I thought her a pretty and sensible little creature."

"No, no! not Sophie; it's the red-haired cousin," said Mr. Pennington. "It's a very good match. He's quite her equal in birth and position, and a charming fellow, too. Handsome, young, artistic, all the rest of it! She's a lucky girl, I tell her, for an heiress. They generally contrive to pick up the broken stick at last!"

"I remember her," said Hadding. "I thought her very handsome, too, though scarcely so attractive as her cousin. Well, I must say goodbye now, Pennington; I promised to dine at the club with Mulhouse."

They shook hands and parted.

10

Hadding went to his club and talked with unusual brilliancy.

He felt an odd surprise at the genuine interest he took in all he said. He stayed late, and at midnight his splendid paradoxes still kept the guests together. This gayety came without any effort; for Hadding felt the strongest impulse to stave off the moment of deep and sour disgust which was lying already at the bottom of his heart. But the moment came at last when all his friends dispersed. Hadding went home, then, bitter and outraged, to his London lodgings.

He turned up the gas, and drew up a chair; leaning his arms on the table he tried to be calm. Why should he trouble himself because this little girl who called herself his friend had secretly engaged herself and kept him in the dark? All women were like that—heartless, insatiable of *coquetry*, vain. He remembered, what he had quite forgotten, how, long ago, before he had learned to be wary and suspicious, he had been betrayed by a light woman whom he loved. Marian, at that moment, seemed to him no better than this nameless creature, and the sting, the ignominy of being twice deceived stung his too-sensitive vanity to madness. With this there mingled the obscure agonies of jealousy, of thwarted possession; for he had half-begun to love the girl. Then with a sudden swing, his fancy turned to that night in Rome when Marian had promised to love him forever. He had not wished it then. She had revenged herself. She had made him rue it now.

He had seen her three days ago, and she had never told him of her marriage. She had let him think himself her only friend. Ah, that very afternoon how good a right he seemed to have to watch her windows. She had meant to deceive him! She had meant to delude him! She had meant that he should suffer. She had found him a ridiculous amusement. With a sudden shock, Hadding's disgust turned into anger—into a fulgent and terrible anger bent on destroying the wicked. Marian must feel it and learn to respect it: Marian, who seemed to him no longer like her fellows, but a monster of heartless vanity, of infamous feminine treachery. There was no excuse, no pardon possible.

Of course he had no objection to her marrying, notwithstanding the madness of her mother; but he would not suffer the ignominy of a woman's triumph. She must know that he rejected her. Hadding sat up for a moment, pen in hand, rigid with a sort of savage quietness, a concentrated fury such as he had not felt for many years, and which, with a strange pleasure, he allowed to overpower him now. Then he began to write:

I congratulate you on your approaching marriage. I only heard the news this afternoon, and from a stranger. At this moment my one desire is that you may reward your husband's devotion as you have rewarded mine. It is two years now since you declared your friendship for me in Rome. At the end of another two years, I trust that your husband may feel as convinced of your confidence and of your loyalty as I. These are good wishes. Let them end our friendship.

Hadding read over the letter twice. It was not the thing that he had meant to say, this clumsy irony, this melodrama. But, with a choking desire to say something, to let her hear by any means his anger and contempt, he went out and posted the letter.

11

In the middle of the morrow morning Hadding's letter was brought to Marian. She was sitting in her dressing-room sorting the papers in her desk. A large bundle of Hadding's letters took up the greater part of it; on the other side were a few notes from Sophie, and a little packet of letters still fresh in date, but more worn than any of the others.

Marian stopped her business to take the note from the maid, and opened it with a look of pleased expectance. The sight of Hadding had reawakened her friendship for him, which lately had begun to feel the strain of too long an absence. The smile of pleasure suddenly faded from her mouth, and her whole face blanched.

She sat quite still for a time, but at last she rallied and began to excuse herself. Oh, she had not dreamed of any deceit; she had always meant to tell Mr. Hadding. But she had only been engaged three weeks; she was shy, and had seen him so little. Still, to the tension of poor Marian's mind, these excuses seemed feeble and insufficient.

Marian was of an enthusiastic, a chivalrous temperament. The tragic, the heroic, the outrageous even, allured her. She did not resent the violence of Hadding's letter; she did not question its justice. She looked back to those days "when you declared your friendship for me in Rome." How much she had meant then, how little she had done, and oh, how deeply she had changed! A hot wave of shame overspread her face and shoulders as she thought of her affection for Hadding, so warm then, so living and full of emotion; so merely grateful and cut-and-dried today. And he, no doubt, had believed in her. Alas! he had done more, he had loved her. Hadding's letter could bear only one interpretation to Marian's simple mind. The friend she had won against his will had fallen in passionate love with her. And she had forgotten him! And she loved Lewis Banbury! Marian sat still a long time trying to think.

When at last she got up she was crying, but she dried her tears. She had found a way at last; difficult and thorny though it was, it would reconcile her life with a high ideal. She would go to Hadding and tell him that, if he chose, she would break off her engagement. She would do now even more than she had meant to do in Rome. She would think only of friendship, for she had not meant to love Mr. Hadding even then; but, since he loved her, if he thought it right, she would marry him. She would consecrate her life to make him happy and keep him great. That she had meant; and she must keep her word.

Thus, with a mind incoherent but resolved, Marian got up and dried her tears. She remembered that Hadding was lodging in Arlington Street. In a few hours it would all be over. Perhaps he might forgive her—she might still be happy; but Marian put this thought behind her. She would not ask to be happy, she would only ask to be honourable and good.

She tied the strings of her bonnet and went out, a very childish, inexperienced soul concealed under the stately and fashionable disguise of her appearance. She walked quickly, strung up to a definite purpose, and almost insensible to pain. She did not once remember that Hadding had no right to command the issues of her life. For, you see, she was very young, very sensitive. And she was conscious, too, of that change in her own constancy which is so terrible a revelation to the young.

She went on, almost happy that she could expiate her fickleness at once, until she reached Arlington Street. But the maid who answered her summons informed her that, early in the morning, the gentleman, though usually so considerate, had rung them from their beds and told them he must take the morning mail to Rome. He had gone, and left no address, said the girl, divining a tragedy in Marian's swollen eyes. But Marian, of course, knew very well where Hadding lived in Rome.

She left the door, and hurried home again. At lunch she pleaded a headache in answer to Mrs. Cathcart's anxieties. Indeed she felt very ill; impatient, too, that she could not wipe away at once the stain of Hadding's reproaches. After luncheon, scarcely knowing why, she went upstairs and counted her money. She had five-and-twenty pounds in her desk.

Then her desperate resolution strengthened in Marian's mind. She would prove herself sincere; she would make ample atonement. If, by her own act, she had led Vincent Hadding to love her, if her ignorant wish for his friendship had produced this dire result, she would take the blame and the suffering herself. She was, you see, convinced that he passionately loved her. Well she would make amends. She would go to Rome at once and let him marry her!

She sat down on her bed, sobbing silently and heavily. She thought of Lewis Banbury, and, strangely enough, that thought gave her courage to go on. It was better Lewis should suffer now than that he should marry a tarnished woman; and, to herself, Marian appeared no less. A flirt, a jilt, a tarnished woman—it was all the same. No, the woman Lewis loved should never submit to being that. She did not see that, in breaking her own heart, she was difficultly committing the very fault she would avoid.

What though it broke her heart? She would be doing right, and Marian measured right and followed it according to the terrible ideal of youth. The very painfulness of this sacrifice had the attraction of martyrdom. She was giving up everything—happiness, and love, and home, and peace—to do the right thing. Marian's lips grew thin and white, but her eyes shone.

Then she locked up her little desk and slung the key on a ribbon round her throat. She put a few things—a very few—into a little bag she had. "They will not miss me," she said, "till dinner at eight." She wrote a line to her aunt, another to her lover, and, with the bitterness of death in her throat, she slipped from the house unobserved.

12

It was a warm and sunny May morning when Hadding awoke and found himself in his own house in Rome. For some moments he remained confused, wondering why he was back again already. Then he was invaded by an immense impatience against the bitter spleen which had driven him there. Already his own violence appeared to him inexplicable and shocking, as remote as the madness of another man. He resolved to write that very day to Marian and humbly to sue for pardon. He wondered whether it would be possible for her to forgive him. "Yes, perhaps, if she thinks I am in love with her," he said aloud. But he felt he owed her the less dignified, the infinitely difficult explanation of the truth.

Then he pondered how he best could patch together those plans which he had shattered in a moment of madness degrading to remember. He could not afford to go north again for the summer. Why, in the name of Heaven, had he rushed back to Rome in May? Hadding was not rich, and was not strong. Although he could not now return to England, he dared not remain a third summer in Home. "I should die of fever, and perhaps that would be best," he said grimly to himself. Nevertheless, he resolved to start at once for Rocca di Papa; he could live cheaply there, and the air was cool and healthy.

He rose early, and began to pack away in an iron chest some treasures he had bought in London. He was standing by the table, dusting and sorting some broken fragments of a Roman urn, when his man appeared at the door and told him that a *signora* wished to speak with him. Hadding thought, "Some message from the trades-people, no doubt," and was preparing to go and speak to the woman at the door, when Pasquale suddenly retreated with a look of tragic amazement, and Marian Bassett entered the *Salotto*.

It was certainly Marian Bassett; but so pale, so changed, so travel-stained and careworn, that, for a moment, Hadding thought the vision some disordered fancy of his brain. He was still disinclined to believe his senses when she came forward, saying, in a flat and tired voice, "I have come here to ask you to marry me!"

"Marian!" cried Hadding, pale with horror. All the consequences of her flight were immediately apparent to him. Certainly he must marry her, and that at once. He deserved even this, he thought to himself, with a grim bracing of the heart to duty. Yes, his irritable and violent vanity deserved it. He looked at the pale face, with all its radiance gone; at the strange, dull eyes, and disordered hair; and he remembered the madness of her mother. They would be poor, too—very poor. Then it rushed back on his mind that Marian was an heiress. He recalled Mr. Pennington's speech about the broken stick. Surely these were the dregs of his cup!

"You don't welcome me," said Marian, with a wan smile. She was so convinced of Hadding's passion for her that she believed him speechless for wonder and delight. "You don't welcome me," she said, smiling. Then Hadding remembered Sir Lewis Banbury: "young, handsome, her equal in position." He looked again at Marian, leaning wearily against the window-frame, her face turned toward him with a pale, uncertain smile. She seemed very young and helpless.

"Oh, my poor child! my poor Marian!" he exclaimed, as he fell on his knees at her feet. "Ah, Marian, is there anything that I can ever do to make you forget so great a sacrifice "

Marian smiled, and took his hand in hers. Her voice trembled, and she could not speak.

A week after that Hadding and Marian were married. He had taken her to stay with a friend of his, a lady well known in Roman circles; and he telegraphed at once to Mrs. Cathcart, who arrived, mystified and angry, in time for the wedding. Another wedding-guest came uninvited to the church, and when Marian left the door she saw, in the shadow of the porch, a tall, handsome youth who looked at her with a fixed sadness. She said nothing, but tightened her hold on her husband's hand.

It was not a very happy marriage. I saw Hadding two years afterward, and thought him aged and altered. He had a shrunk and common look, which contrasted with his old unruffled air. He was anxious, he said, about his wife, who was delicate and excitable, and would let no care be taken of her. He treated her, I heard in Rome, with an almost extravagant consideration, but she did not seem a happy woman. She disliked that equable routine which was his second nature. She could not live without change and excitement and emotion. Gradually she looked for these away from home, and became the fashionable beauty of the foreign set in Rome.

Hadding has not written anything lately. His time is largely occupied in witnessing the different triumphs of Marian's career. She always tells him that he might stay at home and study. But not for all the laurels on Parnassus would Hadding leave his wife to run the dangerous gauntlet of an unescorted beauty.

Two of a Kind
By Henry Norman

1

It had been a dull Wednesday afternoon session at the House of Commons, and Arthur Galton had spent most of it in the under-ground smoking-room, discussing the Irish question with dull people. Since he had shaken himself free several months before from the cliques that dogged his steps all over the House, and had said a final "Yes" to one of the wire-pullers that used to button-hole him in the lobby two or three times a day for permission to "put you down on my list," and a final "No" to all the others, this question had seemed clear enough to him. The decision had been rather difficult to reach, and the cabals into which every independent member was irresistibly drawn at that time, had gone far to disgust him with political life; but he had reached firm ground at last, and since his North of England constituency had returned him again with a scarcely decreased majority, all remnants of doubt on the subject had vanished.

He was disappointed, therefore, and even irritated, that so many of these men with whom he had spent the afternoon should still be veering about in their opinions. Galton had fancied himself a promising metaphysician while a student at Leipzig, and enough of this conceit had remained to make him believe that he had settled the question in a philosophical manner. But the members in the smoking-room this afternoon would neither convince themselves nor let him convince them; and to add to his annoyance, the distinguished leader of the section which he had not joined had turned his back upon him as they stood near each other in the lobby, although during the period of Galton's indecision they had been on almost affectionate terms.

Politics was no career for a man with earnest aims and any sense of personal independence, Galton reflected as he turned into St James's Street, and by the time he reached the steps of his club he had almost decided to withdraw from it At the club there happened to be nobody whom he knew, so he had to dine alone; and as the fish and the claret were both cold, and the waiter finally set down before him a plateful of damson tart, a fruit for which he had a positive loathing, he was even less amiable after dinner than before. The cigar that he had in his case, however, was a good one, so he climbed to the smoking-room and sat down before his coffee in the easiest chair he could find, determined, like the philosopher he used to be, to make the best of a bad day.

Galton had been steadily smoking for some time, and his gloomy mood was yielding, as such moods will, to the impalpable caress of good tobacco, when he became conscious that somebody was looking at him rather curiously.

"Why, yes, it's Galton all over!" said a pleasant voice. "How are you, old fellow?"

"My dear Hughes," exclaimed Galton, rising quickly as he recognized an old friend and chum, "I *am* glad to see you! When did you get back?"

"Late last night; we had a splendid passage."

"You have dined? Well, then, sit down and have a cigar. I've had a beastly day, and you are welcome as a thaw at Helton. What have you been doing all this time in America—nearly a year, isn't it?"

"Yes," replied Hughes, taking the proffered cigar and sinking back into his chair with the air of a traveller. "Well, I've done what most people do over there, and, luckily for me, a few things that most people don't do. In New York, lots of going about— dinners at Delmonico's, dances with the Seventh Regiment, several capital evenings at a riding-school which is the thing there, the best balls in the world, and some wonderful trotting. In Boston, a great deal of Beacon Street, and tip-top fun at what they call 'Commencement' at Harvard—the University there, you know. In Washington, I shook hands with the President. I hadn't time to go West. Altogether, a first-rate time among thoroughly intelligent, independent, amusing, hospitable people. There—you have my budget now. I suppose it's very much like your own first trip to the States. I've brought back food for years of reflection, and a small case of green cigars."

"Well," said Galton, as he looked at his friend's full round face, which the sea air had made brown in comparison with the light wavy hair and moustache, "you've brought back what you went for—a new stock of health."

"Yes, and I've brought something else, too, that you'll be glad to see."

"A wife?"

"No, worse luck, but I asked her to be."

"But she—you admit the pronoun—she must have consented, or she wouldn't be with you, I suppose."

"Not even that. It is a cousin of mine whose existence I hardly suspected a year ago. You know my father's half-brother wanted to marry his deceased wife's sister, and as the law wouldn't let him do so here, he just went to America, and has lived there ever since. So Miss Ayrton is really an English girl brought up in the States."

"Ayrton; it's a pretty name," remarked Galton.

"Yes, and she's a pretty girl," replied Hughes, warmly. "In fact, she's the prettiest girl I ever set eyes on, or expect to. Pretty, though, is not the word—she's really a splendid woman."

"Poor fellow!" said Galton, in the same reflective tone. "Receive my sympathy."

"Hang your sympathy!" retorted Hughes, with a laugh. "I tell you seriously, Miss Ayrton is the most perfect creature I ever saw. That's the general opinion over there, too, I can tell you, for every man in her set has proposed to her, or meant to before she left. I never saw such a sorrowful crew in my life as they are. Two men whom she refused have buried themselves in Mexico, another threw up everything in New York, went West, and is now driving a coach in Texas, and people say there was a suicide, too, but that I doubt She keeps the names in a book."

"Including your own!"

"I dare say," returned Hughes, in a more serious tone, knocking the ash from his cigar. "I did fall in love with her, and I asked her to marry me, and I am not ashamed to confess it You would have done the same thing."

"Oh, of course," replied Galton blandly. He was finding an antidote for his melancholy in returning to the old habit of teasing his younger and more impulsive friend, as he had done ever since they were schoolboys together.

"It's all very well for you to sit there, Galton," retorted the young man with some warmth, "and chaff me, and say smart things, but I tell you that if you had known her as long as I have—"

"Six months!"

"Never mind how long—you would have proposed to her, too."

"My dear boy," said Galton, with assumed deliberation, "your enthusiasm is very pretty and very natural, and I wouldn't throw cold water on it for the world, but you forget that you are addressing a wizened old politician. Such things are not for me."

"Bosh,!" exclaimed Hughes. "I should like to have a wager with you on it"

"I don't bet, either," said Galton solemnly.

"Well, then, my Dutch uncle," replied the other, rising and stretching himself like a man who knows that what he is going to say must necessarily conclude the argument, "I'll tell you something else that I've learned in America, and that is, when an offer is made to me such as I've made to you, either to '*put up or shut up.*' Excuse the vulgarity."

"Oh, if that's your view," laughed Galton, rising too, "let's hear the wager."

"I'll bet you a level hundred," replied Hughes, "that if I introduce you to my cousin, within six months you'll ask her to marry you. And I'll even give you a good start by telling her that you are the best fellow I've ever known. There's nothing mean about me—another Americanism."

"All right," said Galton, laughing, "done with you! It will be fun, at any rate, and I had just come to the conclusion that I should never have any more. But I give you fair and deliberate warning that I shall not ask her to marry me, even if she proved to be Venus and Minerva rolled into one, and that you'll lose your money."

"I'll risk it," returned the young man; "'rira bien qui rira le dernier.' It will stop your chaff, at any rate. But now tell me all about yourself. You must have been having exciting times in politics here."

Little was needed to induce Galton to talk about his work and his interests, and for a long time he spoke almost without stopping, interweaving with the narrative of his own intellectual life during his friend's absence all the anecdotes of public men, the jokes, and epigrams that lay so plentifully about the arena of the great Parliamentary struggle. The lighter side of life was not less interesting to him than the serious one, for he was a man prematurely old. A clever schoolboy, an able but restless student at Cambridge, he had passed through all his educational experiences two or three years ahead of most men; and as his father had died while he was at school, and his mother immediately after he left college, he had had both the means and the freedom to indulge his taste for travel and quiet adventures.

He was thirty-two, but passed for much more among people who knew him only slightly. He had a broad, fine forehead, above which the hair was getting thinner every year; his eyes were of the blue which is called steely, probably because it seems a surface-colour only, and tells nothing of the temperament behind it; and his thick but carefully trimmed light-brown beard gave him almost a foreign air. In his time he had been a moderate athlete, had played cricket and rowed and sparred and fenced a little, and ridden a great deal, so that his tall figure was supple and well-proportioned, and his skin had a pleasant, healthy look.

All his life his two tastes had been for study and the open air; one or two of his years on the Continent had been what is called rather "wild," but he had spent them so chiefly because the men with whom he lived had professed to know no pleasures except in bright eyes that easily reflected an easy affection, in long nights at the card-table, and in all the associations that are symbolized by the kiss, the wine-glass, and the song. If he did not regret these years for ethical reasons, it was only because of the experience they left, which is not otherwise easily obtained, and which had, as he knew, this particular value, that if one is without it one is quite sure to be ceaselessly fidgeting after it.

On his return to England he had fallen among politicians, and being a good-looking man, of a certain social position, a fluent speaker, and able to pay his own election expenses and a little besides, he had found himself in Parliament almost before he had made up his mind to settle down anywhere. Now he felt as if he had been cheated, as it were, out of some of his youth; he had always meant to be a boy again for a while after he had been a man for a few years, and politics threatened to put an extinguisher on that light-hearted intention. He always welcomed, therefore, such a talk with a younger man, and he was by no means averse from playing the fool a little now and then—that was why he had made the bet with Hughes. Of course, he did not in the least mean to take his friend's money, but it would be fun, and would render his relations with the wonderful Miss Ayrton highly amusing.

The talk about politics lasted till Hughes began to feel tired, and at last he took advantage of the clock striking eleven to rise and plead fatigue from his recent voyage, make an appointment for the next evening, and go home. Galton said "goodnight" to him at the door of the club, and then strolled slowly down the street to his chambers, absorbed in the solution of the knotty questions he had himself raised. He had still a couple of hours' work to do before he went to bed, to finish an article on "The Sphere of Sentiment in Economics," which he had promised to the editor of the *Fortnightly* for the next day; so he lighted a pipe and the candles at his writing-table, put on his slippers and velvet coat, and settled down over the last pages of his manuscript. Once he rose to refill his pipe, once to drag a big blue book from under the table, and once to take down a volume of Mill from the shelf. Occasionally the clatter of a rickety hansom disturbed him for a moment, but his pen went steadily on as the candles burned nearer and nearer to their sockets, and it was almost one o'clock before he dashed his pen across the foot of a page in the welcome scrawl which means "*Finis*" in the compositor's hieroglyphics. Then he flung down his pen and rose with a fervent "Thank goodness, that's done!"

His room was lighted by a large copper lamp hanging from an iron chain stretched from wall to wall. The flame itself was hidden in a copper bowl, and only the warm reflected light was thrown down, filling the lower part of the room with a peculiar soft shimmer, which Galton's friends chaffingly called his "dim agnostic light." The furniture was of dull green stained wood, in old plain shapes which he had mostly designed himself; for a dado the walk were covered with wine-red Bengal matting up to the book-case, which ran all round the room, and above there was a tint just the colour of the beams that fell from the copper lamp.

Without being esthetic, he had discovered the beauty of some of Mr. Morris's designs, and his easy-chair and sofa were of sap-green chintz, and the curtains that covered his windows were of the same wild-tulip pattern, but blue. In niches in the book-case little Tanagra statuettes lounged gracefully, and sat reading in their exquisite drapery; a few water-colours, in broad gilt frames, stood about; a couple of old brass lamps that he had picked up in the Borgo Vecchio hung on each side of the fireplace, and over it a tall Venus of Milo, with a little silver crucifix hanging upon her perfect breast, was half hidden in gray velvet folds. The whole room bespoke the traveller who has kept the best place in his heart for his home, and who has affectionately and almost selfishly brought back to his hearth the things that have given him happy hours abroad; and Galton, standing upon his big iron fender and leaning back upon the low mantel, smiled quietly to himself as he saw how good it was, and recalled one by one the associations of the things that surrounded him.

The red-and-white cap and long pipe of his German student-days, the bust of Kant above his philosophical books, the two big beer-mugs with the inevitable "Z. fr. Erg." round their rims, the hunting-crop which hung across the lamp-chain, on the top of a book-case, the big nickel-plated stirrups with their india-rubber bottoms which he had bought in Denver, the tomahawk which an old "forty-niner "had given him; and more than all, the rows of books, old and new, in dirty paper and rusty cloth and pomp-ous leather and gold, picked up here and there and everywhere, and at last united in one family. "The dear old things," thought Galton, as his eyes ranged slowly over his surroundings; "how like old friends they are, or brothers, or even like a wife, they rest so cosily at one's fireside!" And then suddenly he remembered Hughes, Miss Ayrton, and his bet.

The recollection startled him not a little, and gradually, as his imagination clothed the skeleton of a few minutes' careless talk, it became irritating to him, and at last even repulsive. Why should the thought obtrude itself like a falling shadow at such a moment? His home was his own, sacred to him by its associa-tions and by tha hopes which cling around them—who was this woman, that her name should spring up to dissipate his happy memories? It seemed to him as if the mere thought robbed him of half his claim on these old friends and companions. The ir-ritation, however, passed away in a moment, but it left behind a calm disdain of its train of reflections.

No, he would not place his peace of mind in any woman's keeping; the years that were gone had given him a fair share of profitless excitement, and all the shallow satisfactions of "love"; that was all past, and now his work, and even his own personal independence, barred the way to its renewal. His habits and his ambitions were peculiarly his own, and they must be kept as inviolable as his fireside itself; no rustling skirt should quicken his pulse there, and as for the others, they should be securely preserved from air fickleness and petty interests, from all the passing joys which make such permanent inroads upon character and work.

In a minute or two Galton had recovered from his false alarm, and as he caught sight of a flower on the wall opposite him he laughed softly. It was a crushed and faded yellow rose, fastened to the wall by a nail through its heart, just out of reach. How well he remembered putting it there! A woman who had promised to be his wife had worn it on her bosom at a ball, and had given it to him with her pledge. In those days he had believed in immortality, at least for such lovers as they were, but he would not have given that rose for the hopes of all the everlasting years. She was false; her pledge had proved less enduring than the pale petals that symbolized it; and when he came back from his long journey he had taken the flower, all bruised and broken with his kisses, and had glued it together and nailed it up for a witness before his eyes.

Now his laugh might be bitter when his eye fell upon it, but at any rate he would be pretty certain not to give it a companion upon his wall. "'Needles and pins,'" he hummed to himself as he blew out the candle, and wrote down at the corner of his blotting-pad the hour at which his servant should call him in the morning—"'*needles and pins, when a man's married his trouble begins.*'"

2

Two days later, when Arthur Galton reached Mrs. Hughes's evening party, he had completely forgotten the talk with her son at the club. The storm of politics which had threatened for so long was breaking now, and few men in the House of Commons had thoughts for any of their ordinary interests or hobbies. Every young man, at any rate, was wholly absorbed by the consciousness of being a maker of history, and sweethearts and wives had fared badly of late. Galton was not so far from the centre of the whirl that he could keep cooler than the others, and his head ached and rang with the echoes of the cheers and laughter and yells of the debate he had just left behind.

It was quite late when he reached Belgrave Square, and two streams of men and women were passing each other on the stairs, some of them cool as they hurried to or from the momentary appearance which satisfied the claims of convention, others hot and flushed from the dance, the women clinging tight to the arms of their partners, the men looking down at their companions with eagerness or tolerance, according as they were pretty or not. It was a chaos formed of chatter and quick laughter, of trampling feet and rustling dresses, and of a hot perfume-laden air, while above the monotone of noise came the scraping of the musicians tuning their fiddles upstairs, and the popping of corks below.

The whole scene jarred upon Galton's over-wrought nerves, as he wearily made his way upstairs, and half-unconsciously he wondered that people should be so gay and should chatter and laugh and long for the glance of an eye or the pressure of a hand, while the fate of a nation, aye, of an empire, was hanging in the balance, and no two wise men could agree upon a course of action. He was thoroughly at home in the house, so with a word to the servants he escaped being announced and turned into a small room, between the front rooms where dancing had begun again and a series of rooms at the back where people were talking and resting in couples and groups.

For a few minutes he watched them mechanically, half rising every now and then to bow to some passing pair, his thoughts still at Westminster. Then suddenly he became conscious that the crowd had rearranged itself in such a way as to leave a lane open between him and a group of four or five persons in a corner of the room beyond him, and that his eyes were fixed intently upon the central figure of the group. Four of the persons were men, but the other was a tall girl with black hair, in a pale yellow gown trimmed with old lace. Her back was toward him, and he was struck with the thickness and gloss of her hair, and the yellow roses that seemed to have been twisted up with it

From the faces of the men he knew that she was beautiful; and he saw with the thrill that comes at the sight of any beautiful animal life, that her whole figure moved with each gesture, as she threw back her head, or swung open her fan, or raised her hand and arm in a curiously foreign manner. Three of the men were laughing and all talking to her at once, while the fourth appeared to be saying nothing, but never took his eyes from her face, and smiled only when she looked directly at him. The more Galton looked at her the more the charm of her mere physical well-being affected him—the tall figure, slender and rounded and strong, swaying slightly as she turned from one of her listeners to another, the poise of her head and neck, the graceful curves made by her hand. He found himself wishing that she would do something to display in its perfection all her grace and vigour—run a race, or ride at a gallop over a rolling meadow, or wrestle with a companion, or dance—that would be best. He had often felt so before, in the galleries of Rome, at the sight of some old Diana or Atalanta—

"A silver image of the Fleet-foot One,"

and he looked at this tall girl in yellow, with her thick shining black hair, with as much of an artist's admiration and as little of a man's desire as he had felt before those immortal marbles themselves.

"You might just as well hand me that check at once, you know," said a mocking voice behind him.

Galton turned sharply, to find Hughes standing at ease with his hands in his pockets, and smiling at the success of his remark.

"Oh, Hughes, how do you do?" he stammered, feeling as confused as if he had been detected in some indiscretion. "I didn't get away from the House until very late, and I was horribly tired and sick of the noise and wrangle, so I just slipped upstairs and into this quiet corner. I really don't feel up to dancing, you know."

"*Connu, mon cher?* laughed his friend; "don't apologise, but come and be introduced to your fate."

"What do you mean?" Galton asked disingenuously.

"Why, I mean, of course, you old hypocrite," returned the other, slipping his arm through Galton's, "that the superb young person in yellow over there, whom you, the wizened old politician, have been staring at for the last twenty minutes like a moon-struck rustic, is nobody else than Miss Isabel Ayrton, of New York, and—you'll excuse me under the circumstances for being a little premature—the future Mrs. Galton."

"Don't be an ass, Hughes," replied Galton, with annoyance. "I wish you would drop that ridiculous chaff of the other night. It's really not very respectful to the lady herself."

"A bet's a bet," said Hughes in a lower tone as they approached the group; "but I'm in no hurry—I can wait." Then passing familiarly by the men, who were rather unwilling to extend their little circle, he said, "Miss Ayrton, will you permit me to introduce my old school-fellow and dear friend, Mr. Arthur Galton, M. P., of whom you most have heard me speak very often? traveller, philosopher, and politician."

Miss Ayrton had turned toward them, as he spoke, and now, as she looked straight at Galton, he saw that her eyes were large and of a pale greenish gray, like the sheen of olive-leaves. Her face was just oval enough to escape being called round; her forehead was low, and the thick wavy hair was brushed straight back from it at each side; her mouth was small, and the rather full and shapely lips seemed in constant motion, answering like a magnetic needle to each passing current of thought. Galton was extremely angry with Hughes for his fatuous introduction, but he still examined the woman before him as if she had been a chiselled thing on a pedestal.

Looked at from his new point of view she was just as strong and fine as she had seemed to him before, but he thought he detected a mocking light in her eyes, and the corners of her mouth quivered as she tried to repress too obvious a smile at his expense. Then her eyes partly closed, the quivering of her lips passed into a set expression which just showed the tips of her delicate white teeth, and with a shyness which seemed deliberate she put out her hand and said simply, "How do you do?" Galton took it and bowed rather lower than was quite sincere. "*Elle pose,*" he said to himself.

"Galton's the best dancer I ever saw," put in Hughes. "I shall come back for my own turn by and by," he added as he left the room.

It was true that Galton was a good dancer, but he was very fastidious about his partners, and he had not meant to dance that evening. These parting words, however, left him no choice, as the speaker of them had intended. "Mr. Hughes is an untrustworthy person, Miss Ayrton," he said, "but I shall be grateful if you have a dance left that I may have."

"I think I'm not engaged for the next waltz," replied Miss Ayrton, looking over her programme. "No—with pleasure."

"Excuse me," said the quietest of the men standing by, "but I *think* this is my dance—unless I've made a mistake."

The girl drew up her programme again, glanced calmly at it, and then said slowly, "No, I've had this dance open ever since I came—nobody would have it! I'm awfully sorry if you've lost a dance by the mistake, Mr. Spokes."

The man bowed rather stiffly, and murmured something in an apologetic tone. He knew perfectly well that the next waltz had been promised to him, but he was not sufficiently a man of the world quite to conceal his knowledge. Men read men's faces and movements with tolerable certainty, and Galton understood perfectly the man's disappointment and the girl's little deceit.

"I have every dance—" he began, without stopping to consider the inference she would draw from his remark if it were completed.

"This is my only one, Mr. Galton," she interrupted him, with a trifle less calmness in her tone. "If you wish it—"

"Oh—if you please," stammered Galton, as he offered her his arm, thankful for the opportunity to repair his blunder in time.

But again his voice and his action were much more deferential than his thought.

During the waltz, like all good dancers, they hardly spoke, and when it was over they found a quiet corner, and Galton set himself to detect in the manner and convesation of Miss Ayrton the qualities which had placed her so high in the imagination of many men, including his friend Hughes. It was a task congenial to his metaphysical habit, and soon he had come to the conclusion that he had seldom undertaken an easier one. Isabel Ayrton was evidently accustomed to talk freely, so he contented himself with a polite accompaniment of murmurs of assent, broken every now and then by some suggested paradox of opinion which piqued her to find its solution. And he could see that she, on her part, watched discreetly but sharply the effect upon him of her conversation.

He turned it gradually toward subjects common only between persons fairly intimate with each other, and she did not attempt to check him. She even made him little confidences upon her past life, its limits and its ambitions; upon the elderly titled diplomat in Washington, who had offered her his hand, his rank, and half of his million of francs a year, and upon the poor medical student who had been the pride of her brother's university, and who had besought her to wait till he returned from his studies in Europe with a reputation to lay at her feet Galton ventured a distant allusion to his friend Hughes. She responded instantly with more confidences. "Charming fellow, isn't he? We were all very fond of him in New York—so enthusiastic and good-natured, and devoted to his friends. Particularly devoted to me, you know—quite a romance, in fact. But of course he's told you all about it."

And she stopped with a burst of frank and half-embarrassed laughter, and the first shade of a blush that Galton had seen upon her expressive face. Extremely becoming it was, too, as he recognized, with mixed feelings. Then, as the musicians began a new dance, she snatched up her programme and exclaimed, "Dear me, I've sat out three dances! Whatever will my partners think? I must dance this one, because it's the Highland Schottische, and I particularly begged Lord Walter to teach it me. Will you please take me back ?" And, as they returned slowly to the front room, she added, in a lower tone, "I'm afraid I've been terribly indiscreet in talking to you as if we had known each other for years."

"I've known you forever," said Galton, in the same tone.

Miss Ayrton looked up at him quickly for a moment to make sure that he was serious. "If that's a compliment," she said, "it's the nicest one I was ever paid. Anyhow, I couldn't help it. You're very different from most men, you know; one can never talk seriously with them, and they don't seem to understand that a woman loves frankness in them above all things."

"I trust I've been frank," Galton almost whispered, releasing her arm as Lord Walter came hurrying up to claim his dance.

"Very. *Au revoir!*"

When she had quite disappeared among the dancers,' Galton gave way to the smile which he had been suppressing for some time. How could Hughes be so blind as not to see through this dashing American cousin? Surely a simpler problem never presented itself to a student of character! Galton had no more doubt of the accuracy of his diagnosis of the woman he had been studying than he had of the solution of the third Kantian antinomy. A beautiful creature, physically; cast by Nature in a splendid mould, and dipped in the colouring of Italy, as exuberant with vitality as the earth in springtime. The self-confidence of her character was conspicuously the complete counterpart of her bodily superiority.

Reared in Arcadian woods, she would have been another pitiless Atalanta, outstripping in the race all who desired her, and looking on unmoved as the sword-bearer exacted from them one after another the penalty of defeat; born today in the New World, she was still a modern Atalanta, with no wish but to remain untrammelled by any sentiment, delighted to match herself against every man who came to challenge her security, and cruelly careless of the suffering to which she consigned them—

the two in Mexico, the stage-driver in Texas, the suicide, and last, poor deluded Hughes. It was all clear enough to Galton, as he stood there, smiling and flattening himself against the wall, out of the way of the dancers.

And now she had actually marked him down, too, for her prey! The fact was a trifle disquieting to Galton, in spite of the flood of light which his brilliant analysis had cast upon it, for she was a very charming person, after all, and he had reason to know how weak men are before a pink-and-white face and a few flattering words. It was not enough, therefore, he speedily determined, to be upon his guard; he must not merely parry, but also thrust back; he must not only avoid the contest with this modern Atalanta, which would bring his neck under the flower-trimmed sword, but he must also devise a scheme which should cause her own pitiless heart to feel its sharp point.

That was the explanation of his compliment—that was why he had already begun to flatter her with his deference. "I have pleased women before," he thought, "and every quality that I have, and every art that I can compass, shall be made to do service now. If I succeed—well, the suicide will be avenged, at any rate." And Galton edged away from among the circling couples, and staid long in the supper-room before he left to go home.

In the days and weeks that followed the dance, Arthur Galton and Isabel Ayrton saw a great deal of each other. A calm followed the political storm, and Galton, like his fellow-members, turned with relief to society and its distractions. The receptions of Mayfair took on a new charm when they followed the debates of Westminster, and lingering memories of the peremptory division-bell made the strains of Strauss only more bewitching. Galton found himself with an unwonted amount of time at his own disposal, and Hughes seemed bent upon making up in a few weeks all they had missed of each other's companionship during his long absence in America.

But the company of Hughes no longer meant the old bachelor habits: Miss Ayrton was now the invariable third. London life was fascinating to her, and she seemed to grow more vigorous under its ceaseless demands. And Galton yielded himself freely to the charm of her fresh young nature. At the back of his mind there was the consciousness that he had chosen a definite line of action, and protected himself in advance from the danger which she personified.

For a time he kept clearly in mind the recollection that he was thwarting the design upon him which he had detected in her mind, by a counter-attack of his own; that he was making an aggressive defence, as it were, and it was with perfect deliberation that he made himself as attractive to her as he possibly could, and paid her that unvarying and unquestioning service which is a man's surest road to a woman's good-will. Little by little, however, the determining cause passed out of his mind, while the resulting behaviour remained unchanged.

It was in itself so pleasant a thing to be gradually growing more intimate with this beautiful girl; to be entering day by day more closely into the enthusiasms and ambitions of her young heart; to be seeing the old things of life, the baseless beliefs, the exploded trusts, the unveiled deceits, through her idealizing and glamour-casting eyes, that Galton let himself drift along the stream of natural inclination, without a trace of his original determination beyond the vague hovering consciousness that his precautions were taken, and that he had nothing to fear. He was like a knight of old who forgot danger so far as even not to recognize it as such, when once the trusted talisman was hung about his neck. Isabel Ayrton, on her part, did nothing to raise in Galton's mind a moment's doubt of the accuracy of his judgement of her character.

To all his suggestions for her entertainment she agreed instantly; she accepted all his invitations, and even anticipated him when, as often happened, he hesitated on the verge of some proposal too American in its scope for the personified chaperon who regulates the intercourse of young people in England. Her programme was freely offered to him when they met at a dance, she was always by his side at Mrs. Hughes's dinner-table, and in the Row their horses almost grew to recognize each other.

Several times Mrs. Hughes allowed Galton to organize little rid-ing-parties like those to which Miss Ayrton was accustomed in America.

Horses for half a dozen young people, one older couple, and a groom, would be sent to some Kentish or Essex village, and next day the riders would meet at Charing Cross or Liverpool Street, find their mounts waiting for them in an old inn yard, and ride for a couple of days before returning to town. On these occasions Galton and Miss Ayrton were always either before or behind the rest, and many an hour's delightful talk they had, riding alone through quiet English lanes. Of course, too, Galton frequently invited his friends to the House of Commons, after which he carried them off to supper in his rooms, and these oc-casions Isabel Ayrton seemed to enjoy most of all. It was a time full of pleasure for them both, and one of those times in which intimacy makes such unsuspected strides.

The autumn had been unusually fine, and one morning when Galton looked out of his window he found St James's Street filled with warm red sunshine, and even its dull pavement covered with the brilliance of autumn leaves. It seemed almost a sin to spend such days in a great city, and he asked himself what proposal he could make that would best employ such rare last summertime. "What shall we do?" was really the form in which the thought occurred to him, and suddenly the inspiration came. The river! Of all the pleasures that he knew near London, the "sweet Themmes "was the only one he had not now shared with Isabel Ayrton, and the Thames is in its perfection only when Cliveden Woods are on fire with red and gold, and when the fast waning summer urges to a double enjoyment of the hours that remain before the bare, blank winter comes.

A couple of hours later he had persuaded Mrs. Hughes to ask the customary little band to make up a river-party for the next day, although it was both Sunday and too late in the season for most people to regard the Thames as a possible place for a holiday. Miss Ayrton had seconded Galton's arguments with her own appeals, and Hughes, of course, had supported his friend. So next morning, at a quarter to nine, several carriages and hansoms came dashing down the long slope into Paddington Station, and a party gathered on the platform, all the merrier for the rather extraordinary character of their excursion. Galton fell naturally into the position of leader, and when he had taken the tickets he was struck by a large and unusually luxurious saloon-carriage attached to the train.

The guard noticed his curiosity, and after passing a few remarks about the weather and the fine season, he volunteered the information that the carriage was put on, according to the company's contract, to take any members of the Guards' Club to their country house at Maidenhead. "But it only wants a few minutes, now, sir," he added, "and it's pretty certain there'll be none of 'em coming this morning. So if you'd like to take your party down in it—" Galton closed with the suggestion without waiting for the end of the sentence, and half a minute before the station-clock marked the quarter, they all scrambled hastily in, and the guard, with one anxious look down the platform to make sure no belated Guardsman was running up, whistled them away.

Two hours later, Galton was rowing Isabel Ayrton slowly down from Marlow in a light skiff which had fallen to their share in the distribution of the party. Others had found the river attractive on such a day, and there would not have been boats enough for them unless some lady had ventured into a narrow outrigger. Isabel had instantly volunteered, and Galton had responded by drawing the frail craft up to the landing. The lunch-basket was placed in the stern, Isabel took the tiller-ropes, and Galton soon pulled out of the others in their heavily-laden boats. After rowing a mile with a strong, easy stroke, he began to let his sculls drag lazily over the surface of the water. She had been lost in reverie for some time, but the musical ripple aroused her, and she looked up with a smile.

Galton, on his part, had hardly taken his eyes from her face since they left Marlow, and her smile faded slowly away before the strange intimacy with which their eyes met. The current carried them along without a stroke of the oars; there was not another boat in sight, and only the great white swans moved silently upon the surface; upon their left the red cattle were grazing peacefully in the meadows, over which came the sound of far-off church bells, and upon their right the blaze of autumn lay upon the cloud-like masses of foliage. As the boat drifted into the reflection of the woods, it seemed to them as if the river were turning to gold as they approached. The perfect pastoral beauty of the scene, and the subtle sense of sympathetic companionship, fascinated them, and seemed to awe them into silence. At last Galton exclaimed in a low tone, "Let us get on— this is too much," and Isabel whispered "Yes." He seized the oars and neither spoke again till the boat shot into Cookham Lock. Then Isabel said, "Shall we not wait here for Mrs. Hughes and the others."

"Must we!" inquired Galton, "We have only a fair share of the lunch, and for all we know they may have stopped to lunch higher up the river. Besides, the cosiest creek in all the Thames is only a hundred yards from here, and I have been promising myself all the morning to take you there."

"I don't wish to wait," returned Isabel, so they passed through the lock, and then Galton turned the boat sharply to the right. A dozen strokes took them out of sight of the main stream, and they made fast to the trunk of a willow, whose branches formed an arbour about them, beside a high bank which sheltered them alike from wind and curious glances.

After they had lunched, Galton took out the stretcher and sat upon the flooring at Isabel's feet.

"Well?" she asked, looking down at him with a smile.

"Well," he replied, teasing her, "what is her ladyship's desire?"

"You know very well—what have you brought to read to me!"

Galton drew from his pocket a little volume bound, in red Russia, and as he turned the leaves she could see that they were scored all over with pencil-marks. "Not long ago," he began, "I

209

had a very dear friend—a man who had seen and known all the good and all the evil in the world. In his old age he began to write poetry, and put into sad songs all that his life had taught him. He didn't publish it, for he knew that people would only laugh at the idea of his turning poet at seventy, but he gave me all his manuscripts, and I compiled this little volume from them. This is the proof-sheets bound together, which he corrected just before he died. I don't often show them to anybody, but I have brought them to read to you now, if you care to hear them."

There was a ring of sadness in Galton's tone that the girl had never noticed before. "I care very much," she said, wondering what they might prove to be.

For more than an hour Galton read. His voice was low and musical, and it blended with the sounds around them—the bubbling of the water at the bows, the rustling of the willow overhead, and the distant bells, and the faint rumble of the weir. The verses were all sad— some passionately so, some tender, some resigned, but all the outcome of a life-long attempt to reach by any path the ultimate and unattainable satisfaction of the soul. One called *The Glass-Blower* told how "with creative hand and fiery breath and magic wand" an artisan succeeded in moulding a microcosmic crystal earth—

> *Where trees spring up, whose foliage, dyed*
> *Unfadingly in Summer's pride,*
> *Rude Autumn's withering breath defied,*
> *And Winter's icy blasts;*
> *And ships, becalmed on wrinkled seas,*
> *Though full their sails, felt not the breeze*
> *That bent their tapering masts.*

And where—

> *In gardens of ungathered fruit*
> *Young lovers sat whose tongues were mute,*
> *Nor thrilled its spell the anxious late*
> *Within the maiden's hands;*
> *They smiled, in bliss without regret*

As only they who feel not yet
The altar's silken strands.

And when the adept's task was done
I saw the boy for whom was spun
That globe, its beauties, one by one,
With childish ardour greet;
Then clutch it with such eager grip
That mountain, city, tree, and ship
Fell shivered at his feet;

And thought—when down shall shade his chin,
And Fancy mould a world akin,
To that bright Earth, unstained by sin,
The adept fingers wrought—
He'll clutch and lose it, as a boy,
The bubbles which he saw with joy
In rainbow meshes caught.

Yet, when his disenchanted eyes
Shall cease to see the mirage rise,
Between him and the desert's skies,
Above the phantom wave,
He'll halt, and kneel, and cross his hands—
Nor long the Simoon's shifting sands
Will mark the new-made grave.

"What a philosophy of life!" said Galton, sadly. "I wonder if it's true, or if it is worthwhile for another man to keep up a ceaseless search for what he with all his years, and gifts, and opportunities could never find. He held the old beliefs, too, for here is a poem which says that—

When it severs Earth's last thread,
The soul pursues its journeying,
And swells, on fleet and tireless wing,
The shadowy army of the dead;
Until it chance a kindred chord
Within some brother's sleeping heart
To wake, and its own life impart

To sage's lips or warrior's sword.
Napoleon fought with Omar's blade;
Dante was god-like Homer's son;
Timoleon prompted Washington;
And Paul stout Luther's fierce crusade.

"Whose spiritual son could he have been, I wonder, and whom is he prompting now? Sometimes his curious verses affect me so much that I begin to think it must be myself. Here, for instance, are some impromptu verses he wrote *To Sibell*, after witnessing the trooping of the colours on the Queen's birthday. They seem to me exactly like my own heart speaking:'

The martial pageant that absorbed our gaze,
And fired my pulses, when the gladdened air
Quickened with joy the sun's majestic rays—
All disappeared! All save thy face so fair,
Which seemed to say, "A desert it the best
Is life, o'er which the floating mirage-gleams
Incite our paces until we find rest
Beside some angel of our better dreams."

"Did he ever find the '*angel of his better dreams*,' and was it worthwhile to find her like this when he was at the edge of the grave? And how could he distinguish between the angel at last and all the mirages which had preceded her! Is there any hope of such peace at last for other men?—these are the questions everyone must feel—where shall *I* find her, how shall *I* know her, what can *I* say to her that she will be sure to understand? Life would be wholly another thing if we had only some such confident hope—if we could only believe that in spite of all deceit and disenchantment and sham, after all pains and all struggles, one will someday be right and safe in saying, 'The angel of my dreams is here, she is beside me, she is listening to me, I may touch her, my life to all eternity is in her hands to be exalted or shattered at her will; I cannot tell her what my longing means, or what is the service I would offer her—I can only beseech her and cry, "Speak, speak!"'"

Galton was carried away by the mingled flood of memories and hopes that the familiar verses had let loose upon him. The words came passionately from his lips, and his eyes were fixed upon some point far away from the quiet, pastoral Thames landscape. But as he finished, he caught a sound which shattered his vision in an instant—the sound of a suppressed sob. He stopped as if he had been shot, and turned sharply toward Isabel. Her face was pressed tightly into her hands, and she was crying violently.

If an avalanche had suddenly appeared over Galton's head he could not have been more shocked. A cold perspiration broke out upon his forehead as he realized what had happened. The situation was clear enough, but how it had come about he could no longer remember; he could only gaze at the sobbing girl by his side in dumb stupefaction. Slowly his senses began to return to him, and his first thought was almost a curse upon himself. What had he done?—how could he ever undo it? Into what a gulf he had blindly walked. Then sorrow for the child before him—she seemed but a child at such a moment—came over him, and he put his hands upon her arm: "My dear Miss Ayrton—Isabel—"

The girl lifted her face, all wet with tears, from her wet hands, and looked at him with a poor sad smile. "Please don't speak to me now—let us row on. Please—*please?*"she begged, seeing that Galton was on the point of beginning afresh.

"As you will," he said tenderly, and picking up the sculls, with a few quick strokes he sent the boat back into the main stream. Then he straightened his back, and for a couples of miles the skiff shot along, till Isabel's hands trembled upon the rudder-lines. Some distance from Maidenhead they overtook the rest of the party.

4

When Galton reached his chambers that night, and locked himself in, he had hardly recovered from the shock of the afternoon. How the party had reached home, and how he had

213

escaped from Mrs. Hughes's house at last, he did not know. He had not spoken to Isabel again, except to say goodnight, and not much more to anyone else. One thing only was in his mind, overwhelming and obscuring every other thought and interest—the consciousness that he had committed a deliberate, stupendous, and probably fatal folly. And as he paced up and down his room, that one fact seemed to surround and choke him like a fog.

An hour passed before his conduct appeared to him in any new light, and the clearer it became to him the worse it looked. Led away by a foolish joke of a man much his junior, he had let himself drift into a course of action of the most dishonourable kind. He had systematically exhibited an affection he did not feel; and though it was true that, after the first few days, he had done this unconsciously, that did not make it any the less deceptive to others. On the basis of some probably absurd analysis of a woman's character, he had allowed himself practically to make love to her; he, a man of knowledge and experience, of position and fortune, had played upon the mind of this high-spirited, innocent girl as one might play upon a fife.

He had flattered her, he had entertained her, he had instructed her, he had opened up to her new ideas of life, and had inspired in her a wider ethical faith. And he had done this without real affection for her, and even any of those subtle suggestions which constitute the foredawn of love. Now, at last, the natural result had come. She had judged his character according to his own professed standard, she had taken him at his word, she had fallen deeply in love with him, she had believed him to be thinking of herself when he was addressing some abstract ideal of his own; she had betrayed her love for him in return, as clearly as if she had said, "Yes, I will marry you." Fool that he was!

For hours Galton continued to pace his room in a state of mind bordering on despair. All the familiar objects which generally gave him such satisfaction only deepened his anger and alarm now. As he looked at them they seemed to recede from him—they seemed to be no longer his old friends, the landmarks of his travels, the remnants of his adventures. He felt as if he were becoming another person, to whom they were all strange: the old Galton had given himself to other associations. Then his room seemed to be invaded by strange figures, the old furniture to disappear, the very faces in his picture-frames to change—he himself seemed on the point of expulsion.

At last he stopped short in the middle of the room, and dispelled these wandering fancies by an effort of will. "What's done is done," he said to himself. "Now the only question is, what remains to do." He reflected that he was an honourable man, and that all his life his strongest views of personal honour had been those which insisted upon the absolutely straightforward and chivalrous relations of a man with a woman. Only once had he given up a friend, and him he had deliberately and even insultingly sent adrift because he was, to Galton's certain knowledge, trifling with the love of an innocent and unsuspicious girl. Now he himself had sunk to what had always been the level of his own supreme condemnation.

At last he blew out his lamp and drew back the curtains, for the day was breaking, and, as the clear white daylight flooded his room, a light entered his troubled mind. "Yes," he said aloud, "I must do it." His duty had grown clear—it was to become the thing he had pretended to be. To go to this girl and say, "I have been playing with you, deceiving you—flirting," would subject him forever, and properly, to his own contempt. He had been a lover in jest, he would become one in earnest; he had practically pretended an offer of marriage, he would make one. He did not love Isabel Ayrton, that was true—but he had learned to admire her and to respect her. She loved him, and he could insure her happiness; and he knew himself well enough to be sure that he would always act with scrupulous fidelity to the decision he was now making.

He would have preferred to remain single, unless the angel of his better dreams had unmistakably appeared, for he had planned many other things to do with his life. All this, however, was as nothing when compared with the retention of his self-respect—with the consciousness of having acted honourably at the supreme trial of his character.

This decision once reached, the instincts of human nature began to assert themselves, and Galton reflected that, after all, his was not a very hard fate. He thought of Isabel Ayrton as he had first seen her—of her beautiful hair, of her olive-tinted eyes, of her strong, youthful figure, and of the grace which always seemed to be flowing over her. "A man may well be thankful for such a wife, and proud to serve her," he thought; "perhaps, after all, this is the 'kindred chord' in me responding to some note struck by one in the 'shadowy army of the dead.'"

He was already back again in his metaphysics.

5

At eleven o'clock Galton knocked at the door of Mrs. Hughes's house. "Miss Ayrton, if you please," he said with emphasis, to the man who showed him in. And he sat down in the library with something of his old calmness.

When Isabel Ayrton entered, the first thing he noticed was that she wore a yellow gown, and that there was a rose upon her breast. She smiled familiarly, and put out both her hands with a simple "Good morning!" and then Galton led her to the sofa and sat down upon an ottoman by her side.

"I have much to say to you," he began, "and as I hardly know how to say it, you'll forgive me for being abrupt. But after yesterday, it must be said at once." A curious expression passed over her face, but, as Galton did not see it, he went straight on: "We are no longer strangers; in fact—" and he laid his hand upon hers—"I think we are very good friends. You know me well—what my life has been, and what it is; and I know you. Why, don't you remember I told you I'd known you forever the first time we met?" Isabel laughed a trembling little laugh. "I cannot make a pretty speech, and I cannot even say what I really mean; but, Isabel, will you be my wife? I have never in my life done anything to make me unworthy of the love of a good woman, and for the future I promise you that my first thought, as long as I live, shall be for your happiness and your honour. Isabel," he added, almost in a whisper, as he took her hands, "you do love me? You will say 'Yes'?"

For a moment there, was complete silence between them, then Isabel said: "My dear Mr. Galton, I have learned to know you well, as you say, and to esteem and respect you as much. And I think I could never respect you more than I do at this moment. But I will not marry you, and for two very good reasons: first, that I do not love you; and, second, that you do not love me. Hush!" she added quickly, as Galton was about to speak; "I will show you." And disengaging one of her hands she put it behind her into her pocket and produced a scrap of paper, the half of a single sheet of note-paper, torn diagonally across and evidently trampled upon. "Read this," she said, and she held it on a level with his eyes. And Galton read it—an incomplete sentence in Hughes's large handwriting—"*as well send me that hundred at once; I saw you and the fair cousin cooing away this afternoon. I shall win that bet like old—*"

"I think you will know me even better now."

"But—Isabel—yesterday—" Galton stammered.

"I know what you are thinking of," she interrupted. Then with a shy smile she added, while a blush crept over her face, "Why did I cry while you were talking to me? Well, to be frank, I wasn't thinking of you at all just then!"

As Galton entered his club that night he caught sight of a man just going upstairs.

"Hughes!" he called after him. "Wait a moment, will you? Here—" and he produced an envelope from his pocket—"I have something for you. That cheque, you know."

"My dear fellow, how glad am I!" exclaimed Hughes, suddenly seizing his friend's hand; "I knew how it would be, and I do congratulate you both with all my heart!"

"Shut up! Let us go and dine."

Juliet

By Louis F. Austin

And so the new Juliet charms you—her beauty has set you ablaze?

And were you a critic (God save us!) what columns and columns of praise!

But now you complain of the scribblers, whose spite is the curse of the press,

Because they seem eagerly banning what you are so eager to bless;

Or else they are nicely adjusting proportions of merit and blame,

While you want to take a great trumpet, and fill all the world with her fame.

And this is her picture? Well, truly, heaven favours so winning a face;

Her tresses, you say, are like sunbeams, her figure a vision of grace;

Her eyes are as wells in the desert to travellers faint and forlorn,

And love on her lips has been playing since sighs in her bosom were born.

Yet never for me is the glamour that makes your poise hurriedly beat—

Though planets re-echoed her praises, and the world were a slave at her feet,

I never could look on your Juliet—your homage could never

be mine,

For there lives a dead face in my memory that holds all my soul in its shrine.

The years have slipped by—nearly twenty—since I saw in the spring of success

My Juliet, happy and peerless, whose whisper was like a caress;

Her hair took its hue from the woodlands, when their auburn was glinted with gold;

Her eyes stole the dew from the violets, as they slept in the moss on the wold;

And even the veriest dullard on whom fell that rapturous glance

Has felt all his spirit transfigured by love and the glow of romance.

"Ah, Romeo, envied of mortals, leave idle lamenting and sighs!

"Away from this cruel Verona you should bear so precious a prize!"

How often like this have I murmured, as night after night in my stall

I watched that sad story unfolding—from the kiss in the Capulet's hall

To the last and terrible meeting, when they, who bright paths should have trod,

In death and the grave were united, and together ascended to God.

One night I shall ever remember, as captives remember their chains,

A strange and subtle foreboding ran icily cold through my veins,

When Juliet, drinking the potion in a frenzy of longing and dread,

Imagines her solitude peopled with horrible shapes of the dead;

And day after day was I haunted as if by the coming of woe—

I dreamt of her stretched in a charnel, arrayed for some terrible show;

But still to the world not a shadow had darkened that splendid career—

My Juliet, happy and peerless, what evil to her could be near?

'Twas Paris, one morning in spring-time, and over the street's human stream

Her radiant face for a moment had passed like a silvery gleam;

I thought of the gloomy foreboding that once through my blood sent its chill,

And smiled at the strange superstition that fancied such horrible ill;

And all the day long in the sunlight I mixed with the carnival throng,

I laughed at the gambols of children, I listened to music and song. . . .

What is that? A hush—then a murmur—some gossip is tickling the town—

The last escapade of a beauty, a scandal that kills some renown!

But no; it is something that saddens this thoughtless, mercurial mob;

Men's eyes with teardrops are glistening—the women beginning to sob.

What is it? "Ah, *monsieur*, what pity! To perish so young and alone,

And lie in the Morgue like an outcast, to all human kindred unknown!"

Who is it? "The great English actress—" I paused not a breath for the name,

For horror's fell hand seemed to choke me, and my brain was filled with a flame!

In the Morgue! My God, it was true then! The fate of my vision had come!

The dew had gone back to the violets—that voice so caressing was dumb!

And only the light of the woodlands still clung to that delicate head,

Like rays of the bounteous sunshine that play on the vaults of the dead.

The Morgue! How I reached it I know not, but I broke through the curious crowd,

Who shrank from me, pallid and startled, as if from a ghost in a shroud!

And I found her, so fair and so dainty, surrounded by horrible clay—

The ghastly account of self-slaughter, the victims of feud and affray;

And here was the clutch of the river, and there was the hideous stab!

Ah, tragedies never were written like those on that sorrowful slab!

But oh, for the spirit so tender that never again would illume

The form that lay solemn and silent, forever bereft of its bloom!

Midst aliens mortally stricken, just Heaven, 'twas cruel to die—

No friend her last look to remember, to catch her last shuddering sigh!

And now it was only a stranger who mourned o'er that still lovely face,

And kissed the cold hand of sweet Juliet, as he knelt in that heart-chilling place!

The years have gone by—nearly twenty—and yet all the grief of that scene,

As though it were yesterday's anguish, still lives in my memory green.

I know that the world has been busy in smirching a dead woman's fame,

But for me that fair face in the charnel can never be shrouded in shame!

LEONAUR

ALSO FROM LEONAUR

AVAILABLE IN SOFTCOVER OR HARDCOVER WITH DUST JACKET

THE COMPLETE FOUR JUST MEN: VOLUME 2 *by Edgar Wallace*—*The Law of the Four Just Men & The Three Just Men*—disillusioned with a world where the wicked and the abusers of power perpetually go unpunished, the Just Men set about to rectify matters according to their own standards, and retribution is dispensed on swift and deadly wings.

THE COMPLETE RAFFLES: 1 *by E. W. Hornung*—*The Amateur Cracksman & The Black Mask*—By turns urbane gentleman about town and accomplished cricketer, life is just too ordinary for Raffles and that sets him on a series of adventures that have long been treasured as a real antidote to the 'white knights' who are the usual heroes of the crime fiction of this period.

THE COMPLETE RAFFLES: 2 *by E. W. Hornung*—*A Thief in the Night & Mr Justice Raffles*—By turns urbane gentleman about town and accomplished cricketer, life is just too ordinary for Raffles and that sets him on a series of adventures that have long been treasured as a real antidote to the 'white knights' who are the usual heroes of the crime fiction of this period.

THE COLLECTED SUPERNATURAL AND WEIRD FICTION OF WILKIE COLLINS: VOLUME 1 *by Wilkie Collins*—Contains one novel 'The Haunted Hotel', one novella 'Mad Monkton', three novelettes 'Mr Percy and the Prophet', 'The Biter Bit' and 'The Dead Alive' and eight short stories to chill the blood.

THE COLLECTED SUPERNATURAL AND WEIRD FICTION OF WILKIE COLLINS: VOLUME 2 *by Wilkie Collins*—Contains one novel 'The Two Destinies', three novellas 'The Frozen deep', 'Sister Rose' and 'The Yellow Mask' and two short stories to chill the blood.

THE COLLECTED SUPERNATURAL AND WEIRD FICTION OF WILKIE COLLINS: VOLUME 3 *by Wilkie Collins*—Contains one novel 'Dead Secret,' two novelettes 'Mrs Zant and the Ghost' and 'The Nun's Story of Gabriel's Marriage' and five short stories to chill the blood.

FUNNY BONES *selected by Dorothy Scarborough*—An Anthology of Humorous Ghost Stories.

MONTEZUMA'S CASTLE AND OTHER WEIRD TALES *by Charles B. Cory*—Cory has written a superb collection of eighteen ghostly and weird stories to chill and thrill the avid enthusiast of supernatural fiction.

SUPERNATURAL BUCHAN *by John Buchan*—Stories of Ancient Spirits, Uncanny Places & Strange Creatures.

LEONAUR

ALSO FROM LEONAUR

AVAILABLE IN SOFTCOVER OR HARDCOVER WITH DUST JACKET

MR MUKERJI'S GHOSTS *by S. Mukerji*—Supernatural tales from the British Raj period by India's Ghost story collector.

KIPLINGS GHOSTS *by Rudyard Kipling*—Twelve stories of Ghosts, Hauntings, Curses, Werewolves & Magic.

THE COLLECTED SUPERNATURAL AND WEIRD FICTION OF WASHINGTON IRVING: VOLUME 1 *by Washington Irving*—Including one novel 'A History of New York', and nine short stories of the Strange and Unusual.

THE COLLECTED SUPERNATURAL AND WEIRD FICTION OF WASHINGTON IRVING: VOLUME 2 *by Washington Irving*—Including three novelettes 'The Legend of the Sleepy Hollow', 'Dolph Heyliger', 'The Adventure of the Black Fisherman' and thirty-two short stories of the Strange and Unusual.

THE COLLECTED SUPERNATURAL AND WEIRD FICTION OF JOHN KENDRICK BANGS: VOLUME 1 *by John Kendrick Bangs*—Including one novel 'Toppleton's Client or A Spirit in Exile', and ten short stories of the Strange and Unusual.

THE COLLECTED SUPERNATURAL AND WEIRD FICTION OF JOHN KENDRICK BANGS: VOLUME 2 *by John Kendrick Bangs*—Including four novellas 'A House-Boat on the Styx', 'The Pursuit of the House-Boat', 'The Enchanted Typewriter' and 'Mr. Munchausen' of the Strange and Unusual.

THE COLLECTED SUPERNATURAL AND WEIRD FICTION OF JOHN KENDRICK BANGS: VOLUME 3 *by John Kendrick Bangs*—Including twor novellas 'Olympian Nights', 'Roger Camerden: A Strange Story', and ten short stories of the Strange and Unusual.

THE COLLECTED SUPERNATURAL AND WEIRD FICTION OF MARY SHELLEY: VOLUME 1 *by Mary Shelley*—Including one novel 'Frankenstein or the Modern Prometheus', and fourteen short stories of the Strange and Unusual.

THE COLLECTED SUPERNATURAL AND WEIRD FICTION OF MARY SHELLEY: VOLUME 2 *by Mary Shelley*—Including one novel 'The Last Man', and three short stories of the Strange and Unusual.

THE COLLECTED SUPERNATURAL AND WEIRD FICTION OF AMELIA B. EDWARDS *by Amelia B. Edwards*—Contains two novelettes 'Monsieur Maurice', and 'The Discovery of the Treasure Isles', one ballad 'A Legend of Boisguilbert' and seventeen short stories to cill the blood.

LEONAUR

ALSO FROM LEONAUR
AVAILABLE IN SOFTCOVER OR HARDCOVER WITH DUST JACKET

THE COLLECTED SCIENCE FICTION AND FANTASY OF STANLEY G. WEINBAUM 1—INTERPLANETARY ODYSSEYS *by Stanley G. Weinbaum*—Classic Tales of Interplanetary Adventure Including: A Martian Odyssey, its Sequel Valley of Dreams, the Complete 'Ham' Hammond Stories and Others.

THE COLLECTED SCIENCE FICTION AND FANTASY OF STANLEY G. WEINBAUM 2—OTHER EARTHS *by Stanley G. Weinbaum*—Classic Futuristic Tales Including: *Dawn of Flame* & its Sequel The Black Flame, plus The Revolution of 1960 & Others.

THE COLLECTED SCIENCE FICTION AND FANTASY OF STANLEY G. WEINBAUM 3—STRANGE GENIUS *by Stanley G. Weinbaum*—Classic Tales of the Human Mind at Work Including the Complete Novel The New Adam, the 'van Manderpootz' Stories and Others.

THE COLLECTED SCIENCE FICTION AND FANTASY OF STANLEY G. WEINBAUM 4—THE BLACK HEART *by Stanley G. Weinbaum*—Classic Strange Tales Including: the Complete Novel The Dark Other, Plus Proteus Island and Others.

THE COLLECTED SCIENCE FICTION & FANTASY OF JACK LONDON 1—BEFORE ADAM & OTHER STORIES *by Jack London*—included in this Volume Before Adam The Scarlet Plague A Relic of the Pliocene When the World Was Young The Red One Planchette A Thousand Deaths Goliah A Curious Fragment The Rejuvenation of Major Rathbone.

THE COLLECTED SCIENCE FICTION & FANTASY OF JACK LONDON 2—THE IRON HEEL & OTHER STORIES *by Jack London*—included in this Volume The Iron Heel The Enemy of All the World The Shadow and the Flash The Strength of the Strong The Unparalleled Invasion The Dream of Debs.

THE COLLECTED SCIENCE FICTION & FANTASY OF JACK LONDON 3—THE STAR ROVER & OTHER STORIES *by Jack London*—included in this Volume The Star Rover The Minions of Midas The Eternity of Forms The Man With the Gash.

THE CRETAN TEAT *by Brian Aldiss*—The Cretan Teat is a wry and comic novel that interweaves its own fiction with an inner fiction about the discovery of a Byzantine painting of the Mother of the Blessed Virgin Mary suckling the infant Jesus and a fake ikon that becomes an instrument of Nemesis.